Freaky Crypts

A MYSTIC CARAVAN MYSTERY BOOK 14

AMANDA M. LEE

WINCHESTERSHAW PUBLICATIONS

Prologue

THIRTEEN YEARS AGO

S idney Parker sat in the uncomfortable office and studied the posters decking the walls. Happy children everywhere. That's all he saw, except when he thought about the child he'd left with a neighbor to babysit. No, that child wasn't happy. Why would she be?

Laura Carter entered the office wearing the sort of suit that made Sidney itchy just looking at it. She attempted a smile, but it only served to contort her features. She was blond, from a bottle, and wore far too much makeup. Sidney could only wonder what children saw when they looked at her.

It wasn't a pleasant picture. She was too frightening, with that rigid smile and those dark eyes. Did she not realize that turned off children rather than comforted them?

"Mr. Parker." She held out her hand to shake his. "Thank you for coming in." She sat across from him and opened the file she had waiting. "I understand you're the uncle of Poet Parker. The only relative, as far as we can tell."

"I believe she has an aunt on the other side of the family, her mother's side, but she's been estranged for many years. I don't even know where she is. My sister-in-law never willingly talked about her."

"I do see that there's mention of her here," Laura noted, tapping on the top sheet in the file with her pen. "Both sets of grandparents are out of the picture as well."

Sidney hesitated and then nodded. "My mother died several years ago. My father left when I was a teenager. I haven't seen him since."

"It says here he's dead."

"He might be." Sidney held out his hands. "After he left, I never saw him again. If he died in the intervening years, nobody informed us."

Laura nodded in understanding. That was far more common than she was comfortable with. "All right, well, I don't see a need to contact him now. Finding him would be difficult and if the child has no relationship with him there doesn't seem to be much point."

"Poet has never met him," Sidney confirmed. "She met her mother's parents, but they're both gone too."

"Poet is an odd name," Laura noted. "Do you know how they came up with it?"

"I don't. I laughed about it when they announced her name. It seems to fit her, though, and Poet is fine with it. She's a well-adjusted kid. Well, teenager. I guess she's no longer technically a child."

"She's a kid with a lot of anxiety," Laura said. "She's afraid of being abandoned in a world in which she doesn't know anyone."

The statement was a knife to the gut for Sidney, but it didn't change his plan of action. "I know what you're about to ask of me," he started.

"Do you?" Laura arched an eyebrow.

"You want me to raise Poet."

"Your brother and his wife didn't name guardians. It's likely they didn't think it was necessary, but now we're left with this conundrum. As far as I can tell, you're the only relative available who has regular contact with Poet."

"I believe that's true." Sidney steepled his fingers on his lap and waited.

"Are you willing to take in your niece?"

It was the question he'd been expecting...and dreading. "No, I am not."

Laura blinked several times and then nodded, her gaze moving back to the file. "I see."

"I've been staying with her since the accident, but I can't take her on full time." Sidney knew he didn't owe the woman an explanation, but he couldn't stop from vomiting his guilt all over her. "I love her. I do. But I travel for work. I'm not married. I can't give her the life she deserves."

"And I assume you're either unable or unwilling to change your work situation."

In truth, the possibility hadn't even occurred to Sidney. "No," he said in a low voice.

"All right. Well, at least that clears a path for us." Laura moved her hands to her computer keyboard. "We'll start searching for a foster home. I can clear some time to collect the girl this afternoon."

Sidney balked. "So soon? I haven't talked to her about what's going to happen yet."

"Waiting won't help. It will only delay the inevitable."

"But...the house. We haven't gone through anything. We haven't packed her things."

"You can do that relatively quickly. She can only bring two bags."

Sidney suddenly felt sick to his stomach. "She can't fit everything she owns in two bags."

"She'll have to." Laura was matter-of-fact. "Mr. Parker, your niece is going into the system. Her next living situation will be temporary. Our goal is to find her a permanent home, but that's not happening today. She's older, which means placement will be difficult. If I can keep her out of a group home, I'll consider it a win. She won't be able to take more than two bags with her. The homes she will be living in don't have room for more than that."

Sidney wasn't a crier, but hot tears pricked the back of his eyes. "I didn't realize." He glanced out the window, at the drab expanse stretching toward the trees. It was the end of winter in Michigan. There was no color to be found anywhere, and there wouldn't be until spring arrived in an explosion of green and pink. "What about her parents' things? She'll want those."

"We can't store them for her. If there are items you want her to have, you'll need to find a way to keep them for her until she's an adult."

Sidney hated the woman's tone. Absolutely *hated* it. "I want to do what's right for her," he insisted. "I'm just not capable of giving her what she needs. I'm...lacking." *And Poet has magic at her disposal,* he silently added. He'd seen the girl in action, knew she was a force to be reckoned with. He couldn't deal with that either. The notion terrified him. She terrified him, with her sad eyes and fiery temper. He couldn't risk taking her in. It wouldn't end well.

"You don't have to explain yourself to me," Laura replied. "You didn't plan for a child, and you don't want this one."

"It's not that I don't want her. As I said, I love her. I'm just not the right person for her. She needs someone better at all of this."

"I'll find her a placement," Laura promised. "If you want to remain in her life, you'll have to fill out some paperwork. Hopefully, in a few months when she's settled into a long-term home, we'll be able to arrange visitation."

It was something Sidney hadn't considered. "I don't know," he said finally. "She'll be angry with me. She won't want to see me. I mean...she's going to lose her home and her pretty purple room. She'll lose everything she knows. She'll blame me."

"Likely," Laura agreed. "There's nothing I can do about that. Given what she's facing, she'll need a target for her rage. That will likely be you."

"So you're saying it's best I cut ties with her."

"I can't make your decisions for you," she clarified. "I can only do what I can do for Poet."

Sidney ran his tongue over his lips, debating, and then sighed. "Okay. Can I have a week? I want to go through the house with her and pick the items she wants from her parents. I'll secure storage for them, pay for the storage until she's an adult, and slowly break the news to her. That should give you more time to get her a good placement."

Laura blinked several times and then nodded. "All right. Given the circumstances, I can work with that. Don't expect miracles. Going out of your way for the girl won't mean she'll forgive you. Her life will never be the same."

"Her life was never going to be the same the minute my brother and sister-in-law died," Sidney countered. "I want to do my best for her, but I'm limited in what I can provide. Sorting through the house is some-thing tangible I can do. I won't leave her with nothing from them."

Laura offered up a flat smile. "You have a week. I'll find a home for her. If I can find one in the same school district, I will. She needs to be ready to go in a week." She leaned forward. "You must be ready to let her go. You know you can't take care of her. Right now, you're only holding onto her because you feel guilty. That won't benefit her in the long run."

Sidney swallowed hard. The social worker was right. Deep down, he knew that. Still, he wasn't ready to relinquish Poet today. "I'll have her ready in a week. You have my word."

"Make sure you say your goodbyes," Laura insisted. "She needs to be able to look back and know that you didn't just walk away without any forethought. Let her see the conflict you're struggling with. At least give her that."

"If I could, I would give her the world."

"It's time to acknowledge your limitations and move on."

He pushed himself to a standing position on shaky legs. "I'll be in touch."

"So will I. Good luck, Mr. Parker. Together, we'll try to come up with the best living situation for Poet."

"Thank you. That's all I ask. She's a special girl. I want to make sure she has a chance in this world."

"That's what we all want."

One

PRESENT DAY

"The traffic here is murder."

Kade Denton, my fiancé, kept his focus on the narrow streets as he navigated New Orleans. He often became agitated with traffic in new locations—I chalked it up to the being a man thing—but today he was especially out of sorts. For some reason, the ranting and complaining made me smile.

"Do you want me to drive?" I asked in my most innocent voice. I, Poet Parker, was nothing if not helpful in situations like this.

"Do you think you're funny?" He practically growled. "This is just unbelievable. What are they doing? You can't wander between cars at intersections."

He made me laugh. Always. That was one of the reasons I knew we were built to last. We had passion to last for decades, a relationship built on love and trust, but the most important factor is that we have a good time together. Just now, however, I knew better than to burst out laughing.

"New Orleans isn't easy." I chose my words carefully. "It is one of my favorite cities. You'll get used to it, and once we park, we shouldn't have to use the truck more than a few times."

"That doesn't fix the situation now. Oh, will you look at that?"

Kade threw up his hands and glared at two women as they cut between vehicles, plastic cups in hand. "It's not even three o'clock. What's in those cups?"

I chewed my bottom lip as I stared out the window. I knew how I wanted to respond. I also knew it might not go over well, and I wasn't in the mood for an argument, not with my agenda for later in the evening.

"It's New Orleans," I said finally. "You know what's in the cups."

"But they're jaywalking. You can't jaywalk with alcohol. How is that even allowed?"

It was a fair question. I only had one answer: "It's New Orleans."

Kade growled and gripped the steering wheel so tightly his knuckles whitened. "This is not good."

"Definitely not," I agreed.

"It's stupid. That's what it is."

I rested my forehead against the window and studied the buildings. Visually, New Orleans appealed to me on almost every level. I couldn't get enough of it. Emotionally, my stomach was tied in knots.

"Hey." Kade's voice was soft when he reached over and collected my hand. "Are you okay?"

"I'm fine." I put on a brave face for him and straightened. "New Orleans is one of my favorite cities—and that's saying something, because I've been to a lot of cities. I'm thrilled to be here."

Kade didn't look convinced. "Tell me about where we're staying," he instructed.

"It's great." I smiled. "Thirty-two acres of park and water features. It's basically a refuge in an urban jungle. You'll like it."

He turned his attention back to the road. "I'm listening. I just can't look away from the road because of the freaking jaywalkers."

I grinned. "You'll get used to them."

"I don't want to get used to them. It's too early in the day to get drunk."

"Not in New Orleans. It's never too early here." I let my eyes drift back to the window but forced myself to focus on the park, and more specifically what Kade, as head of security, needed to know about the park. We were one of the few groups allowed to set up shop in the historic space thanks to a deal Max, the owner of our circus, had struck

7

with city officials years ago. More than once, the local council had tried to strip our permit. Louis Armstrong Park was a big deal. Their efforts never worked. We were allowed to take over the park when we were in town, and I loved it.

"It's technically in Treme, but it's right across the road from the French Quarter. We're within walking distance of the best food and drinks you've ever had. We're only twenty minutes from the Mississippi River, too. And have I mentioned how much I love beignets? I'm going to make you walk with me to Cafe du Monde to get beignets at least twice."

"I'm up for that," he reassured me. "I don't know if I've ever had beignets, but I'm not fussy when it comes to food."

"Oh, you're going to love the food." I wasn't certain about much, but I was certain of that. "There's a performing arts building as well as a municipal auditorium. There are trees, but it's still very urban. The best part is that it's fenced in."

Kade's forehead creased. "That sounds like a trap more than anything else."

That was such a Kade thing to say. "We'll have keys. Plus, well, we're magical. We can leave the gate open if we feel like it and not worry about people wandering in."

He swore under his breath again when a man appeared in front of his truck. "Ugh. He has two glasses of beer. Don't cross the road when you're double-fisting it, buddy."

I snorted in delight. "You're going to have a really rough time if you can't wrap your head around the fact that people are allowed to wander around with open intoxicants," I warned.

"I have no doubt." His tone was dry. "Tell me more about New Orleans. What's your favorite thing about the city?"

"It's hard to pin down a favorite thing. I guess the food is my favorite. You know how I feel about good food."

"You are a foodie. I like food just as much as you, so we're a match in that department."

I licked my lips in anticipation. "I also love the architecture. There are creole cottages between bars, and mansions sitting between businesses at certain intersections. It's worth a walk around the Quarter just to see that."

"I love walking, as long as it's with you."

"The music is amazing. I'll take you to Frenchman Street one night so you can hear the best jazz of your life."

"I'm up for that."

"The people are fun. The voodoo culture is delightful. I love all of it."

He didn't reach over and squeeze my knee as he normally would. He was too focused on the traffic. "Just out of curiosity, if you love the city so much, why didn't you choose this as our destination once the circus stops traveling?"

I shrugged. "I gave it some thought. The thing is, New Orleans is the type of city that doesn't need a circus to entertain people. We might be a legitimate attraction for a few weeks, but the locals and tourists would lose interest.

"Visitors come here to drink," I continued. "We have a liquor license when we're here—it's almost impossible not to secure a liquor license in New Orleans—but we would quickly fade into obscurity if we decided this was our permanent location. It's not like Moonstone Bay."

He bobbed his head. "I get it. In Moonstone Bay, the tourist turnover is weekly and there aren't as many things to do. We'll be a destination for almost everybody at least one day a week. New Orleans doesn't need us. Moonstone Bay does."

"Pretty much." I grinned at him and pressed a finger into his chiseled cheek. "I like that you're pretty *and* smart."

"Keep it up," he muttered, shaking his head. "Wait...Rampart. That's where we're supposed to be?" His eyes were on the street sign.

"Yes, but we need to cross over to St. Philip Street. That's where we park. Go left and then left again one street down. It should be pretty obvious from there."

"Awesome."

He was doing his best, I reminded myself. He couldn't help that he was agitated. He likely didn't know the real reason he was worked up, but I did. My uncle was in town. Sidney Parker, a man I hadn't seen since I was a kid, had sent a letter during our seasonal break in Florida.

He wanted to have dinner, catch up, and learn all there was to know about my life.

My initial instinct had been to ignore the letter. Instead, I called him. He gushed on the phone, ignoring my discomfort and focusing on himself. That's what I remembered best about him. He was always more interested in himself. Despite that, I agreed to dinner with him. And because I wasn't the sort of person who liked to delay things, I'd agreed to have dinner with him tonight. After we settled in at the park and handled the initial things that needed to be taken care of, I would have another problem. And because he loved me, Kade was taking that problem to heart. He was keyed up on my behalf. It would've been cute under different circumstances. Today it just made me antsy.

"Do you want to talk about it?" I asked.

"Talk about what?"

"You know what. The letter. Sidney. All of it."

"I don't think there's anything to talk about." He seemed relieved when he pulled onto Rampart. Nobody was crossing the busier road willy-nilly with cocktails. "He's your uncle. You want to see him. That's all there is to it."

"But you don't want me to see him."

"It's not that."

"What is it?"

"I don't want you getting upset. You don't ever talk about this guy. Like...ever. That means you don't have good memories of him."

Ever since I'd gotten word that Sidney wanted to see me I'd let my mind stretch back to so long ago. Some of the memories were easier to conjure than others. "I don't remember him being a terrible guy."

"But?"

"But I'm bitter." There was no sense denying it. The feelings were right there, bubbling at the surface. Kade would understand better than anybody what I felt because he was so firmly in my heart. "I want to know why he didn't even try to keep me."

"He's the reason you ended up on the streets."

"No." I shook my head, firm. "A lot of different things played into that outcome. He didn't choose the group home where I ended up. He had nothing to do with my placement with families so difficult to deal with. I did that. The things I could do ensured that I didn't belong anywhere for a time." I didn't come right out and blame the magic.

"Poet, I have trouble believing you were anything but great, even at that age."

I smirked. "You're looking through the lens of love. You didn't know me when I was a kid, when I was going through my obnoxious period. I never tried to steal your wallet or modify your memories."

"Maybe not, but I know you now and you're great."

"It's good you feel that way, what with us getting married and all."

His grin lit up his entire face as he made the second turn. "That is convenient."

"It is. The entrance is up that way. See the sign?" I pointed.

"Yup."

"As for Sidney, he's the last blood relative I'm certain is still around." I didn't always have the easiest time expressing myself, and this was a prime example of that struggle. "It's not as if I need him in my life. I have everything I want. But it can't hurt to see him. I mean…it's one dinner."

"I'm not giving you grief over wanting to see him," Kade reassured me. "In your position, I would probably make the same decision."

"You're still agitated," I pointed out. "That's why you're so focused on the jaywalkers."

"Hey, jaywalking is a crime."

It took everything I had not to burst out laughing.

"You might be right," he conceded after a moment. "There's very little in this world I can protect you from. We face monsters nearly weekly these days. I don't want you to be hurt by this guy."

"I won't," I reassured him. "I'm not the same little girl from back then."

"I'm still annoyed with him." Kade pulled into the parking lot. Other members of Mystic Caravan Circus were already preparing to unload the things that made up our everyday lives. The trailers we lived in were taking over the parking lot rather than the park, one of the stipulations we agreed to in our contract, and the area buzzed with activity.

"Why are you annoyed with him?" I asked.

"Why do you think? You were a little girl who had just lost her parents. He shoved you into foster homes rather than provide a stable environment for you. That's more than enough reason to hate him."

"I wasn't a little girl, I was a teenager. It wasn't as bad as you're making out. Back then, I hated him for what he did, but he was never going to be able to make me happy."

"Because you lost your parents."

"That, and the fact that I didn't want to leave the house I grew up in. I didn't want to leave my school, even though I hated the other kids. They always thought I was weird and treated me poorly."

"Can we not have this discussion?" Kade sounded pained. "I don't like hearing about how you suffered as a kid. It makes me sick to my stomach."

He was loyal to a fault, only one of the reasons I loved him. "I'm sorry." I held up my hands. "I didn't mean to upset you."

"You're perfect," he said.

"I'll remind you of that next time you get annoyed when Luke paints our toenails, and you can't stop ranting about my poor taste in friends."

"Hey, I'm fine with him painting your toenails. I just happen to disagree that us getting engaged means he can paint mine whenever he wants."

"Fair enough." I rubbed my hands over my knees. He wasn't the only one struggling with how to handle Sidney. "Looking back, I see why he did what he did, and I don't hate him for it." My voice was low.

"He abandoned you, baby."

"I wasn't his child. He stopped in periodically when I was growing up. I lost my parents, but he lost his brother. He was grieving too. He couldn't handle me, and he was honest about that. Isn't it better that he acknowledged his shortcomings rather than overcommit and mistreat me? Things might've ended up taking a tragic turn if he'd gone against his instincts."

"How so?"

"I was forced to toughen up fast in the system. If I'd remained soft I would've been an easy mark when I was forced into the real world." I slid my eyes to him. "I'm a big proponent of life working out as it should."

12

"Fate?" He almost looked amused at the prospect.

"Maybe a little," I conceded. "I believe I was supposed to end up with you...and Luke. Am I wrong to believe that?"

He reached over and collected my hand. "We definitely belong together. We belong with this family we've built. I just can't get over how angry I am with him. He should've been a better man."

"He was the best man he could be. If he'd taken me in and fallen apart, that would've been harder. I have a good life. Maybe we should just take the win, have dinner with him, and say goodbye."

Kade used the hand that wasn't holding mine to scrub his cheek. "I still might be mean to him. I'm guessing I won't be able to control myself. I just want you to be aware."

I snickered. "You can be mean. Truthfully, I'm not certain how I'll react. It's going to be a struggle, but I can handle it. Let's just play it by ear."

"I guess I can live with that." He leaned in to give me a kiss. "I love you, Poet. Whatever you need, I want to give it to you. I can't help being protective. I look at you and wonder how anybody could give you up. I never will."

I beamed at him. "So cute." I pinched his cheek and planted a wet kiss on him. "It'll be okay." I flicked my eyes to the park, a place I genuinely loved. "We're in New Orleans. Even if Sidney turns out to be a turd, this is one of my favorite places. We're going to have a great time."

"I'm looking forward to exploring the city with you and eating my weight in gumbo."

"It's going to be magical."

"You're magical, Poet. That's all that matters to me."

Two

Luke Bishop, my best friend, was already organizing vehicles when we hopped out of the truck. He fancied himself the boss of everything, but because we'd taken over Louis Armstrong Park several times in the past I didn't have a problem letting him lead. I had other things to deal with, and they were more important.

"Hey." I sidled over to Cole Ryan, Luke's boyfriend and the new midway chief. He'd been promoted during our trip to Moonstone Bay ten days ago. This was the first test of his new position. I was prepared to help him in any way possible. "How are things?"

Cole dragged a hand through his hair. "Humid."

I smirked. "It's New Orleans. There's a reason it storms most afternoons. They're just part of the deal."

"I'm aware." He blew out a sigh, and when he turned to face me he looked as if he was in pain. "I'm a little nervous."

"I'll bet. This is your first test. New Orleans is usually an easy gig. You'll be fine."

"I'm not nervous about the guests. I can handle that part of the job. It's the workers. A lot of them are still loyal to Mark and they have an attitude with me."

"I figured." I rolled my neck and shifted my gaze to the park. "We'll handle it together." Other than Max Anderson, Kade's father, I was the head honcho of Mystic Caravan. Max was planning his retirement, and when we moved to Moonstone Bay he would be little more than a figurehead. I would be in charge then, including handling personnel issues. There was no reason not to start now.

"Great." Cole bobbed his head. "Where should we start?"

I looked over the heavy machinery being removed from the semis. New Orleans was different from our other stops, and our standard approach to setting up had to be thrown out the window. "The trailers will be set up on the pavement." I gestured to the parking lot. "It's a pain, but we don't have an option given the space. "The booths will be set up inside the park. The fence makes that easier."

"Okay."

"Take a walk with me." I held out my hand to him.

Cole took it without question. I wasn't sure about him when he'd first hooked up with Luke. I was naturally protective of my best friend. It turned out Cole's elemental powers didn't mix all that well with my powers, whatever they were. We'd been able to correct the problem, and ever since, we'd been tight. There were times I thought I was just as in love with Cole as Luke was, although not in the same way.

I led Cole into the park, breathing deeply. New Orleans had a distinctive smell, but it wasn't always apparent in the park. Still, the ambiance of Louis Armstrong Park was difficult not to love.

"What's this?" Cole asked when we approached a stone bridge that arced high and gave us a fantastic view of the pond. He looked tickled.

"It's a unique park," I explained. "The water features are beautiful, but they make our life more difficult. We have limited space to work with and we have to be careful how we arrange things. In years past, we've kept the midway near the water and spread it out horizontally rather than vertically like we do when we're in a field."

Cole's impossibly handsome face was on full display as he took in the park. "It's beautiful, charming really."

I leaned my head against his shoulder. "I love it here. I think I'm going to have to come back once a year even when we move to Moonstone Bay."

"You're still okay with that decision?" He looked pensive. "I know you said you were, but you're used to a life on the road. I'm afraid you're going to change your mind at some point."

One of the things I liked best about Cole was his honest nature. When he sensed a problem brewing, he attacked it straight away. "I'm fine with it," I reassured him. I meant it. "Moonstone Bay has everything we need. We have an in there now. We have friends. I can see building a life there. Max is ironing out the details for the move. He has some heft he can throw around to get things done."

"You're still going to miss traveling."

I shrugged. "Maybe, but there are trade-offs. We can have homes on Moonstone Bay, places we can decorate, gardens. The idea of not having to drive a million miles every year holds some appeal."

"And we can still take vacations," Cole added. "We can go on trips together."

"And apart," I added. "Kade won't be happy with Luke tagging along on every vacation."

Cole snorted. He loved his boyfriend, but he wasn't oblivious to Luke's faults. "I'm positive something can be worked out." He looked around. "I see what you mean about stringing the booths along the water. It will work."

I glanced over my shoulder to where some of the workers had arrived with the booths' pieces. "You're not just worried about the setup here on your first gig." I opted not to beat around the bush. "Talk to me."

Cole was sheepish. "The workers believe I stole Mark's gig. They liked him a whole lot more than they like me."

I shook my head. "That's not it. He was not beloved, so get that out of your head. Like most people, they simply fear change."

"Better the devil you know," he mused.

"Precisely. They will get used to you. You can't step lightly with them. They'll treat you like a doormat if you allow them. You have to be fair but firm."

"Any suggestions on how I get them to even listen to me?"

"Yeah. We talk to them."

He tapped the end of my nose before breaking into a grin. "Look who's getting pragmatic in her old age."

"Don't call me old." I inclined my head to draw the attention of the construction team. "Go with the normal spread. We want the midway booths arranged along the water. Everything else goes in the park area. Spread it out as much as possible but be aware of the space limitations. The big show is in the auditorium this go-around, not a tent, so keep that in mind when mapping out the space."

"I've got it," one of the men replied.

"Thank you." I drew Cole with me when I started back toward the parking lot. "So, for us, living in the parking lot isn't fun. We don't spend much time in our trailers when we're here. We sleep in them, but our downtime is spent in the outlying neighborhoods. The French Quarter, which is just across Rampart Street, is a big draw."

"Because of the drinking?"

"And the food. We fit in here. Even in his dresses, Nellie isn't an oddity on Bourbon Street. He's not even cause for a second look most of the time. We can be ourselves here and nobody questions it."

"I guess that makes sense." Cole glanced over his shoulder. "Do the pixies spend all their time in the water? That pond doesn't look very deep...or clean for that matter."

I laughed. Only Cole, with his law enforcement background, would worry about such a thing. Nixie and Naida, our resident pixies, were addicted to water. If we visited a location that didn't have easy access to some sort of water—whether it be lake, river, or pool—things often went poorly. That wouldn't be a problem in New Orleans. "The Gulf of Mexico is accessible from here, as is the Mississippi River."

Cole bobbed his head. "I didn't even think about that."

"They love it here. They'll be fine. And if they get caught skinny-dipping in the Mississippi, nobody bats an eyelash."

"That's pretty cool." Cole slung his arm around my shoulders. "So, how are you feeling knowing that you're going to see the uncle who abandoned you for the first time in almost two decades?"

I slid him a narrow-eyed look. "I guess I don't have to ask your opinion on the subject."

"Nope," he readily agreed. "He's a jerk."

"Because Luke and Kade think he's a jerk?"

"No."

"Then why? You don't even know him."

"Because you're one of my favorite people in the world and I can't imagine abandoning you."

"He didn't make the choice to have children. Why should he be saddled with one when he wasn't the responsible party?"

"He was your uncle." Cole refused to back down. "He had a duty to you. If one of my sisters died, I would take her children in as my own, no questions asked."

"And you would be good with them," I said. "You're a great guy. I don't remember Sidney being particularly great with me when I was a kid."

Something I couldn't identify kindled in Cole's eyes. "Did he hurt you?"

"No." For some reason, the notion struck me as preposterous. "I don't even remember spending much time with him. I was tight with both of my parents. Sidney visited my father every couple of weeks. He was hardly close.

"He had a specific life he wanted to live," I continued. "It didn't involve taking care of me. I was angry at the time he walked away, but I understand now. I wouldn't have had a happy life with him. Kids know when they're not wanted."

"Did you have a happy life without him?"

I hesitated and held out my hands. "I wasn't unhappy. And look at me now. I'm in a power position and hoping to move to a tropical island in a year. I'm getting married. I have Luke...and you." I poked his side. "What's not to love about my life?"

"You're amazing." Sincerity shone through as he regarded me. "I love you dearly. I'm glad you turned out to be the person you are, and I acknowledge we probably wouldn't all be together if your uncle had raised you. He's still a jackass, and you're not going to change my mind."

I appreciated his loyalty. "Thank you for saying it, but I'm okay. I expect to sit down across from him, have a nice meal, and then text you guys to see where you are so we can meet for some drinks and fun. It will be fine."

Cole shot me an odd look. Before he could say anything, we

emerged into the parking lot. The trailers had already been lined up and everybody was working overtime to cling to our normal configuration despite the limitations of the park. I looked for the trailer I shared with Kade. It had been set up in the far corner, Luke's trailer (and Cole's by extension) positioned directly next to it. Kade and Luke weren't in front of it positioning furniture, which is where I expected to find them.

"Where are ...?" I trailed off as I searched for them.

"Looks like they're dealing with someone," Cole replied, inclining his head to the right. "Is that a city official?"

I followed his gaze, bracing myself because the man in the suit was likely here to argue about a permit. It had happened more times than I could count. After a moment of studying him, however, I realized that wasn't what we were dealing with. No, the man who looked to be having an uncomfortable conversation with my fiancé and best friend was someone I recognized.

"Sidney."

Cole jerked his eyes to me, fire briefly kindling. "Your uncle?"

I nodded as I licked my lips. My mouth was suddenly dry. "He wasn't supposed to be here for a few hours."

"Well, it looks like he couldn't wait to see you."

"I guess." I rubbed my hands on my capri pants. "How do I look?"

Cole's eyebrows drew together. "How do you always look?"

"It depends on who you ask. Raven says I always look messy."

"Screw Raven."

"Thanks," the woman in question offered as she passed. Raven's silver hair shone under the sun, her gray eyes gleaming with amusement. She didn't look surly, despite Cole's words. "Screw you too."

Cole waved her off. "You look beautiful, Poet. You shouldn't care what he thinks."

"I know. It's still weird. I don't want him taking one look at me and thinking 'I made the right choice.' I can't help it. My feelings are all over the place on this one."

Cole studied me for what felt like a long time and then his gaze softened. He reached over and brushed my hair out of my face. "We're not making this any easier on you, are we? Instead of worrying about what you're feeling, we're projecting what we feel and forcing you to grapple with that on top of everything else."

"I'm fine." I meant it. "This is not a big deal."

"Oh, you're so cute." He grabbed my cheek and gave it a jiggle. "You're covering for a waterfall of conflicting emotions, but it's okay. Let's just get it over with. At least by showing up early he cut down on any anxiety you'd be feeling the next few hours."

"Right." He made sense. "Let's do this." It was with a great deal of determination that I strode toward Sidney. I pasted a smile on my face—one that didn't feel natural—and didn't stop until I was next to Kade. "Hey."

As far as greetings went, it wasn't my finest.

"Poet." Sidney looked me up and down, his eyes wide. "Wow. I'd know you anywhere."

Weirdly enough, even though it had taken me a moment to recognize him, I felt the same about Sidney. "You haven't changed." I grasped for a genuine smile and hoped that was what I came up with. One look at Luke's cringe told me I'd missed the mark.

"You're early," I said. "I thought you were going to text me a location so we could meet for dinner later."

"I couldn't wait." Something akin to awe washed over his face. "We have a lot to talk about, a lot to catch up on."

"We're dying to hear it, too," Luke drawled. "We can't wait to catch up with you."

The look Sidney shot Luke was odd, but he didn't push back. "I know you have some questions, Poet. You probably have some anger you want to express. I want you to know that I'm here for all of it. I understand that this won't be easy for you."

"Definitely not easy," I agreed. "I'm not angry with you."

Behind Sidney's back, Luke threw up his hands in frustration.

I had to force myself to keep from reacting. "Nobody expects you to take care of a child that isn't yours. It's fine. I'm not angry."

Sidney looked torn. "Yes, well, I'm angry with myself. I'm hopeful we can talk about things, that I can maybe explain myself, and we can move forward from there."

"Move forward?" *What did that mean?* "I'm not a kid any longer. You don't have to make an effort to keep in touch with me."

"You're my family."

"Sure, by blood, but I have another family now."

"You're married?" Sidney's eyes immediately went to my left ring finger, to where the amethyst engagement ring Kade had given me sparkled.

"Engaged," I said. "I meant the people here are my family. They're the family I chose, and that's just as powerful, if not more so, than the ties one shares with the family they're born to."

"Especially when the family you're born to doesn't want to take you in and your parents are killed in a tragic accident," Cole muttered just loud enough for Sidney to make out.

"You must be the fiancé," Sidney said, extending his hand. "I understand your annoyance."

"Actually, I'm the fiancé," Kade replied. "Cole is...Luke's friend."

"And I'm Poet's soulmate," Luke said pointedly.

Kade cuffed the back of his blond head. "I'm her soulmate. You're the pain in the butt we're forced to deal with regularly."

"Luke is my best friend," I volunteered. "We've been together since I first joined Mystic Caravan."

"That was when you were a teenager, correct?" Sidney looked troubled now. "I tried to chase you down in Detroit, but they lost track of you."

"That happens when you run away," I said.

A momentary jolt of pain flooded Sidney's features, but he covered quickly. "It seems we have a lot to catch up on."

"Definitely," Cole agreed. "We're all looking forward to it."

"Yeah, we thought we would have dinner as a group," Kade added, catching me off guard.

"We did?"

"We did," he confirmed. "Just one big happy family."

Sidney held Kade's gaze for a long moment and then nodded. "That sounds like a fine idea. If you're Poet's family, you're my family too."

"Let's not get ahead of ourselves," Cole replied as he grabbed the front of Sidney's suit jacket and gave it a tug to straighten it. "Let's start with dinner, progress to conversation, and go from there."

"No promises on how we'll act," Luke added. "We're going to do what we're going to do. You just have to live with it."

Sidney chuckled. "I see why you chose them as your family, Poet. They're loyal."

"They are," I agreed. "We're a package deal."

"I'm fine with that." Sidney looked sincere. "I'm looking forward to getting to know all of you." His gaze was on me. "Especially you."

"Then it's a date." Even as I said it, my stomach constricted.

Three

Kade's concerned expression told me where his head was at as I changed for dinner. We'd left Sidney in the lot—Nelson "Nellie" Adler, our "bearded lady" who was actually a dwarf from another plane, was entertaining him—to get ready before heading out. Kade had questions, but he didn't press me. I wasn't good when it came to expressing my feelings, especially feelings this big and important, so he wisely let it be.

When we regrouped in the lot, Sidney looked more amused than upset regarding his time with Nellie. He was all smiles when he focused on me. "I made reservations at Deanie's Seafood if that's okay with you," he said shyly. "If you're a vegetarian or something we can go somewhere else." He looked momentarily lost. "I didn't know what you would like."

"Deanie's is fine," I reassured him.

"We're not vegetarians," Luke offered on a stern glare. "If we were though, you would be in big trouble."

Sidney slid him a sidelong look and then nodded. "Right."

I shook my head at my best friend and then gestured to the sidewalk. "I think we plan on drinks after dinner, so we don't really want to drive."

"It's about eight blocks or so," Sidney replied. "I figured we would walk."

Kade had his phone out as he fell into step behind me. I didn't have to ask. He was looking up the restaurant. He didn't trust others to navigate for him, which is why I almost never drove when we were moving between locations. That was his thing—as far as I could tell it was a male thing—and it wasn't worth arguing about.

"So, what have you been up to for the past fifteen or so years?" I asked lamely. I had no idea how I was supposed to frame the conversation. I felt awkward, like I was an alien in my own body, and I didn't like it.

Sidney let loose a hollow chuckle. "I sell construction equipment now. When there are big projects, I'm the one who provides the tractors and cranes. I travel a lot."

"You must have a home base."

"I don't right now, but we are in New Orleans for the foreseeable future as I have a project. We're debating where we want to put down roots. For now, we're traveling together."

My eyebrows migrated toward one another. "Are you married?" His ring finger was bare, but I knew plenty of men who preferred not wearing a wedding ring.

"No, but I have a partner. We've been together a few months. It's serious."

"Are you gay?" Luke demanded in a tone I wasn't particularly happy with. "If so, you're sending the wrong vibe. You've got pasty straight dude stamped all over you."

I jabbed a warning finger in his direction but didn't verbally chastise him.

"What?" Luke's expression told me he was ready to fight, and nobody was going to get in his way.

"Ignore him," I said to Sidney. "He's a busybody. He's also feeling a bit protective."

"I can see that." Sidney glanced over my shoulder and took in the three solemn men walking together. "It's almost as if you have your own harem."

"I only sleep with one of them," I replied.

Kade raised his hand to indicate he was the one, which made me smile.

"Luke has been my best friend since I was eighteen. He feels proprietary about me."

"She's my second favorite person in the world," Luke acknowledged.

"Oh, does that make me your favorite person?" Cole teased.

"I was talking about myself, so I guess that makes her my third favorite person. Either way, I love her and I don't like you, *Uncle Sidney*."

I pressed the heel of my hand to my forehead. We hadn't even made it to the restaurant and the conversation was already devolving into something from which we might never be able to return. "I'm sorry. He's just...well, he's Luke."

"What she means to say is that he's gotten away with being rude for the better part of his life and it's easier to ignore his outbursts than correct his behavior," Cole offered. "I've been working on behavior modification, but it's not a smooth transition."

"It's okay," Sidney reassured us as we crossed to Iberville Street. "I don't expect you to fall over yourselves welcoming me. I understand why you're so hostile. In fact, I don't blame you. I've got it coming."

"Well, at least you're not completely obtuse," Luke muttered.

"As for my partner, I'm not gay. You were right about that. Her name is Vanessa Congress. I met her in Boston about eight months ago. I was working a job and we met through business acquaintances. I don't know that I believe in love at first sight, but there was certainly something there right from the beginning."

I'd felt the same about Kade when he joined Mystic Caravan. "I'm glad you found someone. Does that mean you never had children of your own?"

"Not that I'm aware of." Sidney's smile was rueful. "After leaving Michigan, I was feeling a bit guilty about things. Children were never on the radar for me."

"You don't have to feel guilty," I assured him.

Cole growled. "She was your only niece. How could you just abandon her like that?"

"It wasn't what I wanted," Sidney replied. His gaze was focused on the sidewalk, something for which I was grateful. "I didn't think I could raise you, Poet. I know that's a lame excuse, but I felt overwhelmed. I never expected to be put in that position. Your father and I never talked about what would happen to you under those circumstances."

"That was probably a failing on his part," I mused. "You don't have to worry about me. I wasn't a baby when they died. I was old enough to understand that my life would never be the same."

"You were still angry," he pressed. "The day I left, you told me you wanted me to die."

I remembered the scene well. "I was in a bad place," I replied. "I didn't mean it. I just...didn't know how I was supposed to deal with what was happening. My life changed in an instant, and even though I recognized things were shifting, I didn't understand the scope of what that would entail."

"You were angry with me."

"That's true. I was angry with you for a long time. Then, after a few years, I had other things to be angry about and what I felt for you faded. You didn't owe me anything, Sidney."

"Didn't I?" He looked pained. "I can't help but feel I failed you. When I heard you'd disappeared from the system I was truly afraid. I didn't know what had happened and I feared the worst."

"How did you find me? It couldn't have been easy. We're constantly on the road. My place in Florida is listed as my permanent address but you still would've had to do some digging."

"It took some time," he confirmed. "I flew to Michigan when I made the decision to look for you. It had been eating at me a lot longer than I realized. I thought they would be able to put me in touch with you. I was naive. I believed they kept tabs on you. When they pulled your file, all they could tell me is that you voluntarily walked away from a group home."

I pursed my lips. "It was safer on the street than in some of the homes. I don't regret my choice."

Sidney briefly pressed his eyes shut. "I told myself I was doing the right thing for you."

"You very well might've," I acknowledged as we reached the restaurant. "Don't make yourself sick over the past, Sidney. I'm fine. Obviously things worked out for me."

He didn't look convinced. "You ended up with the circus."

"That's where I belong. I'm happy. I'm surrounded by people I love."

He nodded. "I think you're letting me off the hook too easy."

"We all think that," Cole supplied.

Sidney smiled. "At least I have that going for me."

Serious conversation ceased as Sidney spoke with the hostess. Within minutes we were being shown to a table on the patio. There, a well-dressed blonde sat alone. When she caught sight of Sidney, she hopped to her feet and opened her arms.

"I was starting to worry," she said.

"I'm sorry, but I took them by surprise," Sidney explained as he returned the hug. "They needed to get changed because they'd been working. You got my text about the bigger party obviously." He glanced at the table, which could comfortably seat six. "Poet has some friends."

"Of course she does." Vanessa's eyes were full of warmth when they landed on me. "Your uncle said he was convinced you would grow up to be gorgeous. He was right. I'm Vanessa." She extended her hand. "I'm so happy to finally meet you."

All I could think as I returned the handshake was that I was glad she wasn't a hugger. "I wish I could say the same, but Sidney hasn't had much of a chance to fill me in about you. Most of our walk was reserved for talk about me."

"As it should be." Vanessa was matter-of-fact as she sat.

There was a scuffle when it came time for me to sit, Luke and Cole shoving each other to see which sat next to me. Ultimately, Luke won—he wouldn't have shut up if he hadn't—and everybody got comfortable.

"Well, let's order," Vanessa suggested. "Then we can talk."

"They have stuffed mushrooms," Kade noted as he tipped his menu so I could see it.

"I know what I'm getting." I managed a smile, although it felt fake. How was I supposed to focus on food when something so monumental was happening? Thankfully, my three bodyguards weren't suffering the same doubts.

"I want the Giant Seafood Platter," Luke announced.

"Is that for one person?" Cole's forehead creased. "Luke, that's seventy-five bucks. That has to be for more than one person."

"Don't worry about price," Sidney said quickly. "This is on me."

Even though he meant well, the offer irritated me. "We can afford to feed ourselves. Just because we work for the circus doesn't mean we're broke."

Sidney looked taken aback. "I didn't mean that. I just want to buy the meal. I...um...." He started to flounder.

"Your uncle is worried that he's going to say the wrong thing," Vanessa explained. "He doesn't mean to be such a pill. He can't help himself."

I forced myself to relax, or at least unclench. "I'm sorry. It's just that when people hear we work for the circus they assume we live a certain way. Most of them couldn't be more wrong."

"I want to hear about all of it," Sidney said. "I just don't want to say the wrong thing. I'm afraid, and that might make me a little stupid when it comes to saying the wrong thing."

His honesty was enough to earn a grin. "It's fine. We deal with it all the time."

"We do," Kade agreed. "It's okay to ask questions. I haven't been with the circus as long as Poet and Luke. I remember all the questions I had when I first joined the team. It's better to ask than pretend you're not curious."

We placed our orders—Luke did indeed order his huge plate of seafood—and then conversation turned to important things.

"So, you're engaged?" Sidney gestured toward my ring.

I nodded as Vanessa squealed.

"Oh, that's lovely," she said as she captured my hand and giggled. "Wow, that's quite the ring." She shot Kade an approving look. "You did good."

Kade smiled indulgently and yet I could tell he was on edge. "Poet told me amethyst was her favorite stone. She doesn't go in for frilly things—except for Luke—so I wanted to get something unique."

"Who helped you pick that ring?" Luke demanded. "That's right, it was this frilly, silly man."

28

"Don't be you," Cole muttered as he flicked the ridge of Luke's ear. "This is Poet's dinner. It's not about you."

"Whatever." Luke's lower lip jutted out.

"When is the wedding?" Sidney asked. "I would love to help if you would allow me. Not that you need help. I'm sure you can afford your own wedding." He slapped his hand to his cheek. "Am I babbling? I think I might be babbling."

Everybody at the table, including me, laughed.

"It's fine," I said when I'd regrouped. "We haven't set a date. We think it will be sooner rather than later, but it won't be a big affair. All of our family travels with us. We just need to pick a city, get a marriage license, and we'll be good to go."

"Now, wait a minute," Kade countered, "I'm not keen on the idea of a huge wedding, but there's something to be said for tradition. There's nothing wrong with a white dress and flowers."

I had to laugh. "I don't know if a white dress is going to work for me."

"Oh, come on." Kade made a face. "You look good in white. You wear white when you read fortunes. My favorite blouse of yours is the white one with the embroidered collar."

"Oh, she's wearing white." Luke was firm. "If I have to wrestle her down and dress her myself, she's totally wearing a white dress."

Perhaps sensing trouble, Sidney changed the subject. "You tell fortunes?"

I nodded. "I'm second in command, but I handle fortunes and tarot readings on guest days."

"She'll be the top dog in a year," Kade added.

"Officially?" Sidney looked impressed.

"That's the way it seems," I confirmed, suddenly uncomfortable with the direction we were heading.

"My father is the current boss," Kade explained. "He's retiring in a year. Poet will be in charge when we set down permanent roots."

"I didn't know that was a thing," Vanessa said. "I thought circuses had to move to stay in business."

"There are very few traveling circuses still in operation," I offered.

"We're one of the last, in fact. We need to change with the times and are looking for a permanent home. We have a few ideas."

Kade shot me a curious look, likely wondering why I didn't mention Moonstone Bay.

"It's great that you're going to be in charge, Poet," Sidney enthused. "You were always smart, even as a little girl. Given the other stuff, I'm not surprised you're going to be the boss."

I froze. *Had he told Vanessa about me? How much did he even know?* I couldn't remember the specifics, what he'd witnessed during my outbursts. I didn't need him talking about me. I didn't know Vanessa. I wasn't yet sure I wanted her to know me.

"There's a lot to plan," I acknowledged finally, working to keep my voice even. "I have lists. I like lists."

Sidney beamed at me. "Organized people keep lists."

"That's me. Ms. Organized."

Luke made a derisive sound in his throat but fell silent when Cole shot him a quelling look.

"Well, that's very exciting." Vanessa rubbed her hands together before standing. "I hope you land somewhere good so we can visit. I need to run to the ladies' room before the food arrives. Excuse me."

"Of course." Sidney stood, showing off his manners, and when he sat again his smile remained intact. "I'm very proud of you, Poet. That's a big deal."

I decided to approach the problem head on and fixed him with a serious look. "How much does Vanessa know about me?"

Sidney looked taken aback by the change in my tone. "What do you mean?"

"How much does she know about the specifics of my childhood? You know, my abilities."

Realization washed across Sidney's face. "I've kept that vague. I didn't feel it was my place to speak out of turn."

"Keep it that way." I was likely coming across as rude, but I didn't care. "My business is my business."

"Of course." His nod was stiff. "I would never purposely put you in danger. I hope you know that."

I could only hope he meant it. We might share blood, but I didn't consider him the sort of family that could be trusted.

"So, tell us about your time in New Orleans," Cole prodded. "Have you been having fun?"

I was grateful for the diversion, but my mind refused to wander to something new. Just how much of a danger was Sidney? Would it be better to cut ties now? I had so many questions, but no answers appeared forthcoming.

Four

I made it through dinner. I was braced for Sidney to say something about my magic the entire meal. He didn't, but I was incapable of relaxing until we were almost finished. Luke, to everybody's amazement, managed to eat his entire meal, which was no small feat. We said our goodbyes in front of the restaurant.

"You're heading out to party it up in the Quarter?" Vanessa asked, eyes sparkling.

"That's the plan," I agreed. "New Orleans is an amazing city. I want to show Kade my favorite places."

"Sounds fun."

"It does," Sidney agreed. He looked as nervous as I felt as he edged closer. "So, we're going to leave you here. We're not young like you, so we're heading back to our hotel room." He hesitated and then continued. "I'd like to see you again."

"Sure." I nodded without thinking. In truth, I needed time to ascertain how I felt about Sidney being back in my life. I couldn't make up my mind this quickly. I also couldn't admit that in front of Vanessa. It felt somehow cruel. "You know where we are, and you have my number."

"We'll spend the next two days setting up," Kade supplied. "We'll be at the park most of the time. We'll also be exploring the city. Call if you want to make arrangements."

"Great." Sidney's face lit up as he extended his hand. "It was lovely to meet you. I'm glad Poet found someone to love."

Kade shook his hand, his face unreadable.

Sidney turned to Cole next. "I'm still not quite sure how you fit into all of this, but I'm glad you and Poet are so close. You seem the pragmatic sort."

Cole kept a straight face. "I love being known for my pragmatism."

Sidney leaned in to hug me, and even though it felt weird I returned his embrace. "I'm so glad you're doing well," he said. "It puts my mind at ease some. The fear I felt when I heard you'd disappeared crippled me for a bit. Knowing you're doing well eases some of my burdens."

Did I want his burden eased? That was another question I couldn't answer. "It was good to see you." I patted his shoulder and then offered Vanessa a smile. "It was nice to meet you."

"You too." Vanessa waved and then linked her arm through Sidney's.

I watched them meander along the sidewalk, not speaking until I was certain they were out of earshot. "Well, that was...interesting."

Cole chuckled as he slung an arm around my shoulders. "It wasn't that bad. Your uncle is...trying."

"And that's good enough for you?" I asked. "I don't want to be petty, but three hours ago you were ranting about him. My, how things change."

Cole lifted one shoulder in a haphazard shrug. "I believe you said you understood why he did what he did. I still don't understand him, but it's obvious he is trying."

I rubbed my cheek. "He almost slipped."

"On the sidewalk?" Kade asked.

"When mentioning my childhood. He almost brought up my magic."

"When was that?"

"Right before Vanessa went to the bathroom. He insinuated that I had abilities. I can't help but wonder what he's told her."

"Maybe he hasn't told her anything. Maybe you're just hypersensitive because you had to hide who you are."

"It's hard to remember," I admitted. "I was afraid and moving to a new place. I know he was aware I could do certain things. I just can't remember how much he knew."

"You could ask," Cole pointed out. "He seems like a straightforward guy."

"Yeah." I blew out a sigh and then slid my eyes to Kade. "You know what I want?"

"Me?" His grin was flirty.

"Always, but I could really use a good cocktail and some music. I don't want to stay up too late because we have a long day tomorrow, but I would love an hour or two of not having to think about anything heavier than Sazerac and jazz."

"I think that can be arranged." Kade tugged me away from Cole. "You have your boyfriend," he said when it appeared Cole might argue. "I want time with my girl."

"Here comes your boyfriend now," I said when I caught sight of Luke's blond head. "I can't believe he ate all that seafood."

As if on cue, Luke lobbed frowns all around as he held his stomach. "Why did you let me eat so much?" The accusation was aimed at all of us.

"Ah, it's going to be a great evening," Cole drawled. "Big fun in the Big Easy."

I pressed my lips together to keep from laughing. "Let's find a bar."

"You read my mind." Cole darted a warning look at Luke as we grew closer. "I don't want to hear one complaint. You did this to yourself."

"That's not how I remember it," Luke countered.

"Well, that's how it was."

"But that's not how I remember it."

"Do you want me to send you home? Because I will."

"Ugh. You're zero fun."

BOURBON STREET WAS LOUD, AS it always was. Even when it wasn't Mardi Gras—it was still two weeks off—the street was full of revelers. Kade was curious enough that we got drinks from one of the kitschy corner shops, parking ourselves under an awning and leaning against a building to people watch. He seemed fascinated with the revelers, though he was careful not to let them get too close.

"I don't want them to touch you," he explained when I arched a questioning eyebrow.

"Who?"

"The drunks." He inclined his head toward a group of men who had taken to hooting and shouting in the middle of the street. "They keep throwing beads at you. I know what that means."

I laughed because there was nothing else I could do. "Do you think I'm going to suddenly start flashing them for cheap beads?"

"I just want to make sure they don't get overzealous. You're my girl." He puckered his lips and moved them in such a way I dissolved into giggles.

I retreated into my head when I needed to think. He hated that, wanted me to lean on him, and this was his way of making sure I didn't wallow in dark thoughts on a beautiful night. Shedding the shields I'd put in place when growing up hadn't been easy, but thanks to him—and Max, Luke, Cole, Nellie, the pixie twins, and even Raven DeMarco, our snarky lamia—I'd grown into the sort of person who didn't always shut people out. I was glad for the growth, but I occasionally reverted to form and put up walls. He feared Sidney's appearance would cause me to shut down. His way to deal with that was to make me laugh.

I wrapped my arms around his neck and kissed the corner of his mouth. "I'm okay," I assured him in a low voice.

He didn't look convinced, but he nodded.

"You don't have to worry about me flashing people for beads either," I added. "You're the only one I want to flash."

"Stop being gross," Luke ordered as he moved closer to me. He'd stopped complaining about eating too much. "Those men are ogling you and you're ignoring them. I think you're missing out on a golden opportunity."

I shot him a dark look. "How many of those have you had?" I demanded, nodding to the huge drink clutched in his hand.

"Not nearly enough." He lightly bopped his forehead against mine.

"You need to live your life to the fullest before you let this one shackle you to him for life." He jerked his thumb at Kade.

"Keep it up," Kade warned. "You ate too much. That will slow you down when I decide to beat the snot out of you."

"Promises, promises." Luke's hand wave was haphazard. "I'm serious, Poet. I know you don't want to hear it—and I'm loath to admit it —but you're a bit of a prude."

He was trying to irritate me, maybe even push me to the point I considered flashing strangers just to prove him wrong. I'd been dealing with Luke and his shenanigans long enough to recognize when I was being manipulated.

"Maybe you should flash them," I suggested. "Just because the beads hit me in the face doesn't mean they were meant for me. They could've been aiming for you."

Luke glanced over his shoulder, giving the men another look, and then shook his head. "There's no way they're gay."

"How can you possibly know that?"

"I have perfect gaydar."

That was a load of crap. "Do you remember Montana two years ago?"

"Oh, don't even." Luke was firm. "That story is no longer funny. Besides, you can only tell a story for two years before retiring it. I didn't make up that rule. You did, after that really weird beaver shifter you met in Idaho four years ago started gnawing on everything we owned when you dumped him."

"There are beaver shifters?" Kade looked dumbfounded as he sipped his drink. "Is he serious?"

"No," I replied.

"Yes," Luke insisted. "I know just as many embarrassing stories about you as you do about me."

"It's not even a contest," I argued. "You've done far more embarrassing things. I'm a good girl." I said it for Kade's benefit, enjoying the smile that curved his lips.

"You're my good girl," he agreed, flirty intent written all over his face.

"Good grief." Luke looked at Kade with renewed disgust. "You haven't even finished one drink and you're already drunk flirting. Get it together." He gave Kade a hefty thump on the back of the head before turning back to me. "I'm serious, Poet. You need to cut loose. There's no better place to do that than New Orleans."

I stared at him a long time, giving him the impression that I was taking his opinion under advisement. "I'll think about it," I said before turning back to Kade. "Tell me again how I'm your good girl."

"Now you're just doing it to gross me out," Luke complained. "I can't believe how annoying the two of you have gotten. You were supposed to be less schmaltzy after you got engaged. That's the only reason I helped him pick out the ring."

I knew better than that. Despite his bold talk, Luke wanted what was best for me. That included Kade. Before I could respond, two women standing in front of one of the frozen hurricane places started talking in measured tones. Their conversation was far more entertaining.

"I don't like it," the brunette said. She was dressed in a uniform that suggested she worked at the hurricane place, whereas the other woman, a blonde, was dressed in the uniform of the place next door. "The cops say we have nothing to worry about, but when have the police in this town had our best interests at heart?"

I leaned against Kade, my arms wrapped around his waist, and hid my face against his impressive chest so I could listen without the women noticing me.

"Nobody likes it," the blonde agreed. "That doesn't change the fact that they're in charge. You know as well as I do that they're not going to tell us the truth."

"To be fair, how do you think it would go if they went on the news and told the public zombies had broken loose from the cemetery and were hunting in the Quarter?" The brunette gave a hollow laugh as she considered her own question. "Nobody would believe it. What's worse, the people likely to believe it are the crazies. They'd panic, and that wouldn't help anybody."

"I still don't believe that it's just gossip." The blonde planted her hands on her hips. "Lucy at the hardware store swears up and down that three tourists had their throats ripped out by zombies on the riverwalk two nights ago. She said the cops are trying to force them into the river so they'll be washed out to sea and eaten by sharks, but that creates a whole other problem."

"Zombie sharks," the brunette said, nodding sagely. "Yeah, I've heard those stories too. Those bull sharks are mean cusses as it is. I'd hate to see a zombified one."

I rested my chin on Kade's chest and when I looked up I found him staring at me with adoration.

"We should write that script," Luke whispered as he appeared at my back, his chin on my shoulder. "SyFy would be all over zombie sharks."

"What's sad is that I would probably watch it," I admitted.

"Oh, I would watch the crap out of that," Luke agreed. "Smile, you swimming dead fish," he drawled in a fairly good Roy Scheider impression.

"What are they talking about?" Cole asked as he sidled closer.

"Zombies," Kade replied, his hand moving lightly over my back. He was definitely feeling romantic, which meant we would be heading back soon. Romance was better than drunken tourists with beads any day of the week.

"Real zombies?" Cole asked. "Are they serious or trying to be funny?"

"I guess they're being funny," Kade replied. "We would've heard if there was a zombie infestation."

"Not necessarily," Luke countered. "I've watched enough movies to know that people always ignore the initial whispers, wave it off as some sort of hoax. By the time they believe, it's too late. The zombie infestation is unstoppable."

Cole blinked several times and then shook his head, as if dislodging himself from an unpleasant dream. "So, anyway..."

I snorted, delighted in their repartee. Cole hadn't been with us all that long, but I had a difficult time remembering before he was part of our family. "For the record, New Orleans has been home to several zombie infestations over the years."

"I think we would've heard if there was one breaking out now," Cole said. "We all have contacts in the area. Someone would've let us know."

"Yeah." I tapped my fingers in time to the person playing plastic buckets down the street. "It's interesting to think about. I've never been part of a full-on zombie invasion."

"Wait, is that a real thing?" Kade's face had whitened. "Tell me that's not a real thing."

I patted his cheek. "Sorry to be the bearer of bad news."

He closed his eyes and made his "I sucked ten lemons" face. "I'm going to have nightmares."

I snickered at his horror. "Just because they're hearing rumors about zombies doesn't mean the stories are true," I reassured him. "This is New Orleans. Zombies are part of the voodoo culture. You hear stories about zombies all the time."

"And vampires," Cole added. "Everybody who has ever visited New Orleans has a vampire story."

"Yes, but most of those are made up," I pointed out. "All of the real vampires fled once Ann Rice wrote that book. They didn't want to be associated with it."

"You guys are totally freaking me out." Kade was morose when he tossed his empty cup into the garbage receptacle. "Poet. I'll never get to sleep if you don't spend some time tuckering me out."

A giggle erupted and then I blew out a sigh. I finished my drink and then threw the cup into the receptacle along with his. "We can call it a night. We have the rest of the week here. Let's go home so I can make you feel better."

"Oh, don't phrase it like that," Kade complained. "We'll make each other feel better."

I nodded. "We can go for beignets in the morning."

His smile, like his eyes, was soft. "That can be arranged."

"Ugh, you guys are so lame," Luke complained. "We're not going back. We're nowhere near done."

I waved my goodbyes. "Then I guess we'll see you in the morning. Keep your eyes open for zombies."

"We will," Cole said as he waved back. "Have fun being lame-os."

Five

Romance was the name of the game when we got back to our trailer, and when it was time to fall asleep I slid under with ease. He wanted to tire me out, and it worked.

When I woke the next morning, I knew he was awake. He sighed in his sleep—something he accused me of doing as well—so when I rolled to him, I wasn't surprised to find him tapping away on his phone.

"Morning," he said without looking in my direction.

"Morning."

He typed something and then finally turned to me, smile at the ready. "How did you sleep?"

"Pretty well."

"Yeah?"

I nodded. "Your evil plan to wear me out to the point I fell asleep against my will worked."

He became the picture of innocence. "I have no idea what you're talking about."

I laughed. "It's okay to worry about me."

"I can't help it," he said after a moment. "I love you."

"I love you."

"I saw your face during dinner. I don't like thinking about what it must've been like for you to find out the one person who took care of you, the one person left in your family, was giving you away."

I rested my hand on his bare chest. "That's not how it went down."

"No?"

"He took care of me in the immediate aftermath of the accident. He moved into the house and cooked me dinner. He helped me sort through their belongings. He didn't tell me until the day the social worker was due to pick me up that things were changing."

Outrage washed over Kade's face. "He just dropped that on you like a bomb?"

I shrugged. "That's one way of looking at it. The other way is that he saved me from spending a week freaking out. He gave me one last week in my home. I found out when I was near the end of my stay at the group home that the day he informed them he wasn't going to take custody that procedure would've had them taking me right then and not letting me pack anything I wanted. He went out of his way to go back to the house with me and sort through things. He made sure I understood the importance of packing light without telling me why it was important."

"I'm going to punch him," Kade muttered. "I'm just going to punch him in his stupid face."

For some reason, his outrage made me feel better. "Kade, you don't know that things would've worked out if he'd kept me. I don't remember him being a responsible adult. He liked to carouse, and I distinctly remember my father joking about him sleeping around. I didn't know what those jokes meant at the time, but I remember them.

"It's possible things would've been worse with him," I continued. "What would've happened if he'd started drinking and bringing women home? What would've happened if he spent two years with me and then walked away? It was better that it happened when I was already in shock from losing my parents."

"No." A muscle worked in his jaw. "That's not how I see it. He was supposed to do the right thing by you. You were the child. He should've gotten his life together and provided what you needed."

"Maybe he wasn't capable of that. It's not as if he abandoned me and went out and had a bunch of kids. I think he did the best he could."

"And I think I'm going to punch him." Kade slipped his arm under my waist and tugged me on top of him. His fingers were gentle as he scooped my dark hair from my face. "I know I can't go back and save Little Poet. I also know that if things had played out differently we likely wouldn't be here together. But I'm not okay with him abandoning you."

"You can't change it," I pointed out. "All that anger you're hoarding like gold won't make things better. It's wasted energy."

He lifted his head from the pillow and pressed his forehead to mine. "I'm still going to punch him."

"We'll see how it plays out." I pressed a kiss to his lips. "I will say that my childhood taught me one important thing."

"What's that?"

"When we have kids we're going to have a guardianship in place right from the start."

"That's fine, and I agree it's smart, but I'm not worried about our kids ending up in the system if something terrible happens. Cole and Luke will take them. They might learn a few bad habits from Luke, but we wouldn't have to worry about them being loved."

"Oh, they'll definitely be loved," I agreed. "I want to make sure that it's set in stone, though. That means talking to Luke and Cole."

"Do you really think they'd say no?"

"Of course not, but it's different to say, 'Hey, will you take care of some kid I have in the future?' than sitting down after the child is a reality and saying, 'This is what's going to happen if we both die.' I want to be prepared."

Kade nodded. "Luke and Cole will step up. I don't have a single doubt about that. And Max is still around."

"Don't forget Nellie and Raven," I teased. "They could film that configuration for a reality show."

"It's going to be okay." He wrapped his arms around me even tighter. "We'll talk to them, because I want to make sure things are in place when it's time. Just for the record, I plan on living a very long life with you. There will be no dying early, for either of us."

I rested my ear on his beating heart. "Ten minutes of this before we get up?"

He nodded. "Ten more minutes. Then I want to try these beignets you've been raving about."

"I can't believe you've never tried them."

"I'm looking forward to you introducing me to a million new things over the course of our lives."

"Sounds like a great plan."

WE DROVE TO CAFE DU MONDE to get enough beignets for the entire group. When we returned, we found Raven making eggs and hash browns with Naida and Nixie.

"We got beignets," I whined.

Raven arched an eyebrow. "Not all of us want to start our day with refined sugar as our main food group."

"Speak for yourself," Luke said as he swooped in to take the box from me. "Refined sugar is the gift that keeps giving."

Raven pinned him with a dark look. They had a unique relationship, one that usually resulted in them sniping at one another for kicks.

"If I'd known you were going to cook, we would've walked there and enjoyed a romantic breakfast, just the two of us," I groused.

"We're not your babysitters," Raven pointed out. "If you want to play Powder My Doughnut with your boyfriend, there's nothing stopping you."

Now it was my turn to glare. "Don't be gross!"

"I'm with Luke," Nellie said, even though nobody had asked his opinion. "Refined sugar is the way to go. Of course, I won't say no to the eggs and hash browns. I'm an equal-opportunity eater as long as I'm not the one cooking."

"Yes, it's delightful that you're such a misogynist," I said, landing a light slap on the back of his head. "Did anything happen last night?" I decided to change the subject as I moved to the picnic tables. They'd erected umbrellas over the tables to protect them from the sun and inevitable afternoon downpour. "I forgot to ask when we got home last night."

"That's because you were playing Come Get My Gumbo," Nellie said on a wicked grin. "Don't bother denying it," he added when I frowned. "We all saw you come in. You made a beeline straight for your trailer, and we all know what you were doing."

I slid my eyes to Kade and found him smirking. "It's not funny," I complained. "I told you they'd know."

"They're not twelve," Kade argued. "I'm pretty sure they know we have sex."

"I didn't know," Seth the tiger shifter said. "I'll be scarred for life."

"Don't go there," I warned as I sat at one of the tables. "We need to be careful. We can't erect the dreamcatcher here. The fence is nice, but it doesn't offer full protection. I don't want anybody getting complacent."

"Then maybe you shouldn't be juggling Kade's jambalaya every night," Luke suggested. "If you're that worried, you guys should spend the night walking the property to make sure we're safe."

"Stop with the sexual food references," I ordered.

"Oh, there's no stopping us now," Luke noted. "You know that as well as I do."

I turned an imploring look to Cole, but he didn't appear to be taking my side. "Hey, I don't care if you want to be creeping Kade's crawfish every night," he started.

"Oh, geez," I grumbled. Kade laughed as he rubbed my back.

"I am curious about why we can't erect the dreamcatcher here," Cole said, turning serious. "New Orleans is exactly the sort of city where we need the dreamcatcher. It draws in evil paranormals. How is that not necessary here?"

"It's exactly because of that," Raven replied. "This city is teeming with paranormals. Most of them aren't evil. They come here to embrace the openness. We'll be overrun if we use the dreamcatcher. We learned that the hard way long before this trip."

"She's right," I said. "It was about five years ago when we last tried. We had seventy alerts in one night."

"We need our beauty rest," Luke added.

Cole's mouth dropped open. "Seventy?"

"In one night," I confirmed. "It's a high tourist area, too. Not all of the humans are good people. The dreamcatcher is out."

"That's not good." Cole dragged a hand through his hair. "Have you ever had any big problems here?"

I shook my head. "There's always going to be minor issues to grapple with wherever we go. The voodoo people keep the city in check for the most part. This is their turf, and we cede it to them as long as we're not in danger. It works for all parties concerned."

"Okay. You're the boss." Cole winked at me. "That gives you and Kade more time to bang your Bananas Foster."

I wanted to wrap my fingers around his throat and squeeze. "Luke has been a terrible influence on you."

"I think he's fun."

I was determined to change the subject. "Don't forget that the humidity is debilitating in the afternoons. Storms pop up almost daily. On days like today—set-up days—it's better to get as much work done as possible before noon."

"Thanks, Mom," Nellie said dryly.

I ignored him. "One more thing." I was hesitant to bring this up because I knew how they would respond, but I was in charge. "Last night on Bourbon Street, we heard two locals talking. They believe zombies are on the loose."

Everybody around the table started giggling.

I kept my face impassive. "I know true zombie infestations are rare, but this is New Orleans. Be on the lookout."

"What are the odds that a zombie infestation would break out here just as we arrived?" Nellie asked.

I held up my hands in supplication. "I just want everybody to be careful."

"We'll be careful." Luke, powdered sugar all over his face, reached for another beignet. "We know how to do our jobs, Poet. You don't have to worry about us."

"I know. I just thought I should tell you. Have fun laughing about me being a worrywart."

"We always do," Luke reassured me. "Now, eat your beignets." He shoved one in my face. "It's New Orleans. Have fun for a change. It's your favorite city."

I bit into the beignet. I was overreacting, as usual. There was nothing to worry about.

So why is your stomach so tight? an internal voice said. *If you believe nothing is truly wrong, why can't you relax?*

AFTER BREAKFAST, I WALKED WITH Cole to survey the midway booths. Louis Armstrong Park's pathways and water features meant the booths were more spread out than we were used to. This was Cole's first time in charge of the midway, which brought in most of our money.

"Are we sure this is going to work?" he asked as we checked a few of the gaming booths.

"It will be fine," I reassured him, shooting Stan Opdike a warning look when he appeared next to the balloon booth. He was a longtime midway worker, and he looked as if he was about to make trouble. "Everybody knows what they're doing when it comes to the games. They won't be a problem. Isn't that right, Stan?"

He blinked several times, his face impassive, and then lifted one shoulder. "I don't know about anybody else, but I'm good." He shot Cole a deliberate look. "We had a boss who knew what he was doing. Now we don't. That might cause some problems."

He was clearly spoiling for a fight. I was on edge, Sidney's appearance in my life and the zombie whispers combining to agitate me, so I was more than happy to comply with his wishes. "Do you have a problem, Stan?"

"Of course I do." He didn't waste time lobbing complaints. "You might not have liked Mark —and from your perspective I truly do get it, because he was a bit of a turd—but he understood the business side of things. Now we're flying blind with a guy who has never done this."

I slid my eyes to Cole, curious about how he would respond. To my surprise, he didn't look angry. It was resignation—and maybe a little something else I couldn't identify—I found waiting there.

"I plan on having a sit-down with you guys tomorrow," Cole offered. "I know you're concerned. I don't blame you. I have no track record running the midway, but I'm not a complete and total ninny. I want your input. I want to improve working conditions. I want you guys to have a say."

Stan was taken aback. "We're going to run the midway by committee now?"

"Not exactly." Cole managed a brief smile. "There are things I want to improve. There are things we're doing that I don't feel are necessary. As you pointed out, I'm new at this. I want you guys to have a say in how things will be run. I will have the final say, but I won't ignore you."

Stan stood there for a beat and then looked to me. "Is he for real? Mark didn't care what we thought."

"There's a reason Mark's gone," I said. "I wasn't the only one who had a problem with his attitude. All I'm asking is that you give this a try. You might be pleasantly surprised."

Stan rubbed his thumb over his bottom lip and nodded. "Okay. I'm not saying I like this, but I'll talk to the others. We'll sit down and talk to you tomorrow." He gave Cole a wary glance. "Please tell me you're not bringing Luke to the meeting."

Cole chuckled. "That's not on the agenda. I'll keep him away."

"Good. That guy is...a lot of work."

"Try living with him."

That earned a genuine smile from Stan. "You must be some sort of saint."

"I must be," Cole agreed.

I left them to continue chatting—small talk couldn't possibly hurt at this point—and turned to scan the other side of the park. The water served as a divider, and while there were several workers erecting booths across the way, things were relatively quiet.

Still, despite the fact that everything was open, the hair on the back of my neck stood on end. It felt as if someone was watching me. I turned in a circle, extending my magic as I went looking for a source. I didn't find one, but the unease continued through my belly. "That went well," Cole said as he slung an arm around my shoulders.

I forced my eyes to him. "Better than could be expected given the circumstances."

"I think this will work. I'll sit down with them, explain my plans, and listen to what they have to say. They know the business well. I'm sure they can teach me a lot."

"That's more than Mark ever did for them."

"Mark was a jerk."

"They'll forget he was ever part of the team before you know it. They'll be loyal to you."

"I hope so. Let's just take it one step at a time."

"Yeah." I flicked my eyes to the fence as we moved through the park. I couldn't make out anyone watching. Why did I feel like I was missing something?

Six

T hings were well in hand as far as setup went—Kade and Luke jockeyed for bragging rights on who was stronger, which had them both shirtless and toiling hard—so I decided to take a walk and leave them to their mindless competition.

"When they're done posturing, tell them I won't be gone long," I instructed Nellie, who was in a sunny dress and sipping water in the shade beneath the umbrellas. "If a storm rolls through, don't forget to take the umbrellas down."

He shot me a withering look. "Do I look slow?"

"Is that a trick question?"

His eyes flashed with annoyance. "Just out of curiosity, where are you going?"

I could've lied. He would've likely believed anything I told him. My fascination with New Orleans was well known. I often took off just to walk the Quarter. I didn't bother with a lie today. "I'm heading to voodoo central."

"Is this about the zombies?"

"I know you guys think I'm ridiculous, but I think it's a good idea to touch base with our allies."

"Uh-huh." Nellie's brow furrowed. "I didn't ask before because I didn't figure it was any of my business but how was dinner with your uncle?"

"It was fine."

He waited.

"It was a good meal," I added. "He brought his girlfriend."

"Wow. Could you be any less enthusiastic?"

"I don't know how I feel." That was the truth. "It was a good meal. Nothing more."

"Okay, well, if you need someone to talk to who doesn't constantly flex while shirtless, you know where to find me."

It was a sweet offer. "Thanks. Right now, I just want to hang out with some old friends."

"Madame Caroline?"

He knew me well. "She's funny."

"And she makes her own moonshine. What's not to like about homemade moonshine?"

"Nothing in my book. I won't be long. Tell them I'll be back in plenty of time for lunch. They probably won't even notice I'm gone."

Nellie snorted. "Please. Once Kade decides he's thirsty you'll be the only thing on his mind. I'll make sure he knows that the only thing you're in danger of crossing paths with is a hangover."

"Thank you." I patted his shoulder. "I just want some time alone with her."

"Of course you do. She's like a mother figure to you. You adopt men much easier than you do women. That makes her special."

I cocked my head, considering. "I make friends with women," I said. "I love Naida and Nixie. Heck, I love Raven, too, but if you tell her I said so I'll set you on fire."

He chuckled. "I'm not saying you don't like women. You obviously do. You don't have a mother figure. Max is your father figure, which is weird when you think about it because you're marrying his son."

"Don't go there," I warned.

He continued as if he hadn't heard me. "You have this mysterious uncle who popped up out of the woodwork. Your best friend is a dude. Heck, all three of your best friends are dudes. You love me more than anybody." He let loose a saucy wink. "You just bond easier with men. There's nothing wrong with it."

I hated to admit it—he had no idea how much I hated it—but he was right. "I'm going to ignore this entire conversation," I said. "Keep watch over them." I hesitated and then said the rest. "If anything weird happens, I won't be that far away. Don't hesitate to send out an SOS."

"Like...if zombies attack in the middle of the day?"

"Just call me if anything big goes down. Otherwise, Kade is in charge. Do what he says."

"Yeah, when I tell the story, I'm going to be in charge."

"Whatever floats your boat."

MADAME CAROLINE'S HOUSE OF SHADOWS was on Governor Nicholas Street, one block east of the LaLaurie Mansion. I opted for a route that took me down Royal Street, my favorite street in the Quarter, and was smiling as I let myself into the store.

Rather than wind chimes or bells, Madame Caroline had strung together bones above the door, and they clacked together to tell her she had a customer. When she emerged from the back room, her eyes were already on me, her lips curved in greeting.

"Well, I was wondering if you were going to stop in and see your old friend," she said as she wiped her hands on a brown rag. "When I heard you were going to be in town I figured I'd see you right away. You arrived yesterday but didn't come to see me. I had libations ready."

I smiled as I cut through the store. "Sorry. I had an important dinner I had to attend."

"Let me guess. Luke decided he wanted to eat his weight in crawfish."

"You're not far off." I leaned over the counter. "I'm glad to see you."

"Yes, I'm a delight," she readily agreed as she tucked a strand of her gray hair behind her ear. She kept most of her head covered by a scarf. When I first met her, I thought it was part of a costume. Now I realized it was just her. She liked decking herself out in as much color as possible. "Are you ready for some day drinking?"

I glanced at the clock on the wall. The hands were also made of bone. "It's more like morning drinking."

She shrugged. "Does it matter?"

"I guess not." I hopped on one of the stools she kept close to the counter and glanced around the shop as she poured. "I see very little has changed."

"I'm not big on change." She slid a mason jar in front of me, amber liquid sloshing inside. She wasn't the type for fancy garnishes. The moonshine spoke for itself. "I see a lot has changed with you." She nodded to my engagement ring. "Please tell me you haven't decided to give up on love and marry Luke. I know you're fond of him, but he can't give you what you need."

I laughed. She had an interesting relationship with Luke. Much like Raven, she enjoyed messing with him. He gave as good as he got, so their interactions were often loud. Deep down, I believed Luke and Madame Caroline liked one another. "His name is Kade. He's Max's son."

Madame Caroline's eyebrows drew together as she hopped on the stool next to me. "I guess I didn't know Max had a son."

"I didn't either. That lack of knowledge turned into an argument when Max dropped Kade in our laps last year as the new head of security. Kade didn't know about magic, even though he's magical. I was furious because Kade thought he was in charge. We fought hard those first few days."

"And now you're engaged." Madame Caroline's eyes sparkled. "Well, that is just divine. I want to hear the whole story."

I obliged her. Nellie was right, she was like a mother figure. I'd never realized it before but becoming aware of it changed nothing about our relationship. "So, that's it," I said when finishing the tale. "We haven't set a date yet, but we know where we're going to land in a year when we stop traveling."

"Wow. That's a lot." She sipped her moonshine. "Please tell me you'll still visit."

"Oh, yeah." I bobbed my head. "I've already told Kade we need to come here at least once a year. It's only a three-hour flight from Moonstone Bay. He's fine with it, although he would prefer we leave Luke at home when traveling."

Madame Caroline snorted. "Oh, is Luke getting on his nerves? I'm shocked."

One didn't need to be an expert on sarcasm to gauge her response. "They get along...for the most part. Luke irritates him, and Kade has to set ground rules. Things are better now that Luke has found a boyfriend."

She made a face. "What masochist hitched his wagon to Luke?"

"His name is Cole. I'm extremely fond of him. Half the time I go to him to complain instead of Luke or Kade."

"So, it's like a happy quadrangle."

"Yes, except nobody is swapping partners."

"Hmm. That probably works." She clinked her mason jar against mine and took another drink. "How is everything else?"

I knew she'd picked up on my anxiety even though I hadn't said a word about what was bothering me. She was good like that, one of the reasons I loved spending time with her.

"That dinner last night," I hedged. "The important one I mentioned. That was with my uncle."

"Your father's brother?"

I nodded. "He tracked down my address in Florida. I asked last night how, but his answer must've got lost in all the male posturing. Kade, Luke and Cole went with me, so it was hardly a relaxed dinner. Anyway, Sidney sent me a letter. He discovered our schedule for the year and saw we were going to be in New Orleans. He travels for business too and was going to be here, so he asked if we could have dinner."

"Didn't it go well?"

I hesitated. "It's not like there was a big fight. He brought his girl-friend. I had my entourage. Luke and Cole were kind of grumpy. Kade was just standoffish. It was uncomfortable but not to the point of being painful."

"Then what's the problem?"

I held out my hands. "I don't know that there is a problem. It's not as if he wants to set up regular phone calls or anything. He said he just wanted to make sure I was okay. I guess he tried to track me down through Child Protective Services in Michigan. When he found out I disappeared from the system he freaked out."

"He felt guilty," she surmised.

"I think there's some guilt there," I acknowledged. "He pretty much said so. He apologized for leaving, for not being strong enough to raise me. I accepted his apology."

"And yet you're troubled."

"He might feel guilt, but not regret. I'm positive he believes he made the right decision. And looking back, I have to believe he did."

"But?"

"But nothing. I'm not even sure where we stand. Nobody is screaming or pointing fingers. On the flip side, we're not suddenly family or anything. He's my uncle, but he doesn't have a place in my heart. The place he once occupied was filled by others long ago."

"Do you think he realizes that?"

"Yeah. He was surprised when I brought Kade, Luke and Cole. He adjusted fast, and when it was over I think he was relieved. He doesn't have to imagine me curled in a ball and living in a box any longer. He knows I'm not starving, that I'm not alone. He can go on with his life without looking back."

"Can you?"

"I never look back."

"Oh, that's a load of crap." She let loose a harsh chuckle. "I've never met anyone as obsessed with the past as you."

"I'm not obsessed with the past."

"Fine, you're not obsessed with the past. You spend oodles of time wondering what could've been. That's who you are. It's not necessarily a bad thing."

The more this topic progressed, the more uncomfortable I felt. "Can we talk about something else?"

"Of course. We can talk about your uncle again before you go. I get the feeling you're still digesting."

"Great." I had no intention of dwelling on Sidney. "So, we were on Bourbon Street last night," I started.

"Never a solid start to a story," she drawled.

I continued as if I hadn't heard her. "Two women who worked in different bars were talking. They said there's a zombie infestation and the police are trying to cover it up."

"Is that what they said?" Madame Caroline gave a derisive snort. "I love when zombie rumors start spreading across the Quarter. They're always entertaining."

"I take that to mean you don't believe zombies are on the loose."

"Have you seen any zombies since you've been here?"

"No, but that doesn't necessarily mean anything. We had dinner and then spent all of our time on Bourbon Street so Kade could gawk. The zombies could've been in Jackson Square for the evening."

Her laughter ratcheted up a notch. "Oh, you're so funny. Do you want to know what I think?"

"Probably not."

She continued anyway. "I think that you want a magical problem to focus on because that's easier than sorting out your complicated feelings about your uncle. Fake zombies are easier to dwell on than a real uncle you've spent the better part of your life hating."

"We don't know they're fake zombies."

"What about the very real uncle hate?"

I held out my hands on a grimace. "I wasn't lying when I said I didn't know how to feel about Sidney. I don't hate him. The bitterness I felt as a kid has dissipated. I'm not saying I love him, but I don't hate him."

"It would be okay if you did. He abandoned you."

"I was never his responsibility."

"We'll have to agree to disagree on that one. Here in New Orleans, you take care of family whether you birthed them or not. It's just what's done."

I let loose a throaty chuckle. "You sound like Cole."

"I can't wait to meet him."

"I'll arrange for you to meet him and Kade. I just needed a bit of air this morning. Kade and Luke had their shirts off and were competing to see which is manlier."

"Is that the only reason you took off on your own?"

I hated that she could read me so well. "I might've felt something when touring the park with Cole this morning."

"Like what?"

"Like...eyes. I felt someone watching me. When I reached out with my magic, I came up empty."

"But you're still convinced someone was there."

"Yeah."

She nodded. "Well, if you believe it, I believe it. I can't get behind the notion it was zombies. If we did have an infestation, they wouldn't spend their time hiding in the bushes and watching you work."

"I know." I rubbed my cheek and took another sip of the moonshine. "This tastes peachier than usual."

"It's a new recipe. I'm thinking of adding some blueberries to the mix, too."

"Ooh." I brightened at the suggestion. "I love blueberries."

"Then I'll definitely do it." Her eyes were stern when they locked with mine. "I'll also be here when you want to talk about your uncle, even when you leave town. You have my phone number."

"I'm really not stressing out about Sidney. Nobody believes me, but it's true. He's almost a non-entity."

"I think you're making up zombies in your head rather than dealing with him, but it's not my place to judge."

"When has that ever stopped you?"

She laughed so hard I was afraid she'd fall off her stool. "Oh, I love you." She swiped at her cheeks. "Put your mind at rest about the zombies. If there was an infestation I would've heard about it. Two waitresses on Bourbon Street gabbing doesn't make for a legitimate infestation."

She was right. "Tell me about your life," I prodded. "Are you still warring with the other voodoo queens?"

"Always. They're absolute pains in my posterior."

"I want to hear all the stories."

"Strap in. I've got some doozies."

I needed a break from worrying about zombies. "Lay it on me."

Madame Caroline did just that for the next hour. When it was time to leave for the park I was still smiling. I'd promised to pick a time to bring Kade and Cole by so she could size them up—and Luke so she could torture him—but it was getting late enough that my stomach was lodging lunch complaints.

Once on the street, the strange sensation that I was being watched returned with a vengeance. I snapped up my chin, determined to find the source, and discovered a man leaning against the building across the street.

He was Black, gray makeup streaking his face, and a cigar hanging from his mouth. His top hat was ragged and decked out with bone enhancements, and his purple jacket was frayed at the elbows.

I recognized him straight away. Or, I recognized who he was dressed as.

Baron Samedi, the loa of the dead. Loas are very big in voodoo culture, and Baron Samedi was my favorite. I'd read all about him after seeing some of the street art in Bywater during my last visit.

"Hello," I called out before realizing I was going to greet him. "It's a nice day."

When he smiled, his teeth were jarringly white. "It is, isn't it?"

"Are you conducting loa business?"

He bobbed his head and kept his unreadable gaze on me.

"Well, have a nice day."

"You too."

I turned my back on him but couldn't stop myself from glancing over my shoulder after a few steps. He was still there, still watching. I finally had to force my eyes away.

He was just a man, I told myself. He was dressed as Baron Samedi to make a quick buck off the tourists. Then why was I so unnerved?

Seven

Kade and Luke were back in their shirts by the time I returned to the park.

Kade pulled me in for a hug, his eyes searching mine. "Nellie said you went to see your therapist. Are you okay?"

I made a face and immediately started searching for Nellie. "I didn't see my therapist. I went to see Madame Caroline. She's a friend."

"Which is what I told him," Luke offered as he appeared at my side. "I need lunch."

"Just a second." Kade planted his hand in the middle of Luke's face and gave him an unfriendly shove. "You can wait two minutes."

Luke's annoyance was palpable. "I'll beat the crap out of you if you ever do that again. Now I need to fix my hair. You have two minutes to do...whatever this is...and then we're going. I will die if I'm not fed in the next forty-five minutes. You've been warned."

I didn't bother to hide my smile as he stomped off. "I take it you won the competition to see who was faster at setting up," I said.

"Was that ever in doubt?" Kade's fingers were gentle as they combed my hair from my eyes. "Where were you really?"

"I was visiting Madame Caroline. She owns a voodoo store near the LaLaurie Mansion. I got to know her years ago and stop in whenever

58

we're here. We talked about a million things, including you, and drank some moonshine. It wasn't a big deal."

"Moonshine before lunch?"

His tone made me laugh. "Just one jar. I promised to bring you and Cole around later. She's dying to get to know the masochist living with Luke."

"I can see that." He remained intent. "You're sure you're okay?"

"I'm fine." I meant it. "I'm extremely fond of her. I figured that since you were busy playing with Luke that it would be okay if I headed out on my own."

"I don't *play* with Luke." His eyes lit with haughty defiance. "I never play with him. I beat him handily. I do play with you." He poked my side. "You could've told me you were going."

"You were busy."

"You wanted to visit your friend and gossip without having to worry about anybody eavesdropping."

He wasn't wrong. "Let's just say I had fun and leave it at that. I'm ready for lunch. I could totally go for some creole."

He kissed my forehead and released me. "Lunch sounds nice. We're way ahead of schedule. Anywhere specific in mind?"

"I was thinking we could go to one of the restaurants near Jackson Square, one with a balcony."

"I can live with that."

I turned and started searching for Luke. "Where is the king of the haircut?"

Kade chuckled. "Let's just message Cole and have them meet us. That way we don't have to track them down."

WE SETTLED ON TABLEAU, CHOOSING a table on the balcony with a clear view of Jackson Square. I went all out and ordered the duck gumbo and Maison salad. Luke, who refused to eat anything that quacked, indulged in the ribeye, while Kade and Cole selected shrimp and grits.

Once our food was delivered, talk turned to the view.

"What happens over there?" Kade inclined his chin in the direction of the Square. "That's the same area we passed this morning when we were getting the beignets, but the gates are open now."

"It's basically a park," I replied. "There are benches inside."

"Yeah, but what's happening in the courtyard? There are a bunch of people gathered around the area right in front of the Square." He pointed so there could be no confusion.

"It's kind of like a market," I replied.

"A flea market," Luke corrected, his nose wrinkled in such a manner there could be no debate as to how he felt about flea markets.

I jabbed a finger at him. "Don't be you," I warned. "Artists sell paintings and drawings. Some do caricatures while you sit there. Other people read tarot cards. Some play music. There's a hodgepodge."

Kade looked surprisingly interested. "Can we wander around after eating? This whole area was empty when we walked through it this morning."

I bobbed my head. "I love the Square. I wouldn't mind hitting up the fudge place on the far corner before we head back. I love eating fudge in bed at night."

"Sweets for my sweet?" Kade teased.

"Ugh. I really hate you," Luke complained.

"Get over it." Kade was used to Luke's moods. "I can see why you like New Orleans," he said as he slipped his arm around my shoulders. "It's eclectic."

"It's amazing," I agreed.

"These are your type of people."

"We'll visit yearly," I said. "I promised Madame Caroline we would. We can look forward to it as a break."

"Speaking of Madame Caroline, how is the old crone?" Luke drawled.

"She's great. She's been adding peaches to her moonshine and the result is divine. You can taste for yourself when we drop in for another visit. I promised I would bring Cole and Kade by, and she even wants to see you."

Luke wasn't subtle with his eye roll. "I'll pass."

"You don't get to pass."

"And yet I'm in charge of me and I say I'll pass. Funny how that works."

"He'll come, whether he likes it or not," Cole promised. "I'll make sure of it."

I shot Luke a smug smile, which he didn't accept with anything even slightly akin to grace.

"You haven't met her," Luke insisted to his boyfriend. "She's horrible. She makes fun of me."

"Now I really want to meet her." Cole leaned back in his chair and stretched out his long legs. "Don't be a whiner. I bet she's interesting. She would have to be for Poet to sneak away and visit the way she did."

I bristled. "I didn't sneak away."

"Nellie said she considers Madame Caroline a mother figure and wanted to gossip about us," Kade volunteered. "I don't think it was meant to be a slight."

"Oh, I'm going to hurt Nellie so bad," I muttered.

"Now I'm definitely looking forward to meeting her," Cole enthused. "Poet doesn't make friends with women. She must be something special."

It was time to rethink my life choices. I apparently had an attitude with women and didn't even realize it. "Let's just eat and then head over to the Square. I'm done having my life analyzed today."

"Sure. We can wait until you're full of fudge to analyze you again," Cole said. "That promises to be all kinds of fun."

Yup, I was definitely over it.

THE HUMIDITY HAD SET IN LIKE A SOAKED BLANKET by the time we'd finished lunch, ruling out hand-holding as we circled the Square's outer area. Normally I might be bothered by that, but it was too hot to care today.

"Whew, baby," Cole said as he fanned his face. "I'm not used to this. I feel like I'm in a really hot shower."

"Right?" Luke's eyes flashed. "I don't get Poet's fascination with this place. I like to drink as much as the next person, but after two nights Bourbon Street loses its appeal, and everything grows tiresome."

"You focus on the drinking," I argued. "I focus on the culture."

"Yes, you're a high-society gal," Luke agreed dryly. "Seriously, this place is like a sweaty armpit sometimes. It grosses me out."

"You'll survive."

"You'll survive." He mimicked my voice before turning to Cole. "Do you want to get our fortunes read?"

"Poet reads fortunes," Cole pointed out. "If you want your fortune read, why not just ask her?"

"Because she tells the truth. I want a fake who will tell me I'm going to be rich and famous."

"Then you should've just said so." Cole winked at me. "I think we're going to get our fortunes read. Are you guys sticking around?"

"We're going to finish the circle," I replied. "I want to take Kade across the road to see the riverwalk."

"Okay. We'll just meet you back at the park if we get separated."

"Sounds like a plan," Kade said as he bumped fists with Cole.

I pressed my lips together at the male gesture and then shook my head as Kade and I started across the Square. "That fist-bumping is such a man thing. It's all kinds of weird."

"You just don't get the nuance," Kade said. "There's a reason fist-bumping is so popular."

"It's nuanced?"

"A million emotions can be conveyed depending on how you bang knuckles."

"If you say so." We reached Decatur Street. "They have horse-drawn carriage tours," I noted.

Kade followed my gaze. "Is that something you want to do?"

"Luke and I have done it three times. I'm good, but if you want to go I won't put up a fight."

He cocked his head, considering. "If we do it, I want to go in the morning or at dusk. It's too hot in the middle of the day."

"I can live with that. Come on." I urged him to cross the street. We sidestepped the line at Cafe du Monde and kept going up the steps. When we reached the top, I breathed in the fresh river air and then slid my eyes to Kade. "Pretty, huh?"

He nodded, his lips curving. "This is the Mississippi River?"

"Yeah."

"It's really cool." We moved to the railing to enjoy the view. "I thought New Orleans was on the Gulf of Mexico."

"It is, but you have to follow the Mississippi around to get to it."

"I guess I always pictured the city looking out on the gulf."

"The river is better."

"How so?"

"I like the energy of it." My eyes slid to the left when I caught a hint of movement out of the corner of my eye. A man who appeared drunk stumbled along the riverwalk. "The only thing I dislike about New Orleans is the humidity. It does get oppressive in the middle of the afternoon."

"We're going to have to learn to deal with the same humidity when we move to Moonstone Bay."

"I know, but it's somehow different when you're living on a tropical island with sandy beaches."

"True. I...what is that guy doing?"

A quick glance told me Kade was looking in the direction of the riverwalk. The man who had garnered my interest seconds before was moving in on a couple as they snapped photos of themselves in front of the river. "He's probably panhandling," I said just as the man lunged at them.

I reacted without thinking, running toward the couple. I couldn't watch a mugging take place and do nothing about it. The woman screamed as I drew closer, and I grabbed the back of the man's collar in an attempt to pull him back. He was foaming at the mouth and snapping his jaw.

"What the...?"

"He tried to bite me!" the woman screeched, holding up her arm for proof. There wasn't a mark on her but that didn't stop her from carrying on as if death—or at least permanent disfigurement—was imminent.

Kade pushed the couple to the side as I adjusted my grip on the man's collar. His teeth were broken in several places, and a thin film covered his eyes.

"What's wrong with him?" Kade demanded as I studied the man's face. He leaned forward and sniffed. "He smells sick."

It wasn't sickness, it was death. "There's no fixing what's ailing him." I held out my left hand in front of the man's face and he immediately snapped at it with his teeth. I was agitated when I pulled it back and turned to Kade. "We have a problem."

"Oh, don't tell me he's a zombie," Kade whined. He already looked resigned to his fate.

"Fine. I won't tell you." I didn't have many options, so I pulsed a burst of magic into the man. In the middle of his snapping fit, he went ramrod straight, his eyes rolling back in his head. When I released him, he tumbled backward onto the ground so hard his head separated from his body.

"Oh, geez." Kade sidestepped the rolling head as the couple I'd forgotten about started making ungodly noises behind us. The woman was screaming, and the man looked to be struggling mightily not to vomit.

"He's dead!" the woman yelled when she'd grown tired of shrieking. "He's tried to eat me, and he's dead!"

Kade's eyes were full of fear. "What did you do?"

"He was a threat. I couldn't release him."

"But now there will be questions about how he died."

I caught sight of a man heading in our direction. He wore a cheap suit—the type of polyester that made Luke melt down when he accidentally brushed against it—and his eyes were focused on us. I knew beyond a shadow of a doubt what we were dealing with. "There are definitely going to be questions," I agreed. "Let me do the talking."

"That's not some random uniform," Kade warned about the approaching officer.

"I've got it."

"He'll want answers that make sense."

"I've got it," I insisted darkly. "Believe it or not, I can handle this."

Kade didn't look as if he did believe it, but he snapped his mouth shut.

"What happened here?" the man demanded.

"I'm not quite sure." I wrung my hands together, feigning discomfort. If I was too calm he would be suspicious. "I just...don't know."

"It's okay, ma'am." His tone was clipped. "I'm Detective Andrew Crowder. Just take your time and tell me what happened. It's okay if you feel faint."

Faint? Ugh, there was little I loathed more than a man who assumed women fainted at the sight of death, but I played the part he wanted me to play. "Thank you. I don't know what happened. We came here to see the river and we noticed that couple." I pointed to the screamer and the cursing man. "They were being loud, and when we looked there that man was moving in on them. I assumed he was trying to mug them and grabbed the back of his shirt."

Crowder held up a finger to still me. "You tried to stop a mugging?"

"It was instinct," I replied. "I wasn't thinking."

Crowder shot Kade an "I can't believe you regularly put up with her" look and then smiled for my benefit. "Please continue."

"There's not much to tell. I grabbed the back of his shirt and noticed there was something wrong with his eyes. They were like white on top of brown. What's the word I'm looking for?"

"Drunk?" Crowder asked.

"Filmy," I replied. "I think he was sick. He acted like he was going to bite me so I kind of pushed him back. The next thing I knew, he hit the ground."

"And his head just popped off?" Crowder looked incredulous.

"I don't know how it happened."

Crowder turned to the still-complaining couple. "Is that what you saw?"

The man nodded. "Pretty much. She was trying to help and she kind of shoved him away. Then he hit the ground." He pointed to the mess that was the body.

"Lovely." Crowder planted his hands on his hips. "I can't wait to explain this to my lieutenant."

"Can we go?" the man asked. "This is ruining our vibe."

"No, you can't go," Crowder snapped. "I need to hear this story again, from the top. After that, I'll tell you when you can go."

"We didn't do anything," the woman whimpered. "We were just taking photos by the river."

"Well, now you're answering questions about a dead guy." Crowder was blasé. "You can spare ten minutes for a man who lost his life, can't you?"

The woman was petulant. "It's so gross."

I glanced at Kade. His expression was unreadable.

"We'll answer questions," I volunteered. "We don't have anything to add, but I would like to get this over. I'm feeling a bit queasy."

"That's normal for a woman when she's been through a trauma," Crowder explained. "I won't push you too hard."

It took everything I had not to explode at him.

Eight

"What was that?" Kade asked when Crowder finally let us go.

"What was what?" I wiped my hands on my capris and then swiped my forearm across my forehead. The heat and humidity were brutal. "We should go to the store."

He frowned. "What was that act you just put on for him? That's not like you, acting like an innocent dimwit. You usually put your brains on display when the police question you."

I rolled my neck until it cracked. "What was I supposed to do?" I asked. "There was nothing I could tell him that made sense. It was better to play dumb."

"But that was a zombie?"

I expected the question, but not for him to ask it so loudly. "Kade." I grabbed his arm and tugged him away from the crowd, not stopping until we were in the shadow of one of the corner trees in Jackson Square. "You need to be careful."

"It's New Orleans. If somebody asks why I dropped the Z-word I'll just say I'm drunk. Nobody will bat an eyelash."

I hated that he had a point. "It *was* a zombie," I hissed, my eyes drifting to the right when I heard Luke's voice. He and Cole were talking to a gentleman selling his art. "I'm not sure what kind. It's not as if using my magic to scan him was possible given where we were and how many people were around."

Genuine puzzlement washed over Kade's features. "There's more than one kind?"

"Yup."

"Well, crap." He dragged a hand through his damp hair. He'd been letting it grow longer. When he first joined Mystic Caravan, he kept his hair much shorter. It fit his rigid, by-the-rules personality then. Now he was calmer, coming into his own. His hair seemed to be following suit. "What are we going to do?"

"We're going to stop at a store, get stuff for dinner, and talk to our people. That's what we always do."

"I thought you wanted to eat out when we were here. That's what you kept saying."

"One group meal won't hurt." I looked back to the riverwalk, where the coroner's office was collecting the body and Crowder was talking to anybody who passed. "We can't ignore this. Where there's one, there's bound to be more."

He nodded, his fingers moving to my cheek. "I'm sorry that this is happening."

The apology surprised me. "It's not your fault."

"You wanted a quiet week. You just wanted to enjoy yourself. That doesn't appear possible now."

"Don't get ahead of yourself." I opted to be practical. "If we can figure out what's going on we might be able to stop it before it gets out of hand."

"What are the odds of that?"

They weren't great, so I shrugged. "We don't know anything yet."

"Here's the thing." Kade was intense as he leaned close. "I don't like zombies."

I studied his face for hints of what he wasn't saying and came up empty. "Nobody likes them. They smell. They bite. They're like babies, but nowhere near as cuddly."

He barked out a hollow laugh. "That's not what I mean."

"What do you mean?"

"I mean that I don't like them."

It took a moment to sink in. "You're afraid of them," I said finally.

"They're zombies. They eat people. Have you even seen *The Walking Dead*?"

"Yes. It won't be like that. I promise."

"How can you be sure?"

"I've seen zombies before. It's going to be okay."

"I hope so." He pulled me in for a hug. "I don't want to watch a walking dead freak eat my intestines while I'm still alive to watch."

I had to press my lips together to keep from laughing at the ridiculous picture he was painting. "Let's not get ahead of ourselves."

"What aren't we getting ahead of ourselves about?" Cole asked as he joined us, Luke trailing a few feet behind. "We thought you left. Where have you been?"

I pointed to the riverwalk. The coroner's men were navigating a covered gurney down the stairs.

"Do I even want to know what that is?" Cole asked.

"A zombie," Kade replied.

Cole's eyebrows flew up his forehead.

"It's true," I confirmed when he looked to me. "It attacked a couple on the riverwalk. I stepped in and killed it."

"In front of people?" Luke demanded. "Are you stupid? You can't use your magic in front of people."

"I didn't have a choice, and it's not as if anybody around could see what was happening. To them it looked as if he went momentarily rigid before falling to the ground."

"And then his head fell off," Kade added.

"Oh, well, great." Cole rolled his eyes. "This can't possibly end poorly."

"There was nothing else I could do," I insisted.

"I'm not blaming you. I just...crap!" He shook his head. "What are we going to do?"

"We're going to the grocery store to get dinner and then going back to the park."

"So you have no idea." Cole pinned me with a look. "Well, let's go to the store. We don't have a choice but to deal with this. Zombies can overrun an area fast. We need to make sure that doesn't happen."

"You've dealt with them before?" That was good news.

He nodded. "Akron was overrun in 2016."

"I never heard about that."

"That's because I'm good at my job."

I mustered a grin. "You're good at a lot of things."

He slid his arm around my shoulders and kissed the top of my head.

"If it's any consolation, I make a mean crawfish boil."

That had him smiling. "It does soften the blow a bit."

THANKS TO OUR PREVIOUS VISITS, I knew where to find a good market. It was in Marigny and boasted the sort of regional fare that made my mouth water.

"We only need one cart," I said when Cole and Kade both went for their own. "We're not getting food for the entire week. I'm serious about eating out."

"Fair enough." Kade took a step back and allowed Cole to commandeer a cart. His eyes darted from corner to corner of the store.

"What are you doing?" I asked, confused.

"I'm making sure we're not about to be eaten."

"Eaten?" Cole made a ridiculous expression. "Am I missing something?"

"Kade is terrified of zombies," I replied as I nudged Cole with my hip. "Come on. Let's shop."

"You're afraid of zombies?" Luke's tone was light and teasing. "Seriously?"

"Oh, don't say it like that," Kade snapped. "Don't act like it's an unreasonable fear. You can't kill zombies—and they eat you while you're still alive. It's totally normal to fear them."

"They're slow as molasses," Cole pointed out. "You can outrun them. Those fast zombies in the movies? Unrealistic."

"I never thought any of it was real," Kade groused. "While I'm glad they're slow moving, that doesn't make them less dangerous. Have you seen *Night of the Living Dead*?"

I was starting to see a pattern. "Kade, I thought you didn't like horror movies? You begged off on *Friday the 13th* night when Luke and I had all that popcorn last year."

"That's because *Friday the 13th* is stupid. It's not realistic. Who would send their kids to that campground after one or two massacres? Ludicrous."

"Technically there were only children at the camp in one movie," Luke argued. "That would be the sixth one, if you're curious. Otherwise, counselors were at the camp."

"That doesn't make it better."

"A couple of those movies were set in the same few days," Cole pointed out. "I think the second, third and fourth movies were set within five days of each other."

"So why weren't people leaving when they heard there was a machete killer on the loose?" Kade demanded. "*Friday the 13th* movies are just stupid. They're not scary. Zombie movies, however, are terrifying."

"And yet, up until we got here, you didn't think they were possible," Cole said.

"Stop." Kade raised his hand and stormed ahead of the cart. "Crawfish, right? I'll find them."

I exchanged amused looks with Cole and Luke. "He's going to be trouble. I didn't realize he was terrified of zombies. He's going to need constant reinforcement."

"I can see it," Luke said, taking me by surprise. He never took Kade's side. Like, never.

"You can see what?" Cole asked.

"Being afraid of zombies." Luke shrugged. "It's a phobia. Being eaten alive is terrifying to think about. It's no different than that recurring nightmare you have about being eaten by the *Jaws* shark, Poet. You know, where he gnaws off your legs, but you h   keep trying to swim to escape."

I narrowed my eyes. "I shared that secret wi.   ou when I was eighteen," I growled. "You can't use it against me now."

"I thought we were family." He wagged his finger between Cole and himself. "That's what you said. The four of us are family. I have to share funny stories with family."

"Oh, is that the rule?" I placed one hand on my hip.

"Of course it's the rule."

"Fine." I turned to Cole. "Luke didn't find out until he was sixteen that women gave birth through their vaginas. He thought babies were crapped out."

Luke's mouth dropped open. "Harlot!"

Cole's shoulders shook with silent laughter as he dropped his head.

"Poet shaves her upper lip," Luke sneered. "If she doesn't, she can double as Gomez Addams by the end of the week."

I glared at him. "That was low."

"You started it."

"No, you did!"

"Well, I'm going to finish it." His voice was a growl. "Don't push me."

I stared at him for a long time, debating, and then I pushed things to a place I shouldn't have. "Luke used to pretend he was famous and gave fake interviews to Oprah when cleaning his trailer," I said.

Luke's eyes practically bugged out of his head. "Poet once tried to be a lesbian after a bad breakup, and the woman she kissed cried because she was so bad at it."

Oh, well, that did it. "Luke—" Before I could finish, Cole slapped his hand over my mouth to silence me.

"As much as I enjoy you two spilling these delightful secrets, I'm putting a stop to it," Cole said. "This is not the time."

He was right. "I'm mad," I said after slapping his hand away.

"Perhaps you should walk it off," Cole suggested.

"I will. I'll get the corn and potatoes. You guys get the crawfish and butter."

I paused in front of Luke before heading down the aisle. "We'll pick up this discussion later."

Luke nodded. "Oh, we most definitely will."

I was in a foul mood as I moved away from them, although if I was honest it wasn't Luke's big mouth irritating me. It was the entire situation.

I'd had a bad feeling. All day, it had been creeping over me, popping up and then disappearing again. I should've been more proactive. It wasn't like me to let others talk me out of believing what I knew to be true. So, yeah, I was mad at myself.

I hit the produce section with a purpose, grabbing multiple plastic bags and packing ears of corn and potatoes into them. I made a mental note to go to the spice section as I started doing the math. I had no idea how many people would be joining us for dinner. It was enough that I wanted to err on the side of caution though. That meant two ears of corn and two potatoes for each potential person.

"You look intense," a male voice said from the other side of the corn bin.

"Hmm?" I almost jumped out of my skin when I looked up and found the Baron Samedi cosplayer staring at me. "You."

"Me," he agreed in a crisp voice.

"I saw you earlier today."

He feigned surprise. "That's odd. Are you sure you don't have me confused with somebody else?"

"I'm fairly certain it was you."

"Well, then you're doubly lucky." He beamed at me, his ridiculously white teeth on full display. It wasn't unusual for the homeless population in New Orleans to dress up for money. That wasn't the vibe I got from this guy.

"I guess you could say that." I looked him up and down. His clothes were off, as if he hadn't bought them from a local store. They looked homemade...and old. "Who are you?"

"That's not important."

I hated—absolutely *hated*—when people played games with me. This guy looked like he was having a grand time, and it set my teeth on edge. "What do you want?"

"Just to talk." He matched my pace when I moved to the right, being careful to keep space between us. It was obvious he didn't want me touching him.

"So talk," I ordered. If he had a message, he might as well deliver it.

"There's trouble brewing in Crescent City."

"The zombies? Yeah, I know."

He smirked. "Most people wouldn't use that word."

"What word do you use?"

"I'm a big fan of the Z-word, but I'm not picky." He trailed his fingers over the corn. "You're an interesting girl. Has anybody ever told you that?"

"Surprisingly, you're not the first person to say that. Most don't mean it as a compliment."

"I do." His smile was back. "Do you know what I find most intriguing about you?"

"My winning personality?"

"Your blood. You have an interesting combination." He wiggled his finger around. "There's some witch in there. Some faint shifter." He cocked his head. "You have some of my people running through you."

Now he definitely had my attention. "Haitian voodoo or loa?"

"What do you think?"

I had trouble believing he was a mortal man. He was too...sparkly. Could he be a real loa? That didn't seem likely, but the same could be said for zombies. I wasn't ruling anything out. "Just tell me what you want." I glanced over my shoulder for the rest of my shopping party. They were nowhere in sight. "I'm not alone."

"You've got a half-mage, a fire elemental, and a shifter with you." His lip curled into a sneer on the word "shifter." "Some of them are more entertaining than others."

"You're going to stay away from them," I warned.

"I have no interest in them. I'm here for you."

I didn't like the way he said it. "Just tell me what you want." I wasn't one to let fear rule me. If I had to push him, I would. "I don't have all night."

"Actually, you have time to burn until night," he countered. "When it's dark, you need to go to St. Louis Cemetery."

"You want me to go to a cemetery?" I should've been shocked but I wasn't. "Why?"

"You're seeking answers. You'll find them there."

"What do you get out of the deal?"

"My interests are varied, but they're none of your concern. I'm here to help you."

"I'm not sure I believe you." I opted for honesty. "I think you're trying to use me to solve your problem."

"Will that stop you from going to the cemetery?"

"Probably not."

"I didn't think so." He moved toward the door. "Have a nice evening, Poet Parker."

I glared at his back. "There's more than one St. Louis Cemetery."

He slowed his pace but didn't look back. "You want No. 1."

"I guess I should thank you."

"Wait until you see what I've gifted you with before you offer thanks."

I blew out a sigh. "Will I see you again?"

"You'll have to see if the gods bless you a third time." With that, he was gone, and I was left with even more questions.

Nine

I filled in the others on the trip back to the park. Kade was agitated.

"It's going to be full of zombies, isn't it?"

I shrugged. "That would be my guess. He stressed we should go after dark."

"What do you think?" Cole asked.

"If we do nothing and something bad happens, I'm going to feel guilty."

"And if it's a trap?"

"Then I'll be angry and looking to hurt him next time I see him." I paused. "If he really is a loa, though, we'll have other issues."

"Such as?"

"I don't know nearly enough about loas," I admitted. "If they're real, they've been around for a very long time."

"And if they've survived that long they're strong," Cole surmised. "Was he aggressive?"

"Are you asking if I got the feeling that he wanted to hurt me?"

"Yeah."

"No, but he could've been lulling me. He was very careful to make sure that I didn't get close enough to touch him."

"That could mean he fears you," Luke offered. "Maybe you're more powerful."

It was an interesting thought, but one I discarded almost immediately. "I don't think so. He mentioned me being a hodgepodge. He seemed interested in my lineage. He said that I had some of his people in my blood."

"Voodoo people or loas?" Cole asked.

"I don't know." I would be lying if I said I wasn't interested. "We need to talk to the others. Raven might have information about loas. She's been around a long time."

"I just don't want to walk into a cemetery crawling with zombies," Kade complained. "I've seen how that goes in books and movies. It never ends well."

"You really need to stop living your life by what you've seen in movies," Luke chided. "They're fiction."

"Okay, Mr. I've Seen *The Godfather* and Know Everything There Is To Know About the Mob," Kade snapped.

"Hey, I could totally be a mob boss," Luke shot back. "I would have to update the wardrobe choices—nobody needs that much black in one closet—but otherwise I would be good to go."

"Yeah, yeah, yeah."

THE REST OF THE TEAM WAS LOITERING IN THE parking lot. Someone had managed to move the big fans we kept for the midway into the lot. The heat was getting to everybody.

"What's this?" I stood in front of one of the fans and widened my eyes as a huge blast of air rolled over me.

"It's hot," Nellie replied. "There's no reason to suffer. We can always move the fans closer to the water features when we open."

I glanced at his dress, which the fan had fluttering, and shook my head. "Tell me you're wearing underwear."

He winked. "Wouldn't you like to know?"

"If I can make it through the evening without direct proof either way I'll consider it a win."

His smile disappeared. "What's wrong with you? You look like you've seen a ghost."

"Not a ghost." I craned my neck. "Where's everybody else? We have the fixings for a crawfish boil and we need to talk."

"Oh, I hate when we have to talk."

"It's the way of the world for us."

"Ugh. I'll get everybody."

"Thank you." I moved to the kitchen area, where Cole and Kade were sorting through the food. They looked confused by the ingredients I'd collected.

"How do we cook this?" Cole asked. He held up a huge plastic bag of crawfish. "Are these bugs?"

"Think of them as tiny crabs," I suggested.

He made a face. "But are they bugs?"

There was no way I was answering. "Check the park grounds. I'll handle food preparations with Raven."

He stared at me, seemingly considering the order, and then nodded. "Okay, but we want to be included in any decisions."

"I don't plan on making decisions without you." Actually, I'd already made my decision. I was going to the cemetery regardless. I simply hadn't told anybody. We had hours before dusk. My announcement could wait. "I want to talk to Raven."

He kissed the top of my head. "When you're ready to talk about the plan, you know where to find me."

"Thanks." I shucked the corn while waiting for Raven. When she appeared, she didn't look happy. "It's a crawfish boil," I offered before she could unleash her snarky tongue. "You like crawfish."

"It's not the crawfish I'm worried about," she replied. "It's whatever bomb you're about to drop on us while we're eating the crawfish that has me concerned."

"I wouldn't call it a bomb."

"What would you call it?"

"Something that has to be dealt with."

"I just know this is going to suck." Raven reached for the potatoes. "Well, lay it on me."

"Zombies."

"I already told you that's unlikely."

"Unlikely or not, there was a zombie on the riverwalk. It attacked two people, and when I stopped it the head fell off."

Raven's expression twisted into one of disgust. "That is why zombies are the worst. They're so gross. If you're going to create an army for a fight, at least make it a dignified army."

For some reason, her response made me grin. "That is something to consider," I agreed. "There's more." I filled her in. When I got to the part about the loa, she stopped what she was doing and fixed her full attention on me. She didn't look happy.

She swung her head back and forth. She'd pulled her long silver hair into a loose bun because of the humidity, and she looked as if she wished she hadn't so she could drag her hands through it for something to do. She fidgeted and grumbled. "This is not good."

"Well, that answers that question," I said. "Loas are real?"

She nodded. "What have I always told you? Most of the myths and legends have some basis in reality. They're not all correct—in fact, most of them have quite a few details wrong—but that doesn't mean they're completely wrong. The loas are real. They're also asshats."

"Asshats?"

"Yes. They're complete and total asshats, as Percival would say," she confirmed, referring to her boyfriend with the fake British accent who liked to dress as a clown. "I can't stand them. Which one did you run into?"

"I'm pretty sure it was Baron Samedi."

She nodded, thoughtful, and didn't as much as look to her left as Cole, Kade and Luke joined us. "He's a righteous pain, and not because he's bloodthirsty. He likes playing games. If people happen to die as he plays them, he doesn't really care."

"What do you know about him?" Cole asked.

"He's the loa of the dead," I replied. "His claim to fame is that he loves debauchery, rum, and smoking."

"And he curses like his tongue will catch fire if he doesn't," Raven added. "One of his powers is resurrection, so if there are zombies it's not surprising he's involved."

"Oh, there are definitely zombies," Kade intoned. "Trust me."

I patted his arm. "He doesn't like zombies," I explained to Raven's questioning gaze. "Apparently it's going to turn into a thing."

"I didn't say that," Kade growled.

"Zombies aren't a big deal," Raven insisted. "Even if you get bit by one we have tonics to turn back the change. You'll be fine."

"Will I be fine if they knock me down and start eating my intestines?" Kade demanded.

Raven turned to me. "I take it he's seen a lot of zombie movies."

"And apparently *The Walking Dead*," I confirmed. "It's definitely going to be a thing."

Kade threw his hands in the air. "I love how you guys treat me as if I'm the problem when we're talking about freaking zombies."

"Chill out," Cole ordered. "It'll be fine." He wiggled his fingers. "I have fire magic. Zombies burn very easily."

"That doesn't explain why there's an infestation now," Raven noted. "If Baron is behind this, why did he recommend Poet go to the cemetery? Most of the time, when he decides to hang out with the humans, he prefers to drop a chaos bomb and then step back to watch it play out. This isn't like him."

"Are you suggesting he didn't start this?" Cole asked.

She shrugged. "He may be here to manage the chaos. If somebody else raised the zombies, he might be annoyed because they stepped on his toes. Did he seem annoyed?" she asked me.

"He seemed more amused than anything else," I replied. "The thing that threw me was that he suggested I had ties to 'his people.' I don't know if he meant voodoo people or the loas, but he was dead serious about it."

Raven was back to staring at me. "That's...interesting."

"It's freaky," I countered. "Do you think he means I'm part loa? Can they procreate?"

She pursed her lips, considering. "I don't know. Loas keep to themselves. They don't mind interacting with humans, but they could take or leave other paranormals.

"Baron is part of the Gede family of loas. And, before you ask, there are numerous other families," she continued. "The Gede family controls death and fertility."

"So, they're responsible for life and death essentially," Cole mused.

"In a nutshell," Raven agreed. "They're big drinkers, love carousing, but they're also drawn to death. According to legend, Papa Gede was the first. The stories say he's the corpse of the first man who ever died, but that's just him boasting. He's supposed to wait at the crossroads with Baron to sort souls. He would be the good angel to Baron's devil."

"Is it possible they're in some sort of struggle and this is how they've decided to duke it out?" Luke asked.

"Anything is possible," Raven replied. "There are numerous other Gede loas, but most of them step out of the way when Baron and Papa Gede go after one another. There is one notable exception."

The way she was dragging things out told me this wasn't going to be good. "Who?"

"Maman Brigitte. She's Baron's wife. They supposedly loathe one another and fight constantly. She's considered the protector of crosses and gravestones. She's a big rum drinker too and is symbolized by the black rooster. She swears like a sailor on shore leave but is known as a truth-teller."

"As opposed to Baron Samedi, who likes to play games and live in half-truths," I said.

"Pretty much."

"Do we think she's involved?" Cole replied.

Raven shook her head. "We have to go to the cemetery and take a look around. Even if Baron is playing a game, we have to know what we're dealing with."

Cole nodded. "I guess the decision has already been made," he said. "We're going cemetery walking tonight."

Raven held out her hands. "We have to go loaded for bear...just in case."

"Well, that will make Nellie happy," I noted.

Raven's expression darkened. "Yes, there's little I love more than making Nellie happy. Tonight should be delightful."

DINNER WAS GOOD. IT WOULD'VE been better if someone else had cooked it for us, but I was happy for the distraction. When it came time to head out, we dressed for battle. Nellie insisted on taking his axe. It was New Orleans, so I hoped nobody would notice. Everyone else was armed with daggers and magic. We were a force to be reckoned with.

I hoped it would be enough.

"There are three St. Louis cemeteries," I explained to Kade as we walked. I felt the need to fill the silence. "The one we're going to is the oldest and most famous. It opened in the late 1700s as the city's main burial ground."

Kade made a big show of listening, but I could tell his mind was elsewhere—likely on zombies.

"Marie Laveau is believed to be interred here and maybe even Delphine LaLaurie, but there's debate about if she was buried here or overseas," I continued. "The weirdest thing about the cemetery is that Nicolas Cage purchased a tomb that looks like a pyramid for his final resting place."

"Nicolas Cage bought a pyramid for a New Orleans cemetery?" Kade was understandably confused. "Why?"

"I guess because he's Nicolas Cage."

When we rounded the final corner, I held my breath. I had no idea what I expected to find. The quiet of the street threw me for a loop, and I frowned as I slowed my pace.

"Anything?" I whispered.

"The cemetery is shrouded with something," Naida replied, her eyes narrowing. "It's almost like a dampening field."

"Well, awesome." I pressed my lips together and turned to Cole. "Be ready."

"Yes, because nothing says 'tourists out minding their own business' like an inferno," he drawled.

"We don't have many options," I pointed out. "If the cemetery is crawling with zombies we have to eradicate them."

"They eat intestines," Kade reminded everybody for no reason in particular.

"Baby, you need to let that go," I chided. "I won't let the zombies eat your intestines. I promise."

He grumbled, which made Raven smirk.

"Keep the formation tight," I ordered those behind us. "Don't do anything until we have a better picture of what we're dealing with. If you get attacked, you can react, but don't kill something just to kill it until we know more."

"She's talking to you," Luke said in a stage whisper to Nellie. "She doesn't want you swinging that axe around."

"Or maybe she's talking to you," Nellie fired back. "Have you ever considered that she thinks you're a big, fat tool?"

"Of course not."

"Maybe you should."

I tuned out their argument and moved toward the gate. I was twenty paces from it when I saw that it wasn't latched. St. Louis Cemetery No. 1 had been closed to new burials years ago. Only tour companies could pay for passes to visit, so I had expected to have to use magic to gain entrance. The gate was propped open...and there was movement on both sides.

"Holy ..."

"Yeah, that's not good," Raven said. She was calm as she strode forward and lifted her hand above her head, letting loose an arc of magic. When the individual closest to us was illuminated, and the only thing staring back were the same filmy eyes I saw on the riverwalk, I knew we were in trouble.

"How many?" I asked as Cole scurried closer to the gate.

"I don't know," he said, slamming the dagger he carried into the head of the nearest zombie as it came sniffing around to see what new treats had arrived. "How many people are interred here?"

"I have no idea."

"Then it's possible all of them are up and walking around."

My stomach plummeted. "Great." I pressed the heel of my hand to my forehead. "Just awesome."

"What do we do?" Kade demanded in a shaky voice. "Do we run?"

I shot him a sympathetic look. "No, we fight. We can't let them roam free."

Kade said the one thing I didn't want to hear. "I just knew it! I told you this would happen. They're going to eat us all. Are you happy?"

I couldn't take his whining, not when there was so much to do. "Why don't you stay here and keep patting yourself on the back," I suggested. "The rest of us will do something proactive." I glared as I stepped around the gate. "Everybody knows what to do. Don't let any of them escape."

"What happens if they're already out there?" Cole asked.

"Then we have to find them."

Ten

I ignored Kade's complaining as I entered the cemetery and threw up a sparkling net so we could see better. The rest of the team, including Kade, spilled in behind me, and Cole shut the gate.

"They can't get out now," he said. "But others may be trolling the neighborhoods."

"We have to clean up the mess in here first," I insisted. "We'll worry about stragglers when we're done. Break into teams. Nobody does anything alone. Take them out."

"Yay!" Nellie excitedly wiggled his butt as he raced forward. He'd opted for a simple cotton strapless dress, and he moved freely as he swung his axe, decapitating the first zombie he saw. "Let's do this!"

I rolled my eyes before heading to the right. I had no idea who was moving with me but wasn't surprised to find Kade, Luke and Cole rounding out my team. I didn't have time to assuage Kade's fears, so I focused on the fight. He would have to come to grips with his fears on his own.

"Here we go," Cole said as his hands caught fire. He was calm as he moved forward, pulsing fire magic into five zombies before I even unleashed my first burst. Each zombie went rigid and then burst into flames when the fire magic hit. Within seconds, the only thing left was ash.

"That's going to come in handy," Luke noted. He was a shifter, but his wolf genes offered little in the way of protection from a bite. His dagger was slower going, but I was gratified when Cole used his magic to clean up the bodies as they fell.

I was reasonably sure there were no humans in front of us, so I unleashed a wave of magic wide enough to take out a swath of the undead at their knees. It arced out, like a tsunami, and knocked anything stumbling toward us back. Luke and Kade began stabbing the struggling zombies, and Cole cleaned up the mess with his fire. It was slow-going, but we kept plodding forward. I knew that on the other side of the cemetery Nellie, Dolph, Raven, Nixie, Naida and Seth were doing the same.

"It smells like barbecue gone wrong," Luke complained after we'd cleared another area. "The residents in the area will smell this."

He had a point, but I had no idea what to do about it. "*Naida*." I said her name out loud and projected it with my magic at the same time. We needed her.

To give her time to find us, I hopped up on the tacky pyramid to my left and started throwing magic at anything that moved.

"What is that?" Luke demanded when he caught sight of the pyramid.

"I believe it's the tomb Nicolas Cage purchased for his final resting place," I replied grimly. The incline of the tomb was steep enough that I had to strain to stay upright. "Tacky, huh?"

"Um, yes." Luke grabbed me around the waist when I started to slide and used his shifter strength to throw me on top of a neighboring tomb. Thankfully, it had a flat roof, so I wasn't fighting gravity while taking out zombies. "You stay up there," he ordered. "Knock them down. Kade and I will take them out. Cole can handle the cleanup."

I balked. "I was doing fine."

"You were slipping." Luke was stern. "Let's be smart about this."

"He's right," Cole offered before I could respond. "We should do this in an orderly fashion."

My agitation was obvious. "Maybe I want to do it willy-nilly. Have you ever considered that?"

"You guys are quite the pair," Cole said to Kade as he set another two ragged bodies on fire. "You're afraid your intestines are going to be munched on and she's suffering from...whatever it is she's suffering from."

"Yeah, what's up with you, Poet?" Luke demanded as he slammed his dagger into a zombie that was more bone than body. "This is about what the loa said, isn't it? Would it be so bad if you were part loa?"

I glared at him while throwing a huge ball of magic to my left. "Loas aren't human," I growled.

"Technically neither are shifters."

"You're human. You're just an enhanced human. The same goes for Kade and Cole. You both have human in you."

"You think you don't?" When Luke turned, he looked annoyed. "Poet, don't even try to convince me you're not human. Only a human would worry about being human, for crying out loud."

"I just don't want to ever find out I'm somehow soulless or something," I grumbled as I continuously threw out magic.

"Yes, because that's something legit to worry about," Luke groused. "Good grief, Poet. There's no way you're soulless."

"I would like to point out that we don't know the loas are soulless," Cole added. "It's entirely possible you're freaking out about nothing."

"I don't freak out about nothing," I muttered. Movement near the bottom of the tomb I was perched on drew my attention. I expected to find a zombie. Instead, Kade stood beneath me and stared directly into my eyes. "I'm not being a baby," I said automatically.

That elicited a smile from him. "Of course you're not. That's not who you are. You're not soulless."

"I'm not saying I'm soulless," I hedged. "I just...don't ever want to find out that I'm missing something I always thought I had."

"What do you think that could possibly be?" He was earnest as he slammed his dagger into an approaching zombie. He barely looked at it. "What did I tell you when we were driving into New Orleans?" he demanded when I didn't respond to the first question.

"That jaywalkers are stupid," I replied.

He smirked. "What else?"

"I'm not sure. You did a lot of ranting about jaywalkers."

"That's my way. Your way is to love with your whole heart and worry with everything you have. If you were anything less than human, or perfect, that's not how you would react."

That's when I remembered. "I'm not perfect. You only think that because I sleep with you."

He chuckled. "No, I feel that here." He tapped his chest. "Even if you do have some loa in you, that doesn't mean you're somehow less than the person I already know you are. You're the most human individual I've ever met. That's why I fell so hard for you."

I let loose a sigh. "That was pretty impressive," I said. "You made me feel like an idiot and got over your zombie fear at the same time. Maybe you're the one who is perfect."

"Oh, no." He shook his head. "I'm pretty far from perfect. Besides, I'm still terrified of the zombies. I just have a fully-formed survival instinct that refuses to allow me to curl into a ball and cry."

"That's probably good for all of us."

"Yeah."

"Just one thing." I hunkered down so we were almost at eye level with one another. "You have a lot of magic at your disposal. It's possible you could end all the zombies with one blow...at least a lot of them."

"What?" He was taken aback.

"It's worth a try, right?"

He worked his jaw and turned to survey the cemetery. "Why didn't I think of that?"

"Fear doesn't always allow us to think rationally," Cole replied. "I agree with Poet. It's worth a shot."

He raised his hands and I marveled at the green fire he conjured. He was getting better at wielding his magic. It wasn't always his first instinct to use it, but he would get there. For now, it still required work. "Here we go."

I smiled as he unleashed the magic, my eyes drifting to the right as two zombies froze in place. They didn't fall or combust, but it was as if they'd been suddenly caught by sub-zero temperatures that rooted them to their spots.

"Well, this makes things so much easier," Luke said as he slammed his dagger into the head of one of the zombies. It remained upright. "Or maybe it makes things weird."

"I have an idea." Cole strode over to me and lifted his arms. "Come on." He prodded me to jump down and join him.

I followed him to one of the frozen zombies. "What do you want to do?"

He ignited his right hand and extended his left hand to me. "You can amplify my magic."

"And?"

"I think we can take them all out with one blow."

It took me a moment to grasp what he was saying before I gripped his hand tighter. Our magic wove together, creating a strong tapestry, and then I reached over to touch one of the frozen zombies. "Fire in the hole," I whispered. The second I touched the creature, it ignited. I turned to study the other zombies that had frozen in place.

Almost immediately, they caught fire too. All around us, rigid zombies burst into flames. They burned hot for several seconds and then were gone.

"That worked," Kade said when the flames died down.

I nodded as I released Cole's hand and crossed to him. "It worked."

"We won." Kade broke into a wide grin. "They didn't eat us."

I returned his smile. "We won so far. We still have to hunt the ones that escaped."

Kade's smile fell.

"Yeah." I patted his shoulder. "We're not done yet, big guy. Soon though."

WE BROKE APART TO SEARCH the neighborhoods. Raven went with Nellie, a pairing that filled me with fear. Naida went with Dolph, a truly odd couple, which left Nixie to pair with Seth. Luke, Cole, Kade and I crossed Rampart together to search the French Quarter. Once there, we split into twos.

"Just for the record, I know you're human," Kade said as we reached Bourbon Street. It was packed with people, many of them drunk. The street was filled with lurching people, not all of them dead.

"I just had a moment," I reassured him. "I was thrown by what the loa said. I know I shouldn't have let him get to me—he probably did it on purpose because he was playing a game—but I'm better now. You don't have to worry."

Kade grabbed my wrist before I could cross the street. "I know you." His voice was low despite the rowdy music and screaming drunks. "You're not afraid you're not human. You're afraid you have monster in your blood."

I blinked several times. "How ...?" I trailed off. Of course he recognized my true fear. He knew me better than anybody. "I don't think I'm a monster," I said. "I am afraid that there's some ticking bomb inside of me, though. If it goes off, what happens to me in the aftermath? I don't ever want to be the sort of monster that goes after the people I love."

"How could you possibly be when you're already a hero?"

"That's sweet."

"I'm a sweet guy."

He made me laugh. "Seeing Sidney has thrown me more than I thought it would. I always wondered why he couldn't be bothered to keep me. I know I said that I was over it and everything, but that might've been a bit of an exaggeration."

Now it was his turn to chuckle. "I knew that when you were saying it. You were trying to be the bigger person. You didn't want to seem bitter. It's okay to hold a grudge. As for the rest, you're not a monster. He didn't leave you because of something in your blood."

"I don't know what I am. Not truly."

"You're not a monster."

"How can you be sure?"

"Because you're the best person I know." He kissed my forehead. "You have nothing to fear. I've seen your heart. Not literally, because that would be gross, but I know what a good person you are."

"That's a very 'Luke' thing to say," I pointed out. "The gross heart thing, I mean."

"He's a terrible influence."

I hugged him, taking a moment to settle myself, and then pulled back. "Now come on. We have to be sure."

We moved to the corner of Bourbon and Conti to obtain a better vantage point. The music from Cafe Beignet was deafening, but I did my best to tune it out. I was just about to declare Bourbon Street clean when I caught sight of a shuffling figure.

I followed because I couldn't ignore the possibility that there was a zombie about to attack the revelers wandering Conti Street. Kade followed without question. I momentarily lost sight of the figure when we hit Royal Street, so I moved to the middle of the road to search the shadows. Royal Street saw much less foot traffic than Bourbon after dark, but I'd lost sight of the man and it didn't sit right.

"Anything?" Kade asked after a full minute of scanning.

"I...don't...." Then I saw it. The figure was in front of a jewelry store, moving toward a woman. She didn't see it coming. She was focused on the trinkets visible through the glass.

I broke into a run, my feet slapping against the ground. I wasn't known for my athleticism, but I could move when I wanted to, and I slid across the hood of a parked car. I grabbed the man, my fingers gripping tightly around his throat, holding back the snapping teeth.

"Mugger," Kade said to the woman as he blocked off her view of the zombie and me. "You shouldn't wander around after dark on your own. It's not safe."

She let loose the sort of giggle that told me she was drunk, and maybe that she thought Kade was flirting. When she asked him if he wanted to help her find her friends, I knew it was likely both.

"I'm sorry," Kade replied. "I'm otherwise engaged."

"Oh, that's too bad," she pouted.

"Bourbon Street is that way." Kade was forceful as he pointed.

I waited until Kade turned to face me to ask the obvious question. "Are we clear?"

He nodded. "Hurry. Somebody could come by at any moment."

I tightened my grip on the creature's throat, doing the one thing I couldn't do when we were on the riverwalk because there were too many people around. I funneled enough energy into the zombie to destroy the creature from the inside out and within seconds it started to flake away to nothing. Grossed out by the remnants of smelly zombie flying around us, I wrinkled my nose and wiped my hand on my pants.

"Well, that was disgusting," I said.

"Now you know why zombies suck. I was right about that."

I let loose a hollow laugh as I turned. "I do not want to hear another word about zombies tonight. In fact...." My mouth dropped open when I realized we were no longer alone, that two figures had appeared directly to my right. Not only had people somehow found us in the aftermath of the zombie takedown, but the faces staring back at us were familiar.

"Sidney," I said, my mouth suddenly dry.

Fear flushed his features, and I knew he'd witnessed what I'd done.

Vanessa, standing to his right, was much more animated. "I figured you were magical when we met," she said. "That was pretty impressive." Her smile was so wide it threatened to swallow her entire face. "You must have some very cool secrets. I can't wait to get to know you better."

Eleven

I swear I thought my heart was going to beat out of my chest. *Did she just say what I think she said?* I glanced at Kade for confirmation. He looked as befuddled as I felt.

"Don't worry," Vanessa added when I was still searching for a response. "Sidney didn't tell me. I have a nose for these things." She tapped the side of her nose for emphasis.

"Poet." Sidney's voice came out in a strangled grunt. "I...um...."

Kade's phone beeped with an incoming text message. He was grim as he checked. "That was Cole," he said. "We need to go to Jackson Square. They need help."

I nodded. "Okay." *Really, what else was I supposed to say?*

"We'll have dinner again," Vanessa suggested. "You're obviously busy. How does tomorrow sound? I have so many questions."

I had a few of my own. "Sure." I bobbed my head. "Give me a call tomorrow and we'll figure things out." I started to move away.

Sidney, as if breaking from a freezing spell, took two long strides and grabbed my wrist before I could move more than a step. "I didn't say anything to her." He looked frazzled. "In fact, I wasn't going to bring it up at all. I didn't figure it was my business."

That was one of the few things he'd said that I believed. "We really have to go. I guess I'll see you tomorrow."

He released my wrist and nodded to Kade. "Good luck."

"We're fine," Kade assured him as he grabbed my hand. "It was nice seeing you. Have a lovely evening."

We put our heads down and hurried in the direction of Jackson Square. Cole wouldn't have asked for help if he didn't need it. The zombies took priority over my personal life.

Still, the Vanessa issue would have to be addressed at some point.

I WAS EXHAUSTED WHEN WE got back to the trailer. The fight at Jackson Square had been short but fierce. They locked the park at night, so we didn't have to creep around trees and benches to find all the zombies. They were in the courtyard surrounding the park, and the only witnesses to our search-and-destroy mission were the homeless bedding down on the benches for the night. Sadly, nobody was going to believe them if they talked of four magical beings taking out the walking dead, but that worked to our advantage.

Back in the parking lot, we touched base with the others. The zombie search had gone well, which suggested we were in the clear...at least for now. We agreed to talk again in the morning.

"What do you think?" Kade asked as he emerged shirtless from the bathroom after brushing his teeth. He wore a pair of silk boxer shorts, a Christmas gift from me, and looked as if he was going to fight sleep because he was so worked up.

"We got as many of them as we could," I replied, rolling my neck. I'd opted for a pair of cotton sleep shorts and a tank top. Morning would come before we were ready and all I wanted to do was rest my busy brain. "We have to wait it out."

"Not the zombies." He shook his head. "Vanessa."

I shouldn't have been surprised that he'd brought her up and yet I was. "I don't know what to think about her just yet."

"Could Sidney have told her about your abilities?"

"He didn't act like a guy who wanted to talk about magic."

"He might've been uncomfortable talking to you about it, but he could have told her."

I crawled into bed and watched as he flicked off the lights before joining me. He slid his arm under my waist and tugged me closer. My head was on his chest and we were tucked in tight.

"Tell me what you're thinking," he prodded in a low voice.

"I really don't know what to think," I admitted.

"Are you worried?"

"I am...*concerned*." That was the only word I could dredge up to explain my feelings. "If he did blab, we'll have to deal with the fallout."

"You could modify her memory. I've seen you do it."

"I'm not sure I want to do that."

"Why?"

"She sounded as though she's been aware of magic for a very long time. She didn't seem shocked by what she saw me do. She was more excited than anything else. She might not be a threat."

"What if she is?"

I didn't have an answer.

"I just don't know." I rested my hand on the spot above his heart, the reassuring thump lulling me. "Sidney never showed much interest in my abilities. In fact, he looked freaked out the few times I did things that couldn't be explained."

"Did your parents confide in him?" Kade asked. "How did your parents deal with your magic?"

That was another question I didn't know how to answer. "They were afraid of me," I said finally.

"I'm sure they weren't afraid of you. Everything you've said suggests they loved you without reservation."

"Fine," I conceded. "They were afraid of some of the things I could do."

"That doesn't mean they were afraid of you."

"Probably not, but it felt that way sometimes." I shrugged. "I really don't know what to do about Vanessa. I need to sleep on it. Let's table this discussion until tomorrow."

He bobbed his head. "Just one more thing." He held me tighter. "You're the most human person I know. I don't want you thinking otherwise. All of this is stuff we have to deal with, including the loa and what he said, that doesn't change who you are at your core."

I knew he was right, but I remained unsettled. "I'm just tired." I meant it. "We can deal with it tomorrow."

"Sounds like a solid plan."

With that, I drifted into sleep.

I WOKE EARLY THE NEXT DAY FEELING rested if not relaxed. Kade and I played cuddle games beneath the covers before I showered and headed out. I headed for Raven's trailer. "We need to put up a modified dreamcatcher," I announced by way of greeting as she drank her tea at a small bistro table outside of her trailer.

"Good morning to you too," she said dryly, shaking her head.

"Good morning," I replied perfunctorily. "We need to erect the dreamcatcher."

She blinked several times, sipped again, and sighed. "I thought we agreed the dreamcatcher was a waste of time in New Orleans," she said. "There are too many paranormals. It will be alerting constantly."

"That's why it needs to be modified," I said. "We can't do what we normally do because it will be nonstop alerts. We can design it so it only alerts when zombies cross."

Realization dawned on her, and she slowly began to nod. "You're right though. It makes sense. If we can draw the zombies to us, it will save innocents."

"And keep us from running around putting out fires," I said. "It's our best option."

"Agreed. We can do it after breakfast."

I smiled, some of the tension I'd been feeling diminishing. The old Raven, the one I'd lived with for years, would've argued with me just for the sake of arguing. This new Raven, the one embracing the possibility of love and trust, was much more of a team player. It was both jarring and gratifying.

"Thanks," I said in a soft voice.

She slid her eyes to me and then proceeded to roll them in dramatic fashion. "Don't even try to hold my hand and skip through a meadow."

"Excuse me?"

"You heard me." She was firm. "We don't need to get mushy. I don't like it."

"Of course you don't." I had to fight back a smile. "I'll do my best not to get mushy."

"Save it for Kade."

"Kade does like when I'm mushy," I agreed. My mind drifted back to the previous evening. "There's one other thing."

"Oh, I don't want to hear about the mush." Raven screwed up her face. "It's disgusting and I hate it."

I ignored her. "We took out a zombie on Royal Street last night."

"Shall I throw you a parade?" Raven asked. "You can do that here. It's an actual thing."

"My uncle and his girlfriend saw us. She didn't seem surprised."

Raven stopped what she was doing. "You haven't talked much about your uncle."

She almost acted as if she cared. I knew that the minute I pointed that out she would stop asking questions. Instead, I kept my face impassive. "He said he's sorry, that he wants to have a relationship with me. I don't know how I feel. I pushed him away a long time ago. I don't have a burning desire to include him, and yet...."

"And yet you can't bear the idea of pushing your one remaining blood relative completely out of your life," Raven finished.

"I'm still thinking about it," I replied. "His girlfriend is another story. She went out of her way to tell me Sidney wasn't the one who told her I was magical. She truly didn't seem surprised that I took out a zombie in front of her. She wants to have dinner tonight and talk about it."

"Well, if you're asking for opinions, you should do it."

I couldn't contain my surprise. "Why?"

"At the very least you need to get a feel for her. If she's a danger, she'll show her hand eventually."

"I didn't get a magical vibe from her."

"Did you look?"

I shook my head. "It didn't seem necessary."

"Look next time. It's possible she hitched her wagon to your uncle to get close to you."

That seemed unlikely. "She tracked down my uncle months ago in Boston in the hopes that he would lead her to me?"

She shrugged. "Stranger things have happened."

"I guess. I...." Before I could finish, movement at the edge of the parking lot caught my attention. I watched as Luke, Kade and Cole emerged from between two trailers. That wouldn't normally be cause for concern, but the individual with them was another story.

"Oh, crap." I viciously swore under my breath.

"Who is that?" Raven asked, following my gaze.

"Andrew Crowder. He's the police officer called to the riverwalk when I dropped that first zombie."

"I'm guessing the fact that he's here so early isn't a good sign."

"I'm sure word of last night's zombie hunt has spread. He's here because he doesn't understand what he's dealing with."

"You would think a police officer in New Orleans of all places would have gotten the zombie memo," Raven complained.

"You would think, but that's not the way it works." I blew out a sigh. "I need to handle this. Then we'll get Naida and Nixie on the dreamcatcher modification. They'll do the heavy lifting on the spell."

Raven continued staring at Crowder. "He has 'schmuck' written all over him."

I didn't disagree. Still, when I left Raven and headed toward Crowder I pasted a welcoming smile on my face. "Detective Crowder, this is a surprise. Is there something we can help you with?"

Kade stood behind Crowder. "Detective Crowder has some questions," he volunteered. "Apparently there was an incident in the French Quarter last night. He believes we know something about it."

I forced myself to remain calm. If I had to modify his memory, I would. I wouldn't like it, but I would do what was necessary to keep my team safe. "What sort of incident?"

"Ma'am." Crowder tipped his hat in deference to me. Southern manners were alive and well in the New Orleans Police Department. He fancied me a helpless female, so he was playing a game with this conversation.

"Last night we received multiple reports from a number of different neighborhoods," Crowder started. "Treme. Marigny. The French Quarter. We even followed a complaint in Bywater, but that turned out to be a homeless drunk with a can of spray paint and a feather whip."

Laughing at the visual he was painting wouldn't be a good look considering his dour demeanor.

"What does that have to do with us?" I asked.

"You don't know?"

"Sorry."

He was slyer than he looked. He'd purposely omitted details, expecting me to fill in some of the blanks. He'd even thrown in the funny story about the drunk in Bywater to put me at ease. He was much smarter than I initially thought.

"We're not quite sure what we're dealing with," Crowder replied. "It's been described as a contagion of individuals who have trouble staying on their feet."

"Isn't that just a drunk?" Luke asked. "I mean...it is New Orleans. That's hardly out of the ordinary."

"Some of these 'drunks' were trying to bite people," Crowder said. "We also have multiple witnesses claiming that superheroes appeared out of the darkness to attack the 'drunks.' When they were done, there was nothing left."

"Superheroes?" I couldn't stop my lips from curving.

"I'm not saying the story makes sense," Crowder reassured me. "But I have questions, especially given what happened on the riverwalk."

"I'm more than willing to answer your questions. It's just...well...I don't have any answers. I'm not sure what you want from me." I darted what I hoped was a "come save me" look toward Kade. I was determined to keep up the ruse.

Kade strode to me and slid his arm around my shoulders. "It's okay, baby." He pulled me in for a hug and fixed Crowder with a serious look. "Are you blaming her for these people being on the street? How is she responsible?"

"It's always a woman's fault," Luke sneered from behind Crowder. "The male patriarchy always blames women. It's who they are."

Crowder shot Luke a quelling look. "That's not what's going on here."

"That's what it feels like," Cole countered. "There's no other reasonable explanation for why you're here."

"I'm here because Ms. Parker was involved in an incident on the riverwalk yesterday," Crowder replied. "She claims she did nothing but grab a man and pull him away from another couple, but I have a headless body and the coroner says that there's no way this person died during the incident."

"Meaning?" Kade asked.

"Meaning that he'd been dead for quite some time before the riverwalk scene played out."

Cole slid forward. "He's saying that he thinks we created zombies."

Crowder balked. "I am not saying that."

"What else could you be implying?" Cole demanded.

"I'm just trying to find answers. Everybody in my department is baffled."

"We don't have answers," Kade said. "I don't understand why you think we would."

"Some of the descriptions of the 'superheroes' from last night match your group." Crowder used air quotes.

"Descriptions?" Kade asked.

"A tall man, dark hair, with a beautiful woman with black hair."

Kade chuckled. "That's a bit vague." He grinned at me as I continued to play helpless female. "I always knew you were beautiful, baby."

Frustration rippled across Crowder's face. "Two men together, one with dark hair and one with light hair." He jerked his thumb at Cole and Luke.

"Well, that's certainly damning," Cole drawled.

"A woman with teal hair in Marigny," Crowder snapped. "You have two women with teal hair. I saw them on the other side of the parking lot."

"I've seen at least fifty people on Bourbon Street alone with teal hair," Kade said.

"I know it was your group," Crowder insisted.

"We don't know what you're talking about," Cole shot back.

Crowder ran his tongue over his lips. "Fine. I guess we'll have to do things the hard way."

I had no idea what that meant, but I wasn't hopeful.

"We have nothing to offer you," Kade replied.

With that, a line had been drawn between law enforcement and us. Crowder was annoyed, but he didn't continue to press us. Instead he smiled. "I guess I'll be seeing you folks."

Kade kept his hand on my back. "I'm sorry we couldn't be of more help."

"The day is young," Crowder called back. "You might help yet."

I had no doubt, if he had his way, we would be singing songs of death and destruction by the end of his shift. He couldn't know that we would wipe his memory before we even considered something like that. For now, we were at a standoff.

Twelve

Erecting even modified dreamcatchers had become old hat to us. Still, we were careful when working.

"Look there," Raven instructed as we tightened the dream-catcher lines. "The margins are funny."

I narrowed my eyes at the spot she'd indicated. "Well...that's weird." I flicked my eyes to Kade. "Do you see that?"

Kade might've been new to the magic game, but he had a good idea what we were trying to do as long as he could watch us work. His magic was instinctive, and we were working at making him more proactive. It was an ongoing project, but today he seemed to understand the importance of what we were trying to build with little explanation.

"It's because you didn't fill in the gap there," he said as he moved behind me. He pressed his chest to my back and ran his hand down my arm. It was almost sensual when he twined his fingers with mine and changed the flow of the magic.

Warmth washed over me when our magic joined, and I found myself looking over my shoulder at his face rather than at the weaving magic.

"Do you feel it?" he whispered as he started tightening the magical strings.

"I definitely feel it." My stomach did a somersault as another wave of magic washed over me. "It feels nice."

"Oh, I think I'm about to have a secondhand orgasm," Luke said, snapping me back to reality. "That's pretty hot, guys...and I don't even get the whole woman-man thing."

I scowled at him. "We're working here."

"Please." Luke let loose a disdainful snort. "The only thing you two are working on is figuring out a way to disappear to your trailer for the rest of the day. That's not allowed. It's New Orleans, which means group outings, not...whatever it is you two want to do."

Kade's lips quirked as he regarded me. "Just how attached to him are you?" he asked. "You can always find a new best friend."

I chuckled as Luke growled. "I heard that."

"I think you were meant to," Raven said as she studied the settling dreamcatcher. "What did you do there, Kade?" She was much more interested in the magic than the innuendo. "You smoothed everything over and enhanced it."

Kade looked caught off guard. "I don't know. I didn't really think about it. I just knew it wasn't quite right and fixed it." Now he seemed uncomfortable. "Was that wrong?"

"No," I reassured him quickly. "It was exactly the right thing to do."

"It was," Raven readily agreed. "I've never seen anything like it before, though. I'm curious how you managed it."

"I don't know how. I just did it."

Raven swung her gaze to me. "You really need to work on training him. He's uber powerful. Being so uncertain has him second-guessing himself too often. We need to fix that."

I agreed, but this was not the time to focus on training. "After we deal with the zombies. If you want to train him, that might be helpful."

Raven's eyes took on a wicked gleam. "Do you really want me training him? He might realize I'm the better magic-wielder and throw you over for me."

"Yeah, that's not going to happen," Kade countered. "You scare the crap out of me."

"And you love Poet," Luke added pointedly.

"And that."

"Stop trying to rile everybody up, Raven," Luke ordered. "We have other stuff going on, and you're making things way too difficult."

"Oh, bite me," Raven muttered, her eyes drifting back to the dream-catcher. "It looks good. It should work for what we need."

As if to prove her right—or perhaps wrong—the dreamcatcher alerted. I snapped up my head, surprised, and then scanned the park for signs of zombies. There was nothing.

"Is it supposed to do that?" Kade demanded.

"I guess it depends on if there's a zombie in the park," I replied. "Break into teams. I want every corner of this park searched. That goes for the parking lot, too. Look under and inside the trailers."

"Be careful," Cole added. His eyes were trained on the trees. "Don't reach in and check areas you can't see. Make sure you don't get bitten."

"Tread lightly," I cautioned. "Noise draws them. If you find one alone try to capture it rather than kill it. I'd like to do some tests and this is a unique opportunity."

There was no backtalk nor questions. Kade, Cole, Luke and I headed for the park. My instincts told me that's where I needed to be, and if I'd learned anything over the years it was always to follow my instincts.

"Eyes open," I barked as we entered the park.

"You're so bossy," Luke lamented. "I don't understand why you have to be such a drill sergeant. We know how to look for zombies. We're not new."

"I am," Kade countered.

"Dude, you've been with us almost a year now," Luke shot back. "You can no longer be considered new. It's time to step up and play with the big boys."

I shot my best friend a derisive look. "That came out dirtier than you thought, didn't it?"

"Pretty much," he conceded. "There's no need to comment on it. We can just let it go."

I was all for that as I hurried up the stone bridge. When I reached the top, I pulled up short, my eyes going wide when I realized we had a visitor.

"Oh, crap," Luke muttered. "That guy must be drunk. How did he get in here?"

"He's not drunk," I replied evenly, never moving my eyes from what I was rapidly starting to believe was a genuine loa.

"He must be drunk to dress in that outfit," Luke insisted. "The hat is a nice touch, but the jacket and that ruffled white shirt scream cosplay, not distinguished gentleman on the make in the Big Easy."

I kept my focus on the loa. "You're the real Baron Samedi," I said.

The loa's smirk told me all I needed to know.

"That's the guy?" Luke didn't look convinced. "Are you sure he's not just drunk and looking for attention?"

Cole slapped his hand over Luke's mouth and dragged him to the left. "Don't be you," he hissed.

"Obviously that's him," Kade noted as he studied the newcomer. "What should we do?"

It was a fair question. Unfortunately, I didn't have an answer.

"I expected you to be alone," the loa said. "I don't suppose I could talk your friends into leaving so we could have a private conversation. No offense, boys, but I'm much more partial to the ladies."

"That's probably good," Luke noted as he managed to dislodge Cole's hand from his mouth. "Wearing that outfit, the only guy you'll attract is a crazy one. Women would be far more likely to find that ensemble charming than a fashion-sensitive dude."

The loa smirked. "Okay, he may remain."

"We're all staying," Kade insisted. "If you have something to say to Poet, you can say it to all of us."

The loa looked resigned. On a sigh, he nodded. "I go by many names depending on your faith, but here I'm known as Baron Samedi. I guess you could say that's my most common name, although I was always partial to my saint name."

"And what was that?" Cole asked.

I answered before Baron could. "St. Martin de Porres."

Baron smirked. "Very good, little loa. You've been doing your homework."

"I knew that long before I met you," I replied. "I've always been fascinated by the loas. I've researched several of them—including you."

"Is that so?" Amusement lighted his face. "Who else did you study?"

"Baron Criminel, although some people believe that's also you. Also Dan Petro, Erzulie, Papa Legba, Loco, and of course Maman Brigitte."

The loa's smile widened. "She is my favorite."

"She's his wife," I volunteered so the others would understand. "If the stories are true, they don't always get along."

"We never get along," Baron agreed. "She's a bit of a pill, if you must know. Just last year she cursed my nether regions to catch fire if I even thought of another woman. It was a hot few months until we reached an agreement to call off the curse."

"That sounds...fun," Cole said. "Why do you stay married if you don't get along?"

"Some bonds can't be broken," he replied. His eyes shifted back to me. "You understand now what I was trying to warn you about, yes?"

"I understand there are zombies on the loose," I replied. "I don't understand why you unleashed them."

"Who said I unleashed them?"

"You're the loa of the dead."

"That doesn't mean I'm responsible for this," he countered. "As much as I would like to claim credit for all things magical, I don't have dominion over all those who enslave the dead. If I did, my life would be much easier."

"You're the reason the dreamcatcher alerted. We modified it for zombies. Why did you set it off?"

"I was playing a game. I assumed your group would break apart to check. I was hoping to talk to you alone."

"Why?" Kade demanded. "Why do you keep approaching her when she's on her own?"

"I already told you. I find much more joy in conversing with women. Men are too...*that*." He moved his fingers in a circle before flicking them in Kade's direction in dismissive fashion.

"What does that mean?" Kade asked.

"He fancies himself a Romeo of sorts," Cole replied. "It's possible he believes females are more malleable."

"Or it's possible I like dealing with my own," Baron replied pointedly to Cole. "Don't try to figure me out, boy. You won't have much luck. Perhaps you should focus on your own. They're scattered and in disarray these days. I thought the loa had drifted too far from their real purpose until I thought long and hard about the elementals. You're so far gone there's no coming back."

Cole's eyes narrowed.

"Why do you keep referring to me as one of your own?" I demanded. "Do I have voodoo or loa in my lineage?"

"Voodoo is not a birthright," Baron replied.

"I think he's saying you're part loa," Luke offered. "Did we know loa could procreate?"

"We didn't know loa were real until yesterday, so I'm going with no," I replied dryly. I didn't know what to say to Baron, what questions to ask.

"You look bothered by the possibility that you're one of us," Baron noted after a few seconds. "Why is that? Given the questions that plagued you as a child, you should welcome the information.

"You're not a full loa," he continued. "No more will ever be born to the true line. But even being a bastard of the line makes you more powerful than most."

I narrowed my eyes. "That's an interesting way to put it."

Baron shrugged. "You're a mutt. There's no getting around it. You have a little bit of everything in you, but it's my people that fuel you."

Kade cleared his throat to draw Baron's attention. "Why would loas procreate with humans?"

"Why would mages procreate with humans?" Baron demanded. "There's no rhyme or reason. You can't control when attraction will take over. I can't speak for why the secondary loa decided to mate with a human in your girlfriend's lineage three generations ago. I only know that it happened. And, because of the other bits of magic that have come together over time—especially the witch—it's made for an interesting individual."

He almost sounded impressed. "What is it you want from me?" I asked.

"You can't take her," Kade added quickly. "She's not going with you."

Baron chuckled. "It's amusing that you think you could stop me if I wanted to take her. You might be powerful, mage, but you're not a pureblood. You have no power over me. But I do look forward to the two of you procreating. The amount of magic that will be funneled into your offspring should make for an exciting new being. I'll definitely be dropping in for a visit."

He'd let a few tidbits slip, but I understood that was by design. He knew much more than he was willing to let on. I didn't understand why he was singling me out. "Let's talk about the zombies," I said. "If you didn't unleash them, who did?"

"Someone with a grudge."

"A grudge against you?"

"It's possible."

That wasn't really an answer. "A grudge against me?" I pressed.

"You as an individual, or you as a group?"

"Either."

"I don't know the answer to that." Baron held his hands palms up. "The magic used to raise the dead is powerful. We're not dealing with a standard witch or bored necromancer. It's a powerful being...and rage fuels its every decision."

I waited for him to expand. When he didn't, I hiked my eyebrows toward my hairline. "That's it?"

"You want more?"

"It would be helpful."

He smirked. "Even though it would be great fun if it were true, I'm not omnipotent. I don't know all. I don't see all. I merely go where I'm called."

"You were called here?" Cole asked.

"New Orleans has been and will always be my home. I live between planes now, but this place has a hold on my soul."

"Loas have souls?" I tried to keep the hope from my voice. "So you're not monsters?"

"Is that what worries you, little sister?" Baron almost looked as if he pitied me. "Is that the source of the fear I sensed when I told you of your loa blood? Monsters aren't born, they're created. If you're worried about being a monster, simply don't become a monster."

"I told you," Kade muttered. "You were worrying for nothing."

I ignored him. "Where do we look to find the individual you mentioned? If somebody is raising the zombies for a specific reason, we have to stop them."

"Oh, I wholeheartedly agree." Baron's teeth gleamed as he smiled. "The situation playing out here is dangerous. It won't improve until you find the instigator. Unfortunately, I don't have the answers you seek. I can't help you."

"Then why are you here?"

"You're the only hope I have to end this. You might be the only one who can track down the guilty party. I'm lazy to my bones, so I want you to do all the work while I sit back and enjoy the fruits of your labor."

"And then?" I asked blankly. "Say I do find the individual responsible for this, what do you want me to do?"

"End the threat."

"That's a given. Other than that."

Suddenly, Baron looked more tired than amused. "I just need you to find the source. What you do after that, as long as the threat is eradicated, is up to you."

"What are you going to do while Poet is doing all the heavy lifting?" Cole demanded.

"Nap and watch from afar. I'm also going to enjoy New Orleans. The city, while modernizing, is still what it was always meant to be — where joy and art meet. I can't help you, at least not the way you desire. All I can do is offer you luck and watch to make sure you don't screw it up."

"That doesn't seem like much," Kade noted. "I mean...you're a loa."

"Alas, like other beings of the old guard, my power is waning. A new power will soon come into being. When that happens, the old guard will retire. That's not as far off as you may think. For now, my job is ensuring you do yours." He offered me a smile, but it was more feral than friendly. "Do your job so I may rest. That is the only task I have for you."

With that, he disappeared. One blink he was there, and the next he wasn't, leaving me with questions. Something told me the answers wouldn't come easily.

Thirteen

After the loa departed, we determined that the dreamcatcher was working as designed. I warned everybody to remain vigilant and then went to my tent, where I spent the next two hours organizing in preparation of guests the following day. I later found Kade and Cole surveying the midway.

"Problem?" I asked as I took in their serious faces.

"No." Cole shook his head. "We were just...talking."

"About what?"

"How lucky I am to have you," Kade replied perfunctorily, sliding his arm around my waist. "We both agree I'm the luckiest man in the world."

I arched a dubious eyebrow. "What were you really talking about?"

"Whether I'm winning over the workers," Cole replied. He rarely played games. "It's a mixed bag."

"I forgot to ask how your meeting with them went. I should've been there."

"No, you shouldn't have been." Cole gave me a fond smile. "You might be the big boss, but I'm now their immediate boss. I have to work out my interactions with them on my own."

"Fair enough. What did they say?"

"There's some confusion," he said. "Mark must have bragged a bit. They believed he was untouchable. Learning he wasn't shook them. There's also concern regarding the move."

I expected that. "We have a year," I reminded him. "Those who don't want to move to Moonstone Bay have plenty of time to find other jobs."

"That's true, but it's not as if there's a thriving circus industry. They have very specific skills."

"There are carnivals if they want to continue traveling. There are amusement parks. We'll make sure they have recommendations. I don't see what else we can do."

"I'm just pointing out that they're fearful. There's not much we can do about the situation."

I huffed out a sigh and nodded. "I'll talk to them if you want."

Cole chuckled. "I just said that I have it under control. If I need you, I'll ask."

"I think he just told you to mind your own business," Kade noted.

I glared at him.

"That's not what I said," Cole said. "I want a chance to troubleshoot on my own. I'm not saying it won't become necessary for you to step in, Poet, but I prefer figuring things out on my own."

I nodded. "Just let me know what you need."

Cole pressed his forehead to mine. "Take Kade and have a good night on the town. And do it in such a way that Luke can't invite himself along."

"And you need that because ...?"

"I want to spend some time alone with Luke. For some reason, he's convinced himself that he needs to stick close to you. I believe the loa has something to do with it, but it's also possible he just wants to irritate Kade."

I could see that. "Well, I was thinking the same thing," I admitted. "We open tomorrow. We'll still get to go out, but it will be different once the circus opens. I would like to take my man out on the town and romance him a bit."

"Sounds great," Kade said.

"Don't you have dinner with Sidney tonight?" Cole asked.

My smile slipped. "Yeah."

"And Vanessa?" Cole's eyebrows rose.

"Unfortunately, that is the case." I let loose a pent-up breath. "I'm not looking forward to it. I don't know what to say to her."

"Treat it as you would any other stranger finding out," Cole suggested. "You don't have to kowtow to her because she's your uncle's girlfriend. If you think she's a danger, modify her memory...and his, for that matter. You could remove yourself from his mind entirely."

My stomach rolled. "I'm not sure I'm comfortable with that," I hedged.

"Because you want to keep a tie to your old life?"

I shook my head. "It's an invasion. Stripping him of his memories is basically an assault. That's an option of last resort for me, and I'd like to keep it that way."

Cole nodded in understanding. "Just remember, it's a trick you always have in your back pocket if you need it. This doesn't have to be a case of you being backed into a corner."

I wanted to believe him. Unfortunately, the sense of dread that threatened to overcome me whenever I thought about Sidney and Vanessa refused to allow me to entertain the idea. "I'll figure it out. As for breaking apart tonight, I'm more than happy to make that a reality. I figured I would take Kade to the Quarter, hang out and have a few beers before dinner. After that, if we want to meet up for a group activity, we can play it by ear."

"Sounds perfect." Cole gave me a side hug. "You don't have to do anything you don't want to do," he said in a low voice. "I understand that you feel you somehow owe this man something because he was your father's brother, but you don't. He didn't struggle with the same loyalty you feel when he left you. Don't let the fact that you're one of the best people I've ever met dissuade you from doing what's necessary if it comes to it."

I nodded. "It's going to be fine."

"It is. You have us. We're your family."

"Forever," Kade agreed as he extended a hand toward me. "Now, come on. I want to get out of here before Luke sniffs out the fact that something is going on. I want a day with my girl."

I grinned. "Can we drink without you reminding me there are zombies on the loose? Just for a few hours?"

"That's the best idea I've heard all day."

I TOOK KADE TO ONE OF MY FAVORITE bars, Bar Tonique. It had a laidback atmosphere and strong mixologists. After that, we hit Bourbon O Bar before taking a breather and checking on the crowd at Jackson Square. It was still early, the sun beating down on us, but I scanned for signs of trouble.

"Anything?" Kade asked, his arms automatically wrapping me tight, a blended Hurricane in hand.

"Another one?" I turned to study his face. He looked a tad flushed but happy. "I thought we decided to sober up."

"We'll be sober in time for dinner," he pointed out. "Then you'll need to be on alert for zombies and dudes in crazy hats. No matter what you say, or what you actually intend, there will be no cutting loose when the sun sets. I've decided to do it now."

I smirked. "How do you know I won't cut loose despite the zombies?"

"Because I've met you." He kissed the tip of my nose. "I don't plan on getting drunk. We're pacing at one drink an hour. That's how I plan to keep things. I'm not going to lose awareness. I just want to have a relaxing time with my favorite person in the world."

"Smooth." I took the Hurricane from him and pressed it to my forehead. It felt deliciously cold. "Why didn't you get one for me?"

"Because I figure we're both going to want to do what you're doing right now. If we share, we'll finish this one before it melts. Then we can get another and it still only counts as one each."

"Good idea." I sipped the Hurricane and thought my eyes might cross. "Wow, that's strong."

He chuckled. "I think we'll be okay." He swayed back and forth, me in his arms, and grinned as the performers across the road danced on the steps to the riverwalk. "It's never quiet here."

I took another sip and then held up the drink so he could do the same. "As much as I love the city, especially the French Quarter, I'm not sure I could live here. I like a little quiet with my culture."

"I'm with you there." Kade took the Hurricane and held it to his forehead for a moment. "We should get a place just outside Moonstone Bay's downtown area. I'm thinking a quiet little cottage with a yard. We can put up a hammock and get our own golf cart. We'll be able to go to town whenever we want but tune out the rest of the world when we need alone time."

"Do you think about that a lot?" I was honestly curious. "Like...do you spend all your time fantasizing what life will be like when we're no longer on the road?"

"Are you worried that I hate life on the road?"

"Maybe a little," I conceded.

"Well, I don't. I have fun on the road. I love seeing the countryside, getting introduced to new places. And there's nothing better than a beautiful view. But I like the idea of having our own house. I like the idea that there will come a time when we don't have to get up at the crack of dawn to head out of town."

I rested my head against his chest. "Still, it's going to be a weird adjustment. I've gotten so used to traveling. It's going to feel awkward when it comes time to stay in one place."

"We still have a year."

I closed my eyes and floated for a few minutes. Then I realized the singers on the steps were belting out a power ballad. "I love this city's unpredictability. Still, when it's time to move on, I'll be ready."

He sipped the Hurricane again and handed it back. "I'm glad we did this."

"A romantic day of just us?"

"Yup." He bobbed his head. "I love Cole, and sometimes I even love Luke, but I need a break from them occasionally. We can't always be together."

"No, and I wouldn't want that." I sipped the drink and placed my back against his chest. I was reminded of the way he'd stepped in to help with the dreamcatcher, the way it had almost turned sexy, and I made a mental note to revisit that feeling later. For now, I wanted to find something fun to do. I immediately hit on a possibility. "How do you feel about having your fortune told?"

Kade followed my gaze. I felt his lips curve against my cheek. "Are you serious? You want to get your fortune told by somebody else?"

"Of course. It's fun."

"Are any of these people the real deal?" He looked dubious. "I don't want to cast aspersions on any of the lovely individuals here, but I have to think if they were genuine they wouldn't be working here."

"Probably not, but that's why it's fun." I grabbed his hand and started dragging him across the courtyard. "Come on. Some of these guys are grifters, but a grifter can be just as entertaining as the real thing."

"In other words you want to mess with them," he surmised.

"Does that make me petty?"

"Yes, but I happen to like you petty." He bopped his hip against mine. "Come on. Let's have our fortunes told. Then we can get another Hurricane."

"And then dinner with Sidney and Vanessa again," I said on a frown.

"Let's not dwell on that before we have to. Let's just keep enjoying ourselves."

"You read my mind."

WE CHOSE THE TELLER NAMED ZELDA, even though I knew she was a fraud the second I laid eyes on her. She was still good at reading people, something I understood from my days on the street, and I was curious how she would play things. She got right to the heart of matters...and went big.

"You'll have three children," she announced.

"Three?" I glanced at Kade. "That seems like a lot given the fact that we already have Luke."

A small smile played at the corners of his mouth. "That won't leave Mommy and Daddy much time to play private games."

Zelda adjusted quickly. "Only if you want three. Otherwise you'll have two."

"More manageable," I said, laughing.

She shuffled the cards and extended the deck to me. "You're the heart of this relationship. Cut the cards."

"Definitely," Kade agreed. "Cut them." He sipped the Hurricane, which was almost gone. "You're definitely my heart."

"So sweet," I drawled, pressing my finger into his cheek before reaching for the cards. I cut them, and when I handed them back my fingers brushed against hers. The spark of magic that galloped between us was intense, and I pulled my hand back a little too quickly.

"We're going to need another drink in a few minutes, baby," Kade said. He clearly hadn't noticed the flare of magic. "We should get the blue one next."

"That sounds good," I said, my eyes never leaving Zelda's. "What do you think about the blue Hurricane?"

"Wasting your time on cocktails when a war is about to be waged on the streets of New Orleans is the sort of thing children do," she said, her voice much different now. Her eyes had gone white.

"Oh, holy hell!" Kade moved to get up from his chair, but I gripped his arm before he could finish the maneuver.

"Don't," I instructed him quietly. "Sit."

Kade worked his jaw and then lowered himself.

"What sort of war are you referring to?" I asked when I was reasonably assured I could speak without coming across as aggressive.

"A war between the living and the dead," Zelda intoned. "A war that's been a long time coming."

"That's sort of vague," I pointed out.

"This isn't your town." Her voice was low, dangerous. "You've made this your concern, so the battle is coming for you."

"Me specifically?"

"Your people."

I leaned back in my chair, debating. "Which side are you on?" I asked finally.

"I'm just here to issue a warning."

"From who?"

"It doesn't matter."

"It does to me."

"Just know that the war is coming," Zelda spat. "Be ready to fight or you'll lose."

I opened my mouth to respond, but whatever I was going to say—and that was still up for debate—died on my lips when Zelda started shaking her head. After a few seconds, her eyes returned to normal, and she stared back at me in confusion.

"Where were we?" she asked in a shaky breath.

"You were about to tell us about our two children," I replied.

"Yes, a girl and a boy." She flashed a wide smile. "You will have a happy life."

"That's the goal," I agreed.

"Some things are meant to be," she said as she flipped the first card. "You and your fiancé were written in the stars. You have no idea how rare that is."

"Oh, I think I have some idea." I sent Kade a reassuring smile as I gathered his hand. Someone was indeed trying to send us a message.

Fourteen

"Was she possessed?"

Kade showed no signs of wanting another Hurricane after the incident with Zelda. Much like him, my taste for alcohol had fled. All I could do was dissect what had transpired...and wonder what it meant.

"I think so," I replied, automatically slipping my hand in his as we walked Conti Street. The heat and humidity were such that hand-holding meant sweating. I didn't much care after Zelda's performance. "She didn't seem to understand what happened, or that anything had gone down, for that matter."

"Could she have been faking?"

I lifted one shoulder in a shrug. "Obviously somebody wants us to be aware that they're coming."

"Baron Samedi?"

"I don't think so. He seems to want to play games up close and personal. I also don't think he's the only loa we're dealing with. It's possible there's more than one hanging around."

"Why haven't we seen any others?"

"Maybe he or she isn't as interested in broadcasting their presence."

Kade gripped my hand tighter. "I don't like this."

He wasn't the only one. "We just have to play it out. We'll figure things out eventually. We just have to be patient."

"That's kind of funny. You're not what I would call patient."

"The same goes for you."

"Does that mean we're going to be impatient together?"

I managed a smile. "There's nobody I would rather be impatient with."

"Right back at you."

WE SPENT AN HOUR WANDERING the French Quarter, even braving Bourbon Street so we could have a full view of what we were dealing with. Nothing seemed out of the ordinary.

When it came time to meet Sidney and Vanessa for dinner, we stopped in Hotel Monteleone to use the bathroom. I splashed cold water on my face—there was no sense wearing makeup in this humidity —and then met Kade in the lobby.

"We should come here after dinner tonight," he said, pointing at the Carousel Bar across the way. "I think the bar actually rotates."

I laughed at his fascination, and it felt good to lighten up a bit. "It *does*, but not so fast that you notice. The drinks are good. Luke and I come here whenever we're in town. He'll be angry if we come without him."

Kade slid his eyes to me. "I don't always want to organize my plans around Luke."

"This is different. He loves this place...and we're here together. Eventually we'll be taking vacations without Luke and Cole. We're not quite there yet."

"Fair enough." He exhaled heavily. "Are you ready to see your uncle?"

I nodded. "Yeah. The good news is that Mr. B's has great food. The bad news is I have no idea what to expect from Sidney."

"Or Vanessa," Kade added.

"She's definitely the wild card." My smile vanished. "The cynical side of me believes that she purposely hooked up with Sidney because of me."

"I can see that," he acknowledged. "But there's no way she could've known—at least before meeting him—that he would be getting in touch with you."

"Maybe it was a fact-finding mission," I suggested. "Maybe she thought he was always in touch with me. Or, maybe when she met him she started manipulating him into reaching out to me."

Kade dragged a hand through his hair. "I'm not sure what I believe."

"I plan to draw it out of her during dinner. You've been warned."

His eyes sparked with mirth as he leaned forward and gave me a quick kiss. "We'll figure it out together. Don't get worked up."

"That's the plan."

SIDNEY HAD MADE RESERVATIONS AT MR. B'S Bistro, so a table was waiting when we checked in with the hostess. Sidney and Vanessa were already seated, and I pasted a smile on my face as Sidney stood to welcome me.

"You guys are early." I worked overtime to keep my voice light. "I wasn't sure you'd be here."

"You're early too." Sidney kissed my cheek, which felt awkward, but his smile was legitimate.

"We were screwing around in the Quarter," I replied as Kade held out my chair. "The circus opens tomorrow, and we finished setting up early this morning. We decided to take advantage of our last free afternoon."

"How does that work?" Vanessa was the picture of polite interest. "Ever since we found out you were a member of a traveling circus I haven't been able to get it out of my mind. Sidney says you sleep in campers."

"Trailers," I corrected. "Although I guess a few people have opted for campers. Kade and I live together. Our trailer has two bedrooms, a full kitchen."

"I've only been with the circus a little less than a year and even I know my way around a move," Kade volunteered. "The locations are still fresh, but the process varies little."

"That sounds interesting." Vanessa bobbed her head. "Are you usually in a park, like here in New Orleans?"

"It depends," I replied. "New Orleans is unique in that Louis Armstrong Park isn't very big. Normally we wouldn't take over the parking lot with our trailers. Depending on the city, we either take over fairgrounds that are set a bit away from the downtown area or parks right in the thick of things. No two venues are the same."

"Wow." Vanessa acted as if this was the most entertaining thing she'd ever heard. "And you go to every state?"

I shook my head. "Our schedule changes every year. Some states we return to on a regular basis. Some states we stagger. Others we go to once and don't return."

"Wow. I just can't imagine living like that." Vanessa made a tsking sound with her tongue. "And how does the magic work?"

My stomach constricted. Thankfully, our server arrived at that moment to take drink orders.

"I think we're ready to order food too," Kade said. I recognized he was buying time for me to decide how I wanted to respond to Vanessa. "We're starving."

"And we'll be buying tonight," I added.

"Oh, no." Sidney shook his head. "This is on me."

"You bought last time," I reminded him. "You even picked up the tab for Cole and Luke."

Sidney was firm. "I'm glad I got to meet them. They're interesting, and I'm happy knowing who your friends are."

"They're very colorful," Vanessa agreed.

I took the opportunity to study the menu. "They have duck spring rolls."

"Let's get those," Kade said. "We can't eat anything that quacks around Luke. Let's take advantage of his absence."

"I also want the honey ginger pork chop."

"I'll have the braised short ribs." His hand landed on my back. "The Blood Orange Margarita, too. You should get a cocktail. Our drinking adventure was cut short this afternoon."

"You had a drinking adventure?" Sidney looked amused. "It is New Orleans. I guess that makes sense."

"We were just enjoying ourselves." I read the list of signature cocktails. "I'll have the Pear Cosmopolitan."

"That sounds yummy." Vanessa was so enthusiastic it was starting to grate. "I'll have the braised rabbit and the eggplant sticks."

"And I'll have the wood-grilled fish," Sidney said. "As for a drink, I think I'll go with the Pimm's Cup."

Once the server was gone I was hopeful Vanessa would have forgotten her question. I wasn't that lucky. "So, let's talk about the magic." She rubbed her hands together like a kid opening an Easter egg. "Sidney has been coy with information. It's almost as if he doesn't want to talk about it."

I flashed a smile I didn't feel. "In our family, we didn't talk about it. I'm sure my father asked him not to say anything."

"Because he was embarrassed?" Vanessa asked.

"Not embarrassed," Sidney replied hurriedly. "He was never embarrassed. He was, however, worried about the wrong person finding out what Poet could do. Her abilities weren't passed from generation to generation in our family. Nobody knows where she got her power."

"You have no idea?" Vanessa looked surprised. "I don't understand how that's possible."

"I just had to accept it," I said. "It's possible that answers could've been found on my mother's side of the family, but most of her family members were scattered or gone before I was born. Once my parents died, I had no means to contact any of them."

"It must've been terrifying to go into the system after losing them," Vanessa agreed. "I'm stunned you made it out alive. I mean...you hear stories about little girls getting ravaged. I'm thankful nothing like that happened to you."

I stared at her hard. It felt like a pointed statement and yet to look at her there was nothing to suggest evil brewed beneath her surface. I was not convinced, even a little. I forced a smile. "The system is designed so it will eat you up and spit you out if you're not strong," I acknowledged.

Next to Vanessa, Sidney looked as if he was going through some sort of ordeal. It made him appear to shrink in his chair. I felt the need to ease some of his burden.

"The individuals with Child Protective Services are good people,"

I offered. "They want to do what's best for their young charges. Unfortunately, they're overworked. Children often fall through the cracks."

"Is that what happened to you?" Sidney asked. "Did you fall through the cracks?"

I debated how to respond. Purposely torturing him seemed unnecessary. Still, lying didn't seem an option. "Okay, here it is." I rubbed my hands on my capris, my palms suddenly sweaty. "I was older when I was put in the system. That meant foster families and group homes. Nobody wants to adopt a teenager."

Sidney looked positively wretched.

"On the flip side, I'd already had a family," I continued. "I didn't want to be part of another. I just wanted to survive until I could strike out on my own. At a certain point, I was able to read the intentions of an individual in one of the homes I was staying in. They weren't good." I didn't want to go into a great amount of detail. "I decided that I needed to control my environment. I left the system and moved to the street."

"How did that work?" Vanessa asked. Her tone was so light it was almost as if she was questioning me about my favorite color.

"There was a group. We took care of each other. We worked when we could. Eventually, I ran into Max on the street. I tried to pick his pocket." I wasn't ashamed of the things I'd done to survive, and I wouldn't sugarcoat it now. "He recognized I was different and offered me a place with Mystic Caravan."

"And you've been with the circus ever since?"

"Yes." I kept my eyes on Sidney now. "I ended up where I was always supposed to be."

"I'm glad." He looked sincere. "The things you went through though...I caused that."

"You did," Kade agreed.

I shot him an incredulous look. "Don't," I chastised.

"I can't help it." Kade was firm. "I love you, Poet, but I'm not going to pretend this doesn't bother me." The gaze he leveled on Sidney was fierce. "She was just a little girl. You abandoned her."

Kade's eyes blazed as he continued. "You don't abandon family. You would never abandon me. If Luke and Cole were to have kids, there's no way you would abandon them."

"It was different," I insisted. "Sidney didn't sign on to raise a teenager."

"He's right," Sidney interjected. "I should've found a way to keep you safe. I didn't, and that's on me."

"You did the best you could, Sidney. It's over and done with anyway. Dwelling on it doesn't do any good." I pointedly glared at Kade. "It's time we move on. I know you want to keep in touch once we leave town, but I need to think about that. We have other things going on."

"Like monsters," Vanessa said.

She wasn't going to let it go. I decide to put things out there and let them fall where they may. "I can't get into specifics because I don't know you." I managed a flat smile for Vanessa's benefit. "You might not understand why I am the way I am, but there are rules in our group. We have to be careful what we tell others."

"Oh, it's like a secret society," Vanessa enthused. "That's so cool."

I wanted to choke her. "Something like that," I said. "I can say that you need to be careful. There are zombies out there. That's what you saw me dealing with last night. We have no idea why they're about, or who conjured them. We only know they're a threat, so be careful."

"Zombies?" Vanessa let loose a high-pitched laugh straight from a sorority soirée, and it set my teeth on edge. "Are you joking?"

I shook my head. "I'm only telling you because I don't want anything to happen to you. You can believe me or not. I would hate for you to get hurt because you think I'm joking."

Vanessa looked momentarily taken aback. "I wasn't trying to be annoying, but I just can't believe zombies are real."

"Well, they are." I flashed a smile I didn't feel. "We're hopeful we can solve this relatively quickly. It's not a widespread problem right now. Just be careful and you should be fine."

"We'll be careful," Sidney promised, planting his hand on top of Vanessa's to quiet her. "We appreciate the warning."

"Sure." I rubbed my forehead.

"I also appreciate you at least considering allowing me to see you going forward," he added. "I know that I let you down, but I was afraid.

And I was mourning them just like you. I convinced myself that you would be better off without me. I told myself that you would be accepted into a home and be happy. Obviously I had no idea...and I'm very sorry."

"You don't have to be sorry," I replied.

"Yes, he does," Kade growled.

I ignored him. "My life is complicated, Sidney. I need to think about how this will work."

"That's fine." Sidney nodded once. "I'll be waiting when you're ready."

I leaned back in my chair and gave Kade a stern look. "Take a breath," I muttered.

Kade looked as if he was going to argue further, but he nodded. "Fine." He glanced at Sidney. "Poet is right. We can't go back in time. I'm going to at least try to let this go."

"Thank you," Sidney replied in a soft voice. "Just know, no matter how much you despise me for what I did, it's nothing compared to how I feel about myself."

Kade blinked several times. "I guess that's a start," he said.

DINNER WAS A TWO-HOUR AFFAIR. Sidney and Vanessa left first because Kade was busy texting Cole. Apparently something was happening, but it couldn't be talked about in front of them. I remained in my chair and waited for him to inform me.

"They want to go to the Garden District," he replied. "Apparently Nellie heard whispers about zombies in Lafayette Cemetery."

I let loose a sigh. I wasn't exactly surprised. "Okay. We can meet them there."

"And here I was hoping for drinks and cuddles with my girl." He kissed my temple. He didn't look any happier than I felt. "Let's get it over with."

I offered up a smile as I stood. "We can cuddle when we get home."

He slipped his arm around my waist and tugged.

I was just about to drag my gaze from the table when I caught sight of something. I leaned forward and snagged it, momentarily confused, and then looked to Kade.

"What's that?" he asked.

"Vanessa's napkin," I replied, my mind working a mile a minute. "She was doodling on it while we were talking."

"Is that important?"

I shrugged. "Normally I would say no, but the pattern is interesting."

"It just looks like a bunch of squiggles," Kade replied. "Do those little drawings mean something?"

"It's a veve."

His expression didn't change. "I have no idea what that is."

"The loas all have a veve. It's kind of like a logo that identifies them."

"Which veve is this?"

"I'm not sure." I stuck the napkin into my pocket. "But I'm going to find out."

"What do you think it means?"

"It might be nothing."

"But you don't think that."

"I just want to look into it a little further." I pasted what I hoped was a believable smile across my face. "Let's worry about the Garden District. This can wait."

Kade didn't look convinced. "Are you sure?"

"It's probably nothing." Even as I said so, I wasn't certain I believed it. "The zombies are our main concern. We don't want your intestines being eaten."

"Oh, did you have to go there?" He screwed up his face. "I was just starting to feel better about zombies."

"I'm sorry. You can punish me for it later."

Fifteen

W e had to drive to the Garden District—the streetcars didn't run late enough—and most of our group was outside the cemetery gate when we arrived. They looked grim.

"The gate is open," Nellie announced, as if we couldn't see that for ourselves.

"Well, great," I said as I poked my head in to look around. Lafayette Cemetery was in a largely residential area. The walls were high enough that nobody could see inside if not immediately located near one of the gates. Our biggest problem was Commander's Palace, a popular restaurant down the road. "I guess we should tackle it the same way we did last night."

"We have no idea if any of them escaped," Cole replied. "We just know that the gate is open, which means this is likely a widespread problem."

"Have you seen any zombies?" Kade asked.

"No, but we decided to wait for you guys. We didn't want you wandering in blind behind us."

"Let's go in." I was braced for whatever was to come. "We'll close the gate behind us, kill anything we find, and then patrol the neighborhood."

"And then hit up Commander's Palace for cocktails," Luke added. "I need something to whet my whistle."

I narrowed my eyes. "Whet your whistle?"

"We watched *Young Guns* in our trailer earlier," Cole explained. "He thinks he's Billy the Kid now."

All I could do was shake my head. "Awesome. Just one more thing before we head inside." I'd debated how much I should tell them before the battle. Ultimately I decided it was best to say it. "Kade and I had our fortune read in Jackson Square this afternoon. In the middle of it, the woman seemed to be possessed by some entity and warned us about an upcoming war. She insinuated we'd stuck our noses into business we shouldn't and now have no choice but to clean up the mess."

"You had your fortune told by one of those grifters?" Luke was incensed. "You can tell your own fortune."

"We did it for fun," I replied.

"Are you sure she wasn't faking?" Cole asked.

"She definitely wasn't faking. Her eyes turned white."

"It was very creepy," Kade agreed. "It ruined my plan to get another Hurricane."

"Poor Kade." Luke clapped his shoulder. "You can whet your whistle with me after we beat the zombies, pardner."

I had to press my lips together to keep from laughing. "We'll worry about cocktails when we're finished with the zombies. Don't get distracted."

"Yeah, yeah, yeah." Luke waved off my worry. "We know what we're doing. Let's just get this over with."

Because I was too tired to disagree, I simply nodded. "Let's see if we can use Kade's trick from last night to take them out quickly. Stick together to start. If Kade can freeze them, cleanup should be fast."

"I'm all for that." Nellie rubbed his hands together. "I want to hit up Commander's Palace too."

"I think they have a dress code," I reminded him.

"So." Nellie glanced down at his sparkly spaghetti-strap dress. "This is a classic."

"Of course it is." I took the lead and crept into the cemetery, going just far enough for the rest of the group to file in behind me. Dolph shut the gate behind us, making sure it latched, and then flashed me a thumbs-up before we continued deeper into the grounds.

It was quiet, eerily so, but when we reached the first ell, I saw it wasn't a wasted trip.

"Look at that," Seth said on an exhale, his eyes going wide at the horde of zombies. They'd congregated in one area wandering in a circle.

"Like rats in a maze," Raven noted, her eyebrows drawn together. "Why are they walking in a circle like that?"

"It's the ground," Dolph replied. "There's a ridge. You can easily step over it if you know to look, but those mindless beings can't puzzle solve. They shuffle, so they can't step over the ridge."

My eyes went to the top of the mausoleums. "You would think whoever did this would hang back to make sure their monsters got to see the light of day."

"That doesn't appear to be the case," Cole said.

I rolled my neck. "Well, it makes it easier to dispatch them."

"Do you want me to freeze them?" Kade asked.

"Please." I watched with unveiled interest as he unleashed his magic. This time, he gave it very little thought. It was almost as if he had sense memory when it came to his magic. Once he learned something, he didn't forget. Even better, once he knew it worked he had confidence enough in himself to make sure it worked a second time.

"That's a neat bit of magic," Raven noted when Kade finished. She gave him a bemused smile. "I'm glad you're not all testosterone and nothing else. It's great you have a working brain."

"Yes, we're both happy about that," Kade drawled, rolling his eyes until they landed on me. "Aren't you glad I'm not just a walking, talking slab of beef, baby?"

"I like your beef." I gave him a friendly pat on his rear end and stepped forward with Cole. "There aren't as many of them as there were last night."

"Could more have escaped?" Cole asked.

"I don't know." Something felt off about the scenario. "Most of them got corralled because of the fluke. We'll check of course, but it's possible we lucked out."

"How often does that happen?" Raven challenged.

Almost never. That's why I was so bothered. Still, we had a job to do. "Are you ready?" I asked Cole, extending my right hand.

He linked the fingers of his left hand with mine and we moved away from the group, approaching the hoard from an angle so as not to expose ourselves.

"Just do it," I said when he gave me a questioning look.

He nodded before resting his right hand on the nearest zombie. "*Combustum*," he muttered, calling on his elemental powers. The fire magic flashed hot and raced through the zombies like a tsunami. I amplified my power, so when the flames encompassed the zombies they flared bright for a few seconds. By the time the fire finished raging, there was nothing left but ash.

Nixie skipped forward, an empty vial in her hand, and dropped to the ground next to the ashes.

"What are you doing?" Cole asked as he released my hand.

"I want to see if I can come up with a spell to lead us to zombies in the future," she replied. "I need the remains to experiment with." Her eyes were clear when they moved to the elemental. "Is there a reason I shouldn't?"

He shook his head. "I was just curious. It's a good idea."

"Make sure you grab any extra you might need," I instructed. "I don't want to come back if we don't have to."

"On it." She sent me a chipper smile.

I moved away from Cole to a spot that offered a clear view of the entire aisle. Nothing moved but our group. Nothing breathed but our group. Utter silence surrounded us, yet I knew we weren't alone.

I stared into the darkness, scanning tombs and mausoleums. Even when I reached out with my magic, the only response was from members of my group. It was odd...and disconcerting.

"Are we ready to drink?" Luke asked, appearing at my side so stealthily I almost jumped when he spoke.

"What?" I dragged my eyes to him.

"Drink." Luke mimed holding an invisible glass and chugging it. "I need to get my drink on."

"One of us has to drive back," I replied. "Kade drove his truck."

"I don't need to drink," Kade offered.

"You need to drink," I countered.

"You could just do that thing you do and use your magic to make the cops think somebody else is driving," Luke suggested.

"How does that work?" Cole asked.

"It's something I figured out when I was on the streets," I said. "We might've stolen the occasional car. It was best to control the car with magic and let the cops see someone else behind the wheel. The spell does all the heavy lifting. No driver. No accidents. No getting pulled over."

"Then I say we do that." He slung his arm around my shoulders. "As Luke so rightly put it, let's get our drink on."

"Yes!" Nellie punched his fist into the air. "Let's do it."

"We have to check the neighborhood for zombies first," I reminded them.

"That will take five minutes. It's obvious the zombies got snagged by that little trap this time. We'll be fine."

I could only hope he was right.

THE SEARCH TURNED OUT TO BE FRUITLESS, and no matter how bothered I was by how things played out there was nothing to be done. That meant it was time to drink. We went as a group. There was no reason I couldn't cast a spell for the rest of the vehicles. That would allow everybody to cut loose.

"I can't believe you paid money to have a rando read your fortune," Luke sneered as he sipped his fancy pink cocktail.

"We were just having fun," I replied. "It wasn't supposed to be a big deal."

"It turned into a big deal," Cole noted, his eyes briefly drifting to the table to our right, where Naida, Nixie, Seth and Nellie were having a good time. "Do you think somebody is watching you?"

I nodded without hesitation. "I felt something in the cemetery tonight."

Kade jerked his eyes to me. "What?"

"And why didn't you say anything?" Cole added.

"There was nothing to say. I used my magic to find whoever it was and came up empty. I had nothing to go on but my gut."

"Your gut has never failed us," Luke pointed out as he kicked back in his chair. "If you say there was something there, I believe you."

"But what?" I asked.

"Maybe it was a loa," Raven suggested as she appeared at the table, chair in hand. She nudged Luke over with a look and plopped down between us. "They're powerful. It's been a long time since I crossed paths with one. I don't remember trying to detect one of the jackholes back in the day, but it's possible they can't be detected. They are ancient. They've managed to survive against all odds."

"I've been thinking about that," I admitted.

"You're in my spot," Luke interrupted, annoyance written all over his face as he glared at Raven.

"Shut up, you big baby," Raven shot back. "Let the adults talk for a change." Her eyes focused on me. "What have you been thinking about?"

"I think the loas are gods."

"Like Heaven and Hell?" Raven made a face. "No."

I laughed at her reaction. "I wasn't talking about the biblical God...or any other biblical god for that matter. I'm talking about the other gods. You know, like Cernunnos...and Pan...and Herne."

Raven's eyes narrowed. She didn't outright dismiss my idea, which I took as a good sign.

"The word 'god' has been thrown around far too many times in history," Cole argued. "I've never met a god—and I don't think they're real."

Raven's chuckle was hollow. "I have some bad news for you. Gods *are* real. The gods of old, the ones who lay waste to the planet and used humans as entertainment, are mostly gone. Cernunnos is still running around. I hear he's practically living in Detroit these days."

That was news to me. "What's happening in Detroit?"

"Gate stuff." Raven shrugged. "The reapers are in disarray. Given the fact that they were never supposed to do what they do, that's hardly surprising."

"I don't understand."

"Death is not supposed to be organized. Either way, that's a problem for another time. The point is that gods are real. As to whether the loas are gods, it's not out of the realm of possibility. I've never really considered it before."

"What about that thing you found after dinner?" Kade prodded me.

I was confused. "What thing?"

"That thing on the napkin."

I'd forgotten. "Right." I dug in my pocket and retrieved the item. "Here we go."

"What is that?" Cole asked when I smoothed out the napkin.

"It's a veve," Raven said. "Maman Brigitte."

I lifted my eyes. "You know it on sight?"

She nodded. "It's the heart. I don't know why it's on a napkin."

"Vanessa doodled it during our dinner."

"Who's Vanessa?"

"My uncle's girlfriend."

"Well, isn't that interesting?" Raven's lips pursed as she stared at the veve. "How long have they been together?"

"Several months at least. Sidney said he met her in Boston."

"Do you believe him?"

"I don't have any reason not to. He's never lied to me before." A strangled sound at my right drew my gaze to Kade. "Do you have something you want to say?" I asked pointedly.

He was matter-of-fact. "He abandoned you. No matter how much you want others to believe that doesn't bother you, I know better. He betrayed you, and he could very well be doing so again."

I had to bite back a sigh. "I'm not an idiot, Kade."

"I never said you were, baby."

"I know that Sidney is...deficient...in some respects, but I don't think he's evil. He's just a man who made a hard decision. It might not have been the decision you'd make, but it wasn't an evil decision."

"It feels evil to me." He folded his arms across his chest. "I'll never be okay with him walking away from you."

"I might never be okay with it either," I said. "He might not be family like we are, but that doesn't make him evil. I feel I would know if he was working against me."

Kade nodded but didn't say anything.

"I trust your instincts," Raven said. "What about the woman? Have you tried to read her?"

"No, and that's a failing on my part," I admitted. "I should have done something the night she saw me take out that zombie. She caught me off guard."

"Can you set up another meeting and read her?" Cole asked.

"Sidney said he wants to keep in touch. I was considering sending some free passes to their hotel. We could draw them into the circus and read her there. She was very interested in the circus. We can promise an in-depth tour."

"Do we think she's working for one of the loa?" Luke asked. "This Madam Brigitte?"

"Maman," I corrected. "I guess that would make the most sense."

"It might all make sense," Raven supplied. "Maman Brigitte and Baron Samedi loathe one another like only a couple married for all eternity truly can. You said you felt he was playing a game with you, Poet. Perhaps the game is with his wife and you're just a pawn."

"I can see him wanting to use us as pawns," I said. "We're magical. If she's unleashing the zombies, he needs us to level the playing field."

"They're both gatekeepers for the dead," Raven added. "It does sort of make sense that this is on both of them."

"If we're nothing but game pieces in a magical marriage meltdown, I'm going to be very unhappy," I complained.

Raven snorted. "You and me both. I swear I'll make them pay."

Sixteen

My spell for camouflaging vehicles worked, but I was riddled with anxiety waiting for the team to pile out back at Louis Armstrong Park. The laughter floating over the parking lot was raucous, but it didn't stop me from scanning the surrounding area looking for potential zombies...or a rogue spy.

"Stop." Kade nudged his hip into me. "We're all home and safe. Your spell worked."

I flashed a smile for his benefit. "Of course it worked. I'm a genius."

He slipped his arm around my waist. "Do you want to show me exactly how smart you are in our trailer?"

He wasn't sloppy drunk but clearly tipsy. "Sure, after you drink a bottle of water and take some aspirin. We open tomorrow. No hangovers."

"I have hangover dust," Nixie announced as she skipped in a circle, wiggling her butt as she giggled and moved her hand as if throwing dust. "I can solve any problem you might have."

I smirked. "You need to douse yourself with that dust."

"I'm good." She grinned at me. "Have I mentioned how pretty you are? You're just so pretty."

"Ugh," Raven complained. "Someone shoot me in the head."

135

Luke's hand shot in the air. "I'll do it. Who has a gun?"

"Don't make me hurt you." Raven's gaze was dark before she slowly tracked her eyes to me. "Do you sense anything?"

I shook my head. "I think we're good."

"Okay, I'm going to romance my clown. I expect it to be a lovely evening."

I had far too many images battling for supremacy in my head to settle on one.

"On that note, thank you for giving us all nightmares, Raven," Kade drawled. "I'm going to take my romantic little flower to bed, too. We'll touch base tomorrow. Until then...have a *lovely* evening."

I let him herd me toward our trailer. "You're definitely drinking water before you put a hand on me."

"You're zero fun tonight," he complained.

"Say that again in ten minutes when I'm rocking your world."

He perked up. "You really are pretty," he said as he paused at the trailer door. "You're my pretty, pretty Poet."

"Oh, geez." I shot a look toward the front door of the trailer Luke and Cole shared and found them making out. Apparently love was in the air this evening. "We'd better hope we're not attacked tonight. Nobody will bother getting out of bed to fight the zombies."

"Screw the zombies," Kade said. "They're not getting anywhere near my intestines tonight. Only you can be near my intestines."

"I don't think that's as romantic as you think it is."

"Maybe not, but I'm still going to offer you some earth-shattering loving."

AFTER KADE AND I WERE DONE PLAYING, he crashed hard. He'd already downed some water and aspirin, but I filled another glass and placed two tablets on the nightstand next to him all the same. You can never be too prepared.

I was tired, in desperate need of sleep, but I couldn't settle. I got dressed and headed out.

New Orleans rarely slept. People said it never slept, but that wasn't entirely true. As far as I could tell, the city slept between six o'clock and eleven o'clock each morning. Otherwise, there was always somebody out and willing to entertain.

After a quick spin around Louis Armstrong Park to make sure everything was quiet and settled, I walked toward the French Quarter, something inside propelling me to the area.

I stopped on Bourbon Street to check the revelers. There were drunks as far as the eye could see, but no zombies. That was a relief, because my backup was otherwise engaged...some with each other.

I was on Conti Street with an eye on checking Jackson Square when I heard the footsteps. I glanced to my left and found a woman with flaming red hair matching my steps. She wore what looked like black leather pants, a low-cut top, and her red waves were tucked under the same sort of top hat Baron wore. As if sensing me watching her, she slowly turned in my direction. I wasn't surprised to find her face decked out in skull makeup, which also mirrored Baron's look.

"Maman Brigitte," I said with a nod. There was no reason to pretend I didn't recognize her. "A nice night, eh?"

She let loose a high-pitched giggle. "Every night is nice in the Quarter."

"It's a lovely city."

"It's home."

I slowed my pace when I reached an intersection, debating. It didn't take long to decide to continue forward. She kept pace but remained on the other side of Conti.

"I met your husband," I said, keeping the conversation light should somebody overhear us. "He's...delightful."

"He has the personality of a bowel after a Del Taco feast."

I almost tripped. "Eat a lot of Del Taco, do you?" I asked.

Her laugh echoed along the street. "I love a good taco."

"You're frequenting the wrong places if you're lumping Del Taco in there."

"I'll take that under advisement."

We walked another two blocks in silence. At Jackson Square I cast an uneasy look at the homeless who had spread out on benches for the night. They didn't stir at the sound of our footsteps. They were probably used to sleeping through much louder, I told myself.

"Do you have something specific on your mind?" I asked as we moved to the benches on the right side of the park.

"I always have things on my mind."

"That wasn't really an answer."

"What answer do you seek, little one?"

The "little one" should've bothered me. It should've been condescending, but it felt endearing.

"You have questions," she noted as she moved to the park's iron fence and waved her hand over it. An opening appeared. "Let's chat."

I frowned as she moved through the opening into the park.

"I'm not here to hurt you," she reassured. "In fact, I can't hurt you. Baron was wise when he picked you as his proxy."

If I thought I was confused before, it was nothing compared to what I now felt. "I don't understand."

"You might never understand," she said. "I'll take a chance on you anyway. Come along."

"Are you taking me to another plane?" I couldn't risk her transporting me to another realm, one from which I might never return.

The question had her belting out a laugh. "I'm taking you inside the park. I don't want to be interrupted by the less fortunate residents."

I worked my jaw, debating, and then nodded. "If you try anything funny I'll fight back."

"I expect nothing less." Her teeth gleamed under the moonlight as she waited for me to join her. "There we go." She waved her hand in front of the opening to close it. "See, we're on the same plane. We can talk here without being bothered. The older I get, the more I find that a little interaction with humans goes a long way – often too long."

"What about the police?" I asked, glancing around. "Aren't you worried they'll hear us and come looking?"

"Not so much." She led me to a bench and made a big show of sitting. "Let's do this like proper ladies, shall we?"

I had no idea what to make of her. She was imperious, but not coldly callous. Calculating? Absolutely. She wasn't what I expected, though. I sat on a nearby bench rather than risk sharing one with her. "What do you want to talk about?"

"My husband."

138

I gritted my teeth. "He seems interesting."

"He's the turd that gets stuck on the bottom of your shoe when walking through a duck waste area."

My eyebrows hiked. "Tell me how you really feel."

"I feel the need to end him."

"Why? If you hate him so, why did you marry him in the first place?"

"I was young and naïve. I thought his magic, so much like my own, indicated we were meant to be." She pinned me with a serious look. "We were not meant to be. Sometimes lust is just lust."

I bobbed my head. "I get that."

"You're with a mage." She leaned back on the bench and crossed her legs. "Is it only lust?"

"It's more."

"Make sure before you yoke yourself to him for life."

"I'm sure. He's my...everything."

"And the elemental? I haven't seen one as powerful in centuries. I thought they'd all retreated to different corners of the world."

"He's my friend, more like a brother."

"You work together."

My forehead creased. "Are you annoyed because I'm working with Cole?"

"I'm annoyed by a great many things. Your relationship with the elemental is merely a curiosity. Did you know, back in my time, loas and elementals fought to the death?"

"I can't say I did." I found the conversation fascinating. "Why?"

"Power makes beings crazy for more. Ask my husband, who I've often wanted to put in a straitjacket and set ablaze. I managed to do it about one hundred years ago. Unfortunately, he escaped unscathed."

"We don't want to fight with you," I noted. "That's not our goal."

"What is your end goal?"

"We want to go about our lives without zombies popping up on every corner to threaten the populace."

"The zombies are no threat to you," Maman Brigitte pointed out. "Why not avoid them and stay out of the fight?"

"That's not what we do."

She wasn't happy with my answer. "This battle you've inserted your-self into is one you shouldn't care about. My dealings with my husband are mine. Once every hundred years we mark the passing of our union with a game of sorts. Outsiders are often included, but Baron outsmarted me this time." She tilted her head. "How did he know that you would be here?"

"I don't understand what you're getting at."

"You're one of our children. Can't you grasp that?"

For a moment I didn't realize I wasn't breathing. I stared at her.

"Perhaps you didn't know." Her eyes glinted with amusement. "There was a time when we loa procreated. Our children were special, but not as powerful. We stopped procreating hundreds of years ago, but the children we did create continued in this world.

"Most of our lines have died out," she continued. "It's rare to find one of our own. Somehow, Baron knew about you. He cheated and tilted our game in his favor."

I swallowed hard. "You don't sound happy about that."

"I'm not. We cannot touch our children."

"By choice or outside influence?"

"Perhaps both. I don't want to kill you. I haven't wanted anything that banal in a very long time. But I don't want you sticking your nose in our business."

"Then stop conjuring zombies," I suggested. "It's an easy solution."

"It's not. This is my game. Baron broke the rules using you as an instrument to bring about my fall."

"Baron sounds like a real jerk," I acknowledged. "He's a game-player and I kind of want to hurt him."

She smirked.

"I can't do nothing when innocent people are being attacked," I insisted. "It's not in my nature. I don't have it in me to be indifferent."

"Is that what you think I am—indifferent?"

I shrugged. "I can't get a feel for you. When I try to read you, there's nothing."

"You're not equipped to read me. This...power you have offers you strength against humans. You're not strong enough to take on a loa."

"I don't have any interest in taking you on." I meant it. "I just wanted to have a nice time with my family in the Quarter. I don't understand why you're insistent on playing a game that puts humans at risk."

"They're like ants to us. There are so many. Why get worked up about losing a few here and there? I don't understand you, just as you don't understand me."

"I'm not going to ignore the problem."

"I didn't think you would suddenly kowtow to my wishes," she acknowledged. "I know very little about you other than you're driven to be a hero."

I balked. "I don't care about being a hero. I care about doing what's right."

"If you say so." She smirked. "Baron has outplayed me at every turn this go-around. I'm not happy."

"What does that mean?" I was instantly on alert. "Are you going to tilt the game back in your favor?"

"I always do." She rose to her feet. "The loa in you shouldn't be as strong as it is. You're...different. Your other blood components are strong, but the loa is growing stronger. I look forward to watching your development." She started to the fence, leaving me to scramble behind her.

"I have questions," I said as she used her magic to open another door.

"I'm not your teacher. As I said, we're far removed from the humans now."

"Except that you want to sacrifice them whenever you're bored."

"Yes, there is that." Her smile was soft as we emerged on the other side of the fence. "What do you know about me?"

"You're one of the most important loa. You're often compared to the Celtic goddess Brigid. You're a powerful healer and can cure myriad ailments. You like to drink and carouse, and you're considered feminine and sensual."

Her smile widened. "Most of that is true. I know Brigid. We're not the same person, no matter what folklore would have you believe. What else do you know?"

"Your devotees offer pepper-infused rum in exchange for you standing guard over them in cemeteries." I searched my memory for tidbits. "There's something about the first woman buried in a cemetery and her ties to you, but I can't exactly remember."

"She becomes one of my soldiers," Maman Brigitte replied. "I have an army at my disposal. What else?"

"Supposedly you were often called on to cure sexually-transmitted diseases," I said, my cheeks coloring under her gaze. "You're supposed to be a powerful force who enjoys doling out punishment to the wicked."

Her smile widened. "There. That's what I'm talking about. What does that indicate?"

"I don't know." I held out my hands. "I don't know what any of this means."

"It doesn't *mean* anything. You just need to know that when it's time to pick a side in this fight, some of us have more altruistic reasons for battling."

"You don't want me helping Baron," I surmised.

"Oh, he's arranged it so you'll have no choice. I'm fully prepared for things to go his way this round. There's something else you're missing."

I was at a loss. "What?"

"This is not a game between two parties. There are three at play. You need to be aware of your surroundings, little one. Just because we can't touch you doesn't mean the third corner of the triangle cannot. Be prepared. Baron has set something dark in motion...and there's no turning back."

With that, Maman Brigitte turned toward the riverwalk.

"Is that it?" I called to her back.

"There's nothing else I can offer you right now. Be alert. Things will happen fast."

My stomach heaved. "Are you on my side?"

"I'm on my side. The side you land on is yet to be determined. I look forward to seeing how it plays out."

I watched her until she disappeared into the darkness. I stared in her wake for another few minutes before heading back to the park. By the time I crawled into bed with Kade, who was softly snoring, the sleep I thought would evade me was ready to be embraced.

Seventeen

K ade woke before me. When I opened my eyes, his back was propped against the pillows, and he was drinking the water I'd left for him.

"Morning."

"Hey." He grinned as I tried to prop myself on an elbow. "How did you sleep? Are you hung-over?"

I shook my head. "There's something I have to tell you."

I could've lied about my late-night excursion, or at least refrained from telling him, but that was never really an option. We'd built our relationship on a foundation of trust...well, after I'd kept Max's secret about him being Kade's father for longer than I was comfortable with. I wouldn't ever break that trust again.

"I couldn't sleep last night after you passed out," I started, choosing my words carefully. "I went for a walk."

"By yourself?" He looked incensed.

"I wanted to make sure there were no zombies chomping on Bourbon Street."

"What would you have done if you found some?"

"Handled it." I had no interest in getting into a debate about my monster-hunting skills. "I didn't find any zombies."

"I guess that's good." He rubbed his cheek. "I still wish you'd awakened me."

"I didn't even consider it. You were down for the count."

"Well, at least you're safe."

"I'm not done yet. I didn't see any zombies. I did, however, have a long conversation with Maman Brigitte."

Kade's mouth dropped open.

I wanted to laugh. "She sought me out. We had a very cordial conversation. Nobody was in any danger. The only magic on display was when she opened a hole in the Jackson Square fence so we could have some privacy. The whole thing, including the walk, lasted about thirty minutes."

"What did she say?"

"She said I'm a descendant of the children she had with Baron Samedi a very long time ago."

"Do you believe her?"

"I have no reason not to. She wasn't aggressive. She wasn't even angry. She was annoyed, but I'm guessing that's normal for her."

"Why would she be annoyed about that?" he demanded. "If she chose to have children with a guy she now hates that's on her."

"I don't think it's that simple. She said that Baron purposely tapped me to use against her. She made it sound as if every hundred years or so they celebrate their anniversary by messing with each other on our turf. Apparently Baron thought ahead strategically when he decided to recruit me. She said that they can't touch me."

"Because you're their great-great-great-however many greats-granddaughter?"

"Essentially." I lifted one shoulder. "She sounded as though she didn't want to hurt me, like maybe they entered into an agreement to protect their line. She also mentioned that she was incapable of taking me out even if she wanted to."

"Is it possible she was trying to lull you?"

"Sure, but I don't see the point in that. If she wanted to kill me I have no doubt she could without breaking a sweat."

"Then what was the point of starting a conversation with you?"

"I've been trying to figure that out," I admitted. "It was almost as if she wanted to feel me out. I made it clear I have no loyalty to Baron, but even though she said some very horrible things about him she didn't harbor much hate or resentment."

"What did you sense?"

"I can't sense anything around her. Or him, for that matter. She wanted me to pull from my knowledge of the loas, asked what I knew about her. She let me meander through it until I got to the part about her being known for unleashing payback on certain oppressors."

He took another sip of water. "Why would she want you to know that?"

"I'm guessing because she wants me to think hard before inserting myself in this battle. I told her we can't ignore the zombies. If she wants to fight with her husband for kicks and giggles, she needs to figure out another way to do it."

"How did she react to that?"

"She said she doesn't care about humans. She actually likened them to ants, which I found a little obnoxious. It was the final thing she said to me that stuck, though."

"Which is?"

"She intimated that there might be another loa involved in all of this, another corner of a triangle. She didn't say who, or why they would be involved, but it felt as if she was trying to include me in something."

"But you have no idea what."

"No."

He was quiet a long time, the only noise in the room from the pedestal fan we slept with and his sipping. "Well, I guess we know more than we did. I'm not sure what help the information is, but it does fill in a few of the gaps, including about you." His gaze was speculative. "How do you feel about all of this?"

I honestly didn't know. "I've always wondered what I am."

"Now you know."

"Well, I know that I have loa in my blood. They procreated a very long time ago. Generations ago. I have other things in my line. She seemed intrigued by that, said she would be watching. She almost seemed impressed that Baron managed to snag me for his team. I don't get the feeling that she likes him, but she may still love him."

"And yet they're trying to destroy one another."

"I think it's just a game to them. I wonder how things would go if someone else posed a threat to either of them."

"What do you think we should do?"

That was easy. "Open the circus."

"Right." He let loose a hollow chuckle. "The show must go on."

"There's nothing we can do until one or both of them shows their hand. They're in control. We're merely pawns. We're going to have to wait it out."

"I can't tell you how much I hate that."

COLE PICKED UP BREAKFAST FROM A restaurant I'd told him about. Oceana was famous for its huge bowls of biscuits and gravy. I was a big fan. The four of us sat at our shared bistro table between the trailers and talked about the day in front of us.

Luke and Cole listened raptly as I related my conversation with Maman Brigitte again. Neither were happy when they heard I'd left on my own, but only Cole kicked up a fuss. Luke knew me well enough to recognize arguing with me about my safety was a wasted effort.

After that, we prepared for our day.

"Call me if you need help," I instructed Cole. "There's no shame in reaching out. This is your first time in charge. If the workers give you grief, tell me and I'll step in."

"As much as I appreciate the offer, I prefer to do this on my own," he said. "We've been getting along. There's nothing to worry about."

I hoped that was true. "Just remember that we're a family and we're in this together."

"Did you remember that when you went wandering around the Quarter on your own last night?"

I narrowed my eyes. "I'm an adult."

"We're a family, something you're constantly telling us. There is no reason to put yourself in unnecessary danger when you have an entire battalion ready to serve as backup."

"I didn't need backup."

"You were lucky. Loas are new to us. They're powerful. I want to keep our family intact."

I hated that he had a point. "Nobody got hurt, and I gained a bit more information. Let's take it as a win."

"Fine, but don't think we're done with this conversation."

"Ugh," I grumbled. "You're worse than Kade sometimes."

"He has to walk a fine line between loving you and not stepping on your toes. I don't have that problem. I can love you and yell. In fact, I'm gifted in that department."

I didn't want to smile—it would only encourage him—but I couldn't help myself. "You're a bit of a bossy pain."

"Then I fit right in with the rest of our quaint foursome." He grabbed my cheek between his fingers and gave it a jiggle. "Don't freak out the people who love you. It's not fair or necessary."

I nodded because there was nothing else to do. "Fine, but you're still not the boss of me."

ONCE THE PARK GATES OPENED, the area filled quickly. The locals, rather than the tourists, were more interested in what we had to offer. That only proved that we'd made the right choice in selecting Moonstone Bay as our permanent home. A city like New Orleans couldn't sustain profitability.

"Come in," I said when I saw someone hovering near the opening of my tent. I'd already given ten readings and expected to barrel through another five or so before taking a break. "Have a seat."

I shuffled my cards and put my face toward the fan Kade had erected to keep me from sweating to death. I was all smiles when I turned to my next customer.

"Should I call you Grandpa?" I asked Baron Samedi dryly.

He grinned as he leaned back in the provided chair. He had a lackadaisical approach to life, and under different circumstances I had to wonder if I would've liked him. As it stood, I definitely didn't like him—mostly.

"I hear you've been talking to Brigitte," he said. "How is my darling bride?"

"She likens you to duck turds."

"She always did have a sense of whimsy. What face is she wearing today?"

I was taken aback. "I...don't...." I trailed off, uncertain. Then I regrouped. "I guess I didn't realize you could glamour. I'm guessing the face she showed last night was her true one, at least if I'm to believe this is your true face."

"We can look as we want," Baron replied. "I've never understood the need for artifice. If you're as handsome as me, you want to show it off."

I extended the deck of cards to him. "Cut."

He eyed the stack in my hand for a long moment, and I thought he would decline. Instead, he did as I instructed. "I haven't been able to track down Brigitte since she arrived in town. I find it interesting that she sought you out when she's hiding from everyone else."

"Maybe she likes my sense of style."

He barked out a gregarious laugh. "I doubt that. You favor my side of the family, not hers."

"She believes you keep coming to me because of some loophole that prevents her from touching me. Is that why you picked me?" I flipped up the first card. The Tower—which could mean death and destruction in certain formations.

"I selected you because I felt a kinship with you. Besides, your circus is famous, something she would know if she bothered to keep her ear to the ground in this realm. She's become disinterested in life. I want her to rejoin the land of the living and to stop spending so much time with the dead."

I studied his face for a long time. "You love her," I said. "After all these centuries, after all the fights and competitions, you still love her."

"My feelings for my wife are complicated. They're also none of your business."

"Oh, no." I wagged a finger. "You brought me into this. You approached me at the store."

"That was only after you fought the zombie on the riverwalk. I knew you were up for the task I had in mind."

"I saw you earlier that day," I countered. "You were outside Madame Caroline's shop. That was long before I saw the zombie on the riverwalk, which means you were monitoring me before I got involved." I flipped another card—the Fool.

Baron's smile widened. It was almost as if he was garnering joy from the reading. "I guess you caught me. I did know you were coming. I keep minions in town to monitor my interests. I've been aware of you for quite some time."

"But why approach me now?

"I didn't need you before. There was no reason to interrupt your life before this visit."

"How about you have answers to my past?"

"That is not my concern. You are responsible for your own destiny."

"I might buy that if you weren't trying to involve me in your fight with your wife." I flipped another card—Death. The odds of these three cards appearing together were long. "Just tell me something: Are you still in love with Brigitte?"

He blinked twice and then held out his hands. "She is my wife. When I married her I mated for life. Our relationship is complicated, as I've mentioned."

"That wasn't really an answer."

"I don't owe you an answer."

My lips curved up at the corners. "You do love her." I was absolutely certain of that. "She loves you. Yet you constantly fight. What's up with that?"

He let loose a hearty chuckle. "You of all people know you can't always control who you love. She is my mate. If life was always happy or simple it wouldn't be worth living. Our games are our business."

"Except she made it sound as if somebody else—a loa, maybe—was sticking their nose in your business."

He sat up straighter, reacting with something other than cool confidence for the first time since I'd crossed paths with him. "Interesting." He darted his eyes to the tent opening and then back to me. "Have you seen anyone else?"

"I don't know. I can't sense you guys. It's not as if there's a void. You just refuse to compute for me."

"Your powers are interesting. You're capable of using them for more than you do, but fear holds you back."

"You think I'm afraid?"

"A healthy dose of fear is fine. But you sometimes let it hold you back, and that's to your detriment. Most of the time you remind me of me."

"Yeah, let's not go there," I said. "I want to know what the ultimate plan is. Why is Brigitte unleashing zombies? Why are you tapping me to eradicate them? If there is another loa messing with your game, who is it? Why would he or she get involved?"

"You ask a lot of questions."

"And you provide scant answers. If you want my help, tell me."

This time when he laughed I knew it was at my expense. "You're so amusing." He clucked his tongue. "You'll help because it's the right thing to do. That's the human in you. You didn't inherit that weakness from Brigitte or me."

"I happen to think it's a strength."

"That's because you don't understand your place in this world." Baron shook his head. "Look at those cards and tell me what you see."

I glanced back at the table. "If anybody else had gotten these cards I would assume a terrible death awaited them," I admitted. "You're not a normal mortal. These cards mean something different for you."

"You're correct. This...game...won't play out as any of us want. If Brigitte is right and there's another player, this could blow up in all of our faces."

"So, what do we do?"

"You don't do anything but what you have been doing. I'll handle the rest."

"You're asking me to put a lot of faith in you when I know you've been playing a game from the start."

"I'm not asking you to do anything. I'm telling you that it will be a waste of time to try to get ahead of us. Our intellect is vastly superior."

"Okay, Khan." My mind immediately landed on the *Star Trek* villain for some reason. "You're entitled to your beliefs, but I'm not backing down."

"I don't expect you to." He pressed his fingers to his lips and offered up a chef's kiss. "Tell Brigitte I admire her most recent move and approve. Also, I'll be seeing her soon."

"Will you be seeing me soon?" I wanted him to say no. The last thing I needed was to be used as a pawn in an age-old grudge between bitter spouses.

"Definitely." He gave a saucy wink. "You're my flesh and blood, and you've proven yourself most intriguing. There's no escaping me now."

"That's a total bummer."

"You'll survive." He paused by the tent flap. "You might learn to love me."

"I don't see that happening."

"Never say never."

Eighteen

I took a break after the loa departed and went to find Raven. She was in the House of Mirrors, looking bored, at the back of the third room.

"He stopped in to see me again," I announced.

Raven arched an eyebrow. "Who?"

"Elvis. Who do you think?"

"There's no need to get snippy." Raven grabbed my arm. "Come on." She led me into her office at the back of the building and shut the door before speaking again. "I don't understand his fascination with you."

"Apparently I'm one of his descendants," I said.

"He told you that?"

"Maman Brigitte did when I was out for a walk last night."

"Oh, geez." Raven rubbed her forehead. "I guess I'm behind. Lay it on me."

I did just that, leaving nothing out.

"Freaking loas," Raven seethed. "They're always so dramatic. Why can't they just be dignified like other gods?"

"Do you know many dignified gods?"

"A few. Then there are gods who live in holes in the ground and charm slugs to follow you around just to mess with you."

I was curious but getting sidetracked when there was so much at stake wasn't an option. "This isn't over, and if there really is a third loa messing with us we need to figure out which it is."

On a sigh, Raven opened her laptop and started typing. "There are a lot of loas. I don't know that we can narrow it down without knowing why this is happening."

"Do Baron Samedi and Maman Brigitte have a common enemy?"

"As far as I know, the loas fight with one another constantly. They make friends for a bit and then become enemies again. There's no reason to the madness."

I pursed my lips. "What about someone with specific ties to New Orleans?"

She shot me an incredulous look. "Are you kidding me? They all have ties to New Orleans, Poet. They follow the people of their faith. Not all of them live here, but back in the day this was the voodoo capital of the world."

"So, what do we do?"

She shrugged. "I'll start digging through the list. We might be able to rule some out simply because of who the loa is. That will still leave a significant number to wade through."

"Well, at least it's a start." I darted my eyes to the door, the sound of laughter on the other side drawing my attention. "You know what really bothers me about this entire thing?"

"I'm sure I have an idea but go ahead."

"It's that these higher beings—that's how they see themselves—feel it's okay to kill others in their search for entertainment. Brigitte acted as if I was the one with the problem when I voiced my concern regarding the zombies killing innocents."

"Are you really surprised?"

"I guess I have trouble understanding why they're like this."

"It's the longevity."

I blinked several times. "Was that you explaining something to me?" I asked finally.

"It's the longevity," she repeated. "If you live long enough, you

153

become jaded to the problems of others. Even your own problems no longer feel dire because there's no fear associated with the day-to-day. At a certain point, you go from fearing death to becoming indifferent. Your view of how others fit into the world changes."

It was a fairly profound thought, although I wasn't certain how I should feel about it. "Are you indifferent to life?" Raven had been alive for a very long time. Maybe not as long as the loas, but not far off. She seemed to understand them.

"I was getting there," she admitted with a half-smile. "I didn't think there was anything worth engaging with for a bit. Then I found something that made me happy to greet the day."

"Are you talking about Percival?" I couldn't understand her relationship with the clown. The man had a fake British accent, for crying out loud. Ever since she'd hooked up with him, there had been a marked change in her attitude. It was almost miraculous.

"I think I'll avoid answering that question," she said on a half-laugh. "I will say that one thing I've learned throughout all these years is that you don't live for the big things. You live for the little things. Like the way you curl up on Kade's lap when we have a bonfire. The way you smile at him when he whispers to you. That's reason to live. The rest of it, the big fight, those are simply details we have to grapple with."

"How did you get so profound?" I asked as I pushed myself to a standing position.

"Practice."

I laughed. "I'm glad you found something to live for." I meant it. "I don't understand why it's a clown, but you do you."

"When you reach a certain age, there's no reason to be anything other than what you are."

"That's a good motto for all of us to live by."

I SPENT THE AFTERNOON GIVING READINGS. By the time my last guest of the day made his way into my tent, I was ready for a meal and a nice cocktail in the Quarter.

"So, you believe women aren't interested in you because of a curse that you somehow managed to contract without your knowledge?" I asked.

Ben Mayer, blond and dour, bobbed his head. "I know who cursed me."

After a few seconds of contemplation, I decided to wade into the mess rather than brush him off. "Who cursed you?"

"Do you really need to know that?" Ben's expression was difficult to read. He was clearly hiding something.

"I really do," I confirmed. For some reason, I was betting on this story being funny. "Was it a former girlfriend?"

"No." He sank lower in his chair, his shoulders drooping.

"Why would someone curse you unless they were angry with you?"

"I didn't say the person who cursed me wasn't angry," he replied hurriedly. "She wasn't a girlfriend."

He was being purposely vague, which made me suspicious. "Was it a woman who wanted to date you, but you weren't interested?" I estimated his age at around twenty-four. The way he kept huffing told me he was a bit petulant.

"No." He pursed his lips and looked anywhere but at my face.

I pressed my palms to the table with a slap, drawing his attention. "You need to tell me what's going on. I can't help unless I know the details."

"Aren't you psychic?" Ben was shrill. "If you have psychic powers you should already know."

He had a point, loath as I was to admit it. "If I use my psychic powers I could hurt you," I lied. "If you're mentally strong—which you clearly are—an invasion could force you to fight back. Your body could react negatively."

He was suddenly suspicious. "How?"

"Your blood flow could be interrupted." I fully embraced the lie. "Your extremities could fall off. I'm talking fingers, toes, and your...um...you know."

It took Ben a full beat to grasp the implication. "My penis?" He screeched it so loud I was certain people outside the tent heard.

"That would be the extremity I'm talking about," I confirmed. "It's really better if you tell me the salient points and don't make me go looking for information."

"Fine." Ben threw his hands in the air, reminding me of a pre-teen gearing up for a fit. "My mother has decided that she doesn't trust me to get my act together and move into my own place, so she cast a curse and now no woman will date me."

Now we were getting somewhere. "Am I to take it that you live in your mother's house?"

"Her guesthouse."

"Your mother has a guest house?" It seemed that if the family was so well off it had a guest house that the mother could afford to help her son rent a place in another location.

"They call it a guest house, but I think they were actually slave quarters at one time. Almost all the creole cottages have them."

I knew that. I'd been way off about his mother's financial status. "You're like twenty-four, right?"

"How do you know that?" His tone turned reverent. "Was that magic?"

"An educated guess, but sure." I tapped my fingers on the table. "Why do you still live with your mother?"

He shrugged. "Why wouldn't I? Rent is expensive."

"Okay, but you're twenty-four. You shouldn't be living with your mother. Do you have a job?"

"Of course. I'm a server at Olde Nola Cookery two days a week."

"Why only two days?"

"Because I need two days buffer between shifts to recover. Work is hard."

I saw where this was going. "You think your mother cursed you so women won't date you because she wants you out of her house."

"Yes. She says I'm lazy. Can you believe that? She's evil."

"Yes, obviously she's the problem," I drawled. "Tell me why you think you're cursed with women."

"The last five I've interacted with have told me to get a job."

"Interacted with? How were you interacting with these women?"

"Well, Penny and I met at a riverwalk concert. We were getting along great and then we decided to get drinks from one of the vendors. I didn't have money—drinks are expensive—so of course she had to pay. She basically told me to take a hike after that. There's no way that's not my mother's fault."

"No way." I shook my head. He didn't pick up on the fact that I was mocking him. "And the other instances?"

"Well, Gina and I made it through three dates before she kicked me to the curb. She said it was because I took twenty bucks from her wallet, but it wasn't that. She makes enough that she shouldn't have noticed the twenty bucks."

"Wow."

"Then there was Vivian." Ben made a face. "I told her she had an old lady name and that she probably had old lady money—that's totally a thing. She slapped me. I've said that to women before and they haven't slapped me. That's how I know this is on my mother."

I stared at him, dumbfounded.

"Do you want to know about the other two?"

"No, I do not." I flashed a smile I didn't feel. "I think it's time for some hard truths, Ben."

"About my mother? She's totally a witch. I've already figured it out."

"I have no idea if your mother is a witch," I replied. "But you, good sir, are a total tool. Your mother isn't to blame. She didn't curse you. It's your fault."

"How can you say that?" Ben's eyes were glassy, as if he was about to burst into tears. "I'm the victim."

"You have a victim mentality," I readily agreed. "You are not the victim, however. Your poor mother is the victim...and those unsuspecting women you tried to romance. You're the common denominator."

Ben squealed. "You're a scammer! You're trying to take my money. Did my mother get to you?"

I was officially at my limit. "Ben, you're a tool. You're lazy, and I'm betting that laziness extends to your prowess in bed.

"You're the problem. You need to get a job," I continued. "A job you go to five days a week and stay there for eight full hours each day. You need to save money so you can get your own place. And, most importantly, you need to get out of your mother's house. You're a man. It's time to act like one."

Ben blinked several times, and I was wondering if he was absorbing what I said. Then he slowly got to his feet. "My mother definitely got to you."

"Oh, grow up." I was about to unload a rude pile of truth on him when I heard a scream from the other side of the tent flap. "Hold that thought." I moved around him and poked my head outside. Screams weren't unheard of when we were on location. Occasionally guests got wound up—and drunk. This scream didn't sound like it was of the fun or giddy variety.

"What's going on?" I grabbed a woman who was hurrying away from the big top by the wrist. "What's happening?"

Her eyes went wide. "Let me go." She slapped at my hand.

"I'm not trying to hurt you," I reassured her. "I'm just trying to figure out what's going on."

"Zombies! That's what's going on."

My heart sank. "Zombies?"

I didn't realize Ben had followed me out of the tent until he lent his imperious opinion. "Zombies aren't real."

I ignored him and kept my focus on the woman. "Where?"

"Over there." She made a vague gesture with her free hand. "Now let me go."

I released her wrist and looked in the direction she'd indicated. Normally I would've chalked up her reaction to drunken shenanigans and called it a day. The dreamcatcher should've alerted us to their presence.

"Stay here," I ordered Ben as I started in the direction of the midway.

"I certainly will not," Ben shot back as he chased after me. "I don't appreciate your attitude, and to let a woman like my mother, who clearly doesn't care about her own offspring, dictate how you do your job...well...that's just unacceptable."

"You're a huge man-child who takes no responsibility for his actions," I said, not bothering to look over my shoulder. "You need to realize that you're an adult and start doing something to fix your situation. Your mother shouldn't have to do all the heavy lifting for you."

"I get too tired if I work two days in a row," Ben snapped. "Do you want me to be tired?"

"I want you to grow up. I—"

A scream interrupted me, and when I rounded the corner by the ring toss I found a woman trying to climb into the booth to escape a zombie. The creature looked to have crawled out of a centuries'-old grave before going on a rampage.

"It's the end of the world!" the woman screeched at me.

I grabbed the creature around the neck. There was very little remaining flesh, and when the zombie started snapping at me it was as if I were fighting a skeleton.

"It's the rapture!" the woman screamed.

I tuned her out and gave the zombie a shake. One of the creature's arms fell to the ground. The fingers clawed at the ground, making the arm appear to crawl toward me.

"Omigod!" Ben screamed. "Did you use your powers on him? How did you really know I was twenty-four?"

Before I could answer, Cole appeared. He had a cut on his right cheek and what looked to be soot on his face. He pressed his hand to the back of the zombie, and I immediately released it as it went up in flames. Then he stomped on the arm crawling along the ground, pulverizing it.

"We have a problem," he announced.

I was incredulous. "Oh, you think?"

"They're everywhere."

"We have to find Kade."

Nineteen

The big top was chaotic. Luke was in the center ring, top hat in hand, arms extended to keep a snarling zombie from encroaching on his space.

"Where's Kade?" I demanded, glancing around.

"I don't know." Cole looked as if he was ready to leap over several bodies to get to Luke, but I grabbed his arm.

"Don't even think about it," I warned. "We need Kade. Luke can handle himself."

I thought Cole would argue with me, but he nodded. We dashed out of the tent, and I almost immediately slammed into a broad chest.

"It's me!" Kade barked when I raised my hands to unleash a burst of magic.

Relief washed over me as I gave him a quick hug. "We need to take them all out at once."

Kade nodded. "How will we explain that to the guests?"

"We'll pretend it's part of the show."

"Freeze them," Cole ordered, his gaze intent. "Do it now."

Kade did as instructed, his hands flaring to life as he reached inside the tent and grabbed the nearest zombie.

Luke, still in the center ring, seemed close to meltdown. Despite

160

that, he did his best to keep the crowd in check. "Everybody remain calm!"

I slid my eyes to Cole, who seemed relieved to find his boyfriend safe, and then extended my hand. "Ready?"

Cole linked his fingers with mine. "Let's do it."

"Go," I said as I held his gaze.

Cole's hand caught fire. He never took his eyes off Luke as he extended it to the closest zombie. The crowd was confused by the frozen zombies.

The zombie nearest us exploded in flames. He was followed by the others in the tent—and likely in the park—in spectacular fashion.

An "ooh" went up from the crowd as the flames rose. As the zombies crumbled to ash and the flames burned out, the noise crescendoed into an "aah." To my surprise, there was a split-second of silence before the crowd broke into thunderous applause.

"Wow," someone yelled. "That was freaking amazing!"

"Do it again," a child insisted. "Make them do it again, Mommy."

Cole released my hand. He looked as flummoxed as I felt.

"It's New Orleans," I said. "Nothing is too out of the ordinary."

"I guess." Cole raised his hand to catch Luke's attention. "He's okay," he said after a few seconds.

"I think everybody is okay," I replied. "We lucked out. In fact—" A frantic voice broke through the protective wall in my head.

Come to the House of Mirrors right now. Bring the pixie zombie tonic.

"Raven," I gritted out as I turned away from the tent.

"What about her?" Cole asked as he and Kade gave chase. "Is she okay?"

"She's asking for the zombie tonic." I ran through the aisles, not stopping until I reached Nixie's booth. She'd left it open but was nowhere in sight. She was likely helping guests. "Here." I grabbed the tonic. "I'll go to Raven. You guys search the rest of the park."

Kade immediately started shaking his head. "You might need us to do the spell again. We're not separating."

"The spell should've knocked out all the zombies in the park," I argued.

"And the dreamcatcher should've alerted the second the zombies crossed it," Kade shot back. "Nothing is working correctly. Suck it up because I'm coming with you."

"He's right," Cole said. "Let's get to Raven."

I grumbled but turned to the House of Mirrors. "We're going to talk about this later," I warned.

We picked our way to the House of Mirrors, peering around every corner and listening for the telltale shuffling. We found the room empty.

"Raven?" I called.

In my office.

I headed in that direction, my senses alert as I searched for stragglers. When I pushed open the door to Raven's office, I found her on the floor. She was cradling Percival in her lap, and I was almost positive she'd been crying.

"Raven?"

"He tried to save me," she said. "I told him it wasn't necessary, that I could take care of myself, but he wouldn't listen. They bit him."

I held up the zombie tonic. "It's okay." I dropped to my knees, skirting a pile of ash. "Zombie?"

She nodded.

"They were everywhere," Percival said. He didn't bother with his fake British accent as I poured Nixie's dust into his open wound, instead grimacing as he tried to pretend he wasn't in pain. "We ran this way, but it was too late."

"How did they get in here?" Kade moved to the door. "I'm going to check the back door."

"I'll go with you," Cole offered, shooting me a reassuring look. "Nobody should be alone right now."

I smiled in thanks and then focused on Percival. "How do you feel?" I pressed my hand to his forehead. He wasn't burning up, which meant the bite had happened recently.

"I'm fine." He lobbed a happy smile at me. "I'm with my beloved. If I should happen to shuffle off this mortal coil, there's no place I'd rather be than in her arms." The accent was back.

I flicked my eyes to Raven.

"He's dramatic," she said to my unasked question. "He can't help himself."

I grinned. "The bite should be gone in an hour."

"It already feels better," Percival said. "Still, if you want to dote on me, my beloved, I won't complain."

"He's a bit of a pain," she acknowledged. "Overall, he's not so bad. The 'beloved' thing is tedious, but he's a jackhammer in the sack."

I couldn't help but smile. "Ah, the little things."

She nodded.

I flicked my gaze to the door as Kade and Cole returned.

"It was open," Kade confirmed. He was calm as he looked me over. "I know you don't want to hear it, but we need to check the Quarter. We may not have gotten all of them."

I pocketed the pixie dust. "There's more in Nixie's booth if you need it."

"Go." She waved me off. "Once I'm sure he's fine I'll handle locking down the park."

"Try to figure out why the dreamcatcher failed while you're at it."

Her eyebrows moved toward one another. "It failed?"

"We need to find out, but first things first. We'll grab Luke and scour the French Quarter. You take control here. We'll regroup when we get back."

She gave me an encouraging nod. "Don't worry about us here. We can take care of ourselves. Protect the innocent. That's the only way we can truly win this one."

LUKE REFUSED TO CHANGE OUTFITS. I didn't bother arguing with him. Instead, we crossed Rampart as a foursome and started searching.

"Where?" Cole asked as I scanned the street.

"Where else?"

"Bourbon Street."

We examined every face. It wasn't easy given the way people were jumping around and whipping beads. Kade caught a set before they whacked me in the face and threw them back at the revelers.

"She's already taken," he said gruffly.

"I don't want to take her from you," the man replied. "I just want to see her boobs."

I drawled, "I think that could be the nicest pick-up line I've ever heard."

The man apparently thought I was sincere because he nodded. He licked his lips, his eyes never moving from my chest. "Go ahead."

Luke stepped in front of me and lifted his shirt. "Mine are better." He flexed for good measure. "Now, go away. Try not to sexually harass women while you're at it. And if you could stop throwing beads at people's faces, that would be great."

The man adopted a downtrodden expression. "You're a bummer." Despite that, he reached out and touched Luke's chest. "Not as good as I expect from her, but I'll take it."

Luke's smile was congenial. "Awesome."

We moved down the street, everybody looking in a different direction. I was about to declare Bourbon Street safe when I saw Sidney coming out of the Royal Sonesta, a smile on his face. He was looking over his shoulder at whoever followed him instead of paying attention to the man darting toward him.

"*Congelo*," I intoned, whipping a freezing spell at the zombie.

When Sidney turned back around, he seemed surprised to find someone near him. Then his eyes went wide, and his mouth fell open as he looked into the zombie's face.

I was about to yell at him to go back when I saw another zombie approaching him from his left. I hurried forward and caught the creature by the throat before it could bite a chunk out of Sidney's neck, my hip slamming my uncle back into the hotel exterior.

Cole walked up next to me and placed a flaming hand on the zombie's head, dropping the creature in its tracks before extending the same hand to take out the one I'd frozen. Within seconds, only a lingering scent of overcooked barbecue remained.

"What was that?" Sidney asked with a gasp.

I flicked my eyes to Vanessa. She'd positioned herself in the entryway to the hotel, where she could easily dart inside if necessary. Why had she slowed her pace? Why hadn't she kept up with Sidney?

"You're fine," Cole replied. "It's just part of the Bourbon Street show."

Sidney didn't look convinced. His eyes sought—and found—me. "What's going on?"

"There's a situation," I replied.

Sidney was incredulous. "You just burned two people alive."

"Not people." I looked back at Vanessa. I could've sworn she had a smug smile on her face. She shuffled it aside quickly and fixed me with a wide-eyed stare.

"This is bad, right?" she asked in an innocent voice.

"It's not good," I replied. "You should go back inside. Don't come out."

"We're going to dinner," Sidney said dumbly.

"Eat at one of the hotel restaurants."

"You have to go outside to access them."

Were we really having this discussion? "Then order room service," I snapped.

"We just want to know what's going on," Vanessa demanded.

"We should let Poet and her friends go back to whatever they're doing," Sidney said. He looked caught. "This is her business."

"It is," I readily agreed. "I'm trying to keep you safe."

"Then we'll do as you ask." Sidney made an attempt at a smile. "We don't need to go out tonight." He grabbed Vanessa's arm and nudged her back toward the hotel. "Please contact me when you can talk. I would like to arrange another meal before you leave town." The request was stiff, as if it took him considerable effort.

"I'll do what I can," I promised. "I'm sorry if I was cold. I just...have things I need to do."

When Sidney smiled this time he managed a wan one. "Go do whatever you need to."

I started moving to my right.

"Be safe," he called after me.

For some reason, the response rankled me. "We know what we're doing," I reassured him, forcing myself to keep from exploding.

With that, I offered the lamest wave imaginable and started down Conti Street.

"That was weird," Cole said.

"The weirdest," Luke confirmed

I did my best to keep my face impassive. "I don't think I'm handling this new family situation all that well."

"You're doing the best you can," Cole countered. "Nobody expects you to forge a relationship with your uncle out of thin air after so many years apart, and so many hard feelings. Do what feels right."

"I have no idea what that is," I admitted on a sigh. "It feels like too much. Life was easier when he wasn't part of it."

"Then don't let him back into your life," Kade said. "He doesn't deserve you."

"If I tell him to go, he will."

"Is that so bad?" Kade asked.

"There's a finality to it that I don't know I'm okay with."

"I'm okay with it," he grumbled.

Cole gave Kade a hard shot to the ribs. "This isn't about you."

"I know. I just...hate the guy. He didn't do what was necessary for Poet. He shouldn't be able to slide back in as if that didn't happen. She deserved more from him."

"I don't think it's about what I deserve," I said as we moved to the intersection of Royal and Conti to scan for suspicious movement. "I either move forward or let him go."

"Do I get a vote?" Kade asked.

I hesitated and then shook my head. "I'm sorry, but no. My relationship with Sidney has to be my own."

"That's how it should be," Cole insisted. "Ignore Kade."

"If anybody is wondering, I agree with Kade," Luke interjected. "Poet is far better than her slimy uncle who abandoned her. We should kick him in the nuts, shave his head, and be on our merry way."

I couldn't help smiling. "I'll take that under consideration."

"You're going to think about how you want things and ignore these two," Cole countered. "They want to protect you. They want to make sure you never feel an ounce of hurt. It's too late for that. You've felt the hurt and now you have to grapple with the aftermath. It's your decision."

Cole stroked my hair, pushing it from my face to stare into my eyes. "They don't get a vote on this. You decide."

"What if I don't know what to do?"

"It's still up to you. Don't let them steal your agency."

"Hey! I was just minding my business here," Luke complained. "Don't give me grief."

Cole ignored him. "We can't make this decision for you. Just give it time. You can't decide when we have zombies on the loose."

"Speaking of that, we need to keep searching. I was about to declare the Quarter zombie-free when they moved on Sidney. We need to keep looking."

Cole pulled away. "Let's go up and down the streets and see what we come up with. After that, we'll regroup with the others."

Twenty

I was exhausted by the time we got back to the park. The rest of our team was gathered, their heads bent together. They looked as tired as I felt.

"How is Percival?" I asked Raven.

"He's fine," she replied. "His arm has nearly healed. No fever. He's in bed. I'll check him again, but I don't expect any problems."

"That's good. What about the dreamcatcher?"

"The threads have been severed on the far side of the park," Naida replied. "It was obviously a magical assault, and whoever did it is powerful. I don't know of any creature who could do that."

"Maybe a loa," I mused.

Raven nodded. "Your grandfather has been by twice that we know of. The first time the dreamcatcher alerted. You said he stopped by today, but it didn't alert."

I nodded. "I realized it at the time, but I didn't dwell on it. I figured he simply found a way around it. I guess it was more than that."

"Maybe he was trying to tell you something," Cole offered. "Maybe he expected you to realize something was wrong with his visit."

"Why not just tell us?" Nellie demanded. He was sweaty and his pink dress had seen better days, which told me he'd been fighting in my absence.

Cole held out his hands. "Maybe there's a rule that you can't tattle on the other loa. It might be an unspoken rule, but it sort of makes sense."

"Not to me." Nellie pouted. "Is anybody else sick of these freaking loas messing with us just because they can?"

Several hands shot in the air.

"We need to figure out how to kill them," Nellie said grimly. "I don't like being played with."

I agreed but killing loas didn't seem an option. "They play by their own rules," I supplied. "Maman Brigitte made it sound as though Baron had somehow changed the rules of the game."

"And we know it's not just the two of them playing," Luke added. "There's at least one more."

"Baron said he and Brigitte do this every hundred years or so to mark their anniversary."

"Some party," Dolph muttered. "Putting people in danger doesn't sound like much of a celebration."

"That's the thing: They don't care about humans. They're not only indifferent to humans, they believe they're beneath them."

"I understand their point of view," Raven said. "They've been around a long time. You become indifferent when you live that long."

It was a continuation of our earlier discussion, and I could only nod. "They need to stop using New Orleans as their murderous playground. Unfortunately, I have no idea how to stop it. Brigitte suggested we're now considered part of Baron's team. Maybe we need to flip the script so there are no teams."

"How do we do that?" Kade asked as he sank onto one of the picnic table benches. "How do we play the game when we don't even know the rules?"

I wished I had an answer for him. I planted my hands on my hips and focused my attention on the park grounds. "The dreamcatcher isn't working. We need patrols to monitor the park at night."

"I'll have my men do it," Kade replied.

"Make sure they're aware of what they're dealing with," I

cautioned. "I don't want anybody getting bitten. If they do get bitten, they need to contact us immediately. We can use the pixie dust to cure them."

Nixie stirred. "That's another problem. We only have enough dust to treat five more people."

I stilled. "What do you mean?"

"It's not like the other dust, which I have a constant pipeline to. This is rare, and we haven't crossed paths with peddling pixies in quite some time. We don't have enough to save people from a massive outbreak."

"Then we need to keep the dust for our people," Raven said. "We can't be doling it out on the street like cocktails."

That didn't feel right. "We can't let innocent people turn into zombies if we can stop it."

"No? What if we use the last of it and Kade is bitten?" Raven's eyes flashed with annoyance. "We need to be smart."

I didn't necessarily disagree, but the thought made me uncomfortable. "Let's not go there until we have to," I said. "How many zombies did you take out?"

"Nellie and Dolph went into the outlying neighborhoods," Naida replied. "They eradicated ten to fifteen. The spell you used when the guests were still here seems to have taken out all the threats here."

"How many in the Quarter?" Raven asked.

"About ten," I replied. "They weren't clumped together. We had to search for them."

"So most of them were here." Raven tapped her bottom lip. "We need to end this. If this keeps up, we'll be stretched too thin and vulnerable."

"Maybe that's what the loas want," Luke suggested. "Maybe the zombies are cover for something else."

"What could they possibly want?" I asked. "Baron sounded as if the entire thing is a game."

"Have you ever asked yourself what the winner gets?" Cole asked.

"No, but... ." It was an interesting question. "I would feel so much better if we knew the other loa," I admitted. "I absolutely hate not understanding how the game is played."

"We all do," Cole said, "but I don't know how we find answers. The loas only seem to care about you, and they're not forthcoming."

"It's almost as if they're testing you," Kade volunteered. "They want to see how you'll react. Maybe this is something else entirely."

"That revolves around me?" I grimaced. "I don't like that."

"I'm just saying it's possible." Kade sighed. "Has anyone seen Max? We could really use his insight. He said he would be joining us."

"You should text him before we go to bed," I said. "We need him."

"I will, but we can't count on him getting here in time to answer our questions," Kade noted. "He may not know either."

"He might've crossed paths with the loa," I pointed out. "They're old and powerful. He's old and powerful. He's our best shot."

"I'll text him," Kade promised. "I have no idea what to do until he responds."

"The only thing we can do is set up regular patrols in the park," I replied. "Breakfast will come soon enough. We'll touch base then."

"Tomorrow is a full day," Raven said. "We need to be better prepared for Armageddon than we were today. There's no way we'll get through a full day unscathed."

"Good luck sleeping," Luke groused. "I don't know about anybody else, but I'll be jolting awake at every sound now that we know the zombies can cross whenever they want."

"Just do your best. Raven is right. Tomorrow is going to get ugly."

"Awesome." Luke shot me a sarcastic thumbs-up. "By the way, your grandfather is a complete and total tool."

I was right there with him.

I DIDN'T EXPECT TO SLIP INTO SLEEP straight away, but I was so exhausted that's exactly what happened. I barely felt Kade climb under the covers and roll up behind me, spooning me tight, before I drifted off.

"You're late." Maman Brigitte stood as I emerged in a hazy dreamscape park. Though I couldn't make out a single landmark, I had to think it was Jackson Square. The fog was so thick I couldn't see more than a few feet.

"Why am I not surprised?" I grumbled as I glared at her. "I just want to sleep."

"I'm pretty sure you are sleeping." She looked amused. "We need to talk."

The last thing I wanted was to talk with her. "No." I vehemently shook my head. "I'm done playing with you and your friends."

Rather than be offended or angry, she merely smiled.

"What?" My temper got the better of me and I tried to set her on fire with my eyes. It was a dream, so anything was possible. Unfortunately, I'd never been very good at controlling my dreams.

"You remind me of me," she said, "back in the days when I cared enough about others to get irrationally angry."

"That doesn't sound like a compliment," I grumbled.

"It wasn't meant as one. I was never known as one of the great thinkers of our time. I was always ruled by my emotions. We have that in common."

"What rules you now?"

"Wisdom."

The snort that escaped was derisive. "If you say so."

Brigitte cocked her head. "What's bothering you, little one?"

"Can you not be so condescending?" I was at the end of my rope. "Between you and your husband, I'm sick of the cutesy names. It's not as if you really care that we're related by blood."

"On the contrary. The fact that we share blood is very important to me. It's how Baron managed to skew the game."

I eyed her a moment, debating, and then decided to pelt her with questions. "You had children with Baron," I said. "I didn't think gods could procreate."

"Who said we were gods?"

"It's the closest comparison we can come up with," I said. "I mean...how long have you been alive? Were you born yourself? How did you come into being?"

"So many questions." Brigitte made a tsking sound. "Does it matter?"

"It does to me."

She let loose a heavy sigh. "I was a mortal once, a very long time ago.

Gods aren't born. They just are. In my case, the gods decided someone had to watch over the Haitian people and their emerging religion. I was born into voodoo, and I was selected because of my magical prowess to serve as an ambassador of sorts."

I pondered the information. "I don't understand how that works," I admitted.

"You're not meant to understand. Suffice it to say that belief systems mature over time. Why do you think zombies are associated so closely with voodoo?"

"Compared to what?"

"Well, let's say Christianity. Jesus was dead for days before rising."

I wasn't certain a theological debate was going to make things better. "But Jesus wasn't human when he rose," I hedged. "He was a god."

"He was *the* God, according to Christianity," she corrected. "He wasn't a god like the gods you're implying."

"Then what was he?"

"Something more, but only for that religion. You need to grasp the distinction."

Something occurred to me. "You're saying you're more for the voodoo faith."

Her smile told me I was on the right track.

"You're saying that your power is related to the belief system." My mind was going a mile a minute. "Baron said he considers this home. That's because he'd be more powerful here than someplace else. There are more believers here."

"Essentially," she confirmed. "It's more convoluted than that, but when you break it down it's simpler than people want to believe. Faith creates gods in this instance...but we're not the gods of old. That's reserved for others."

"Like Cernunnos...and Pan."

"Yes. They were around when the earth was formed."

It was all so much. I plopped down on the bench and rubbed my forehead. "You were once human but were recruited to serve as a spiritual leader for the voodoo believers."

"I would never have thought to phrase it that way, but yes."

"Your powers would've grown with time. The longer you were amongst true believers, the stronger you would've become."

She bobbed her head. "During that transition, becoming a mother was still possible. I did it because I thought that's what was expected of me. It seemed the responsible thing to do. Baron and I had several children. The stronger we grew, however, the more removed we became from those who worshipped us."

"Did you leave your children to be raised by others?"

"No. The separation was gradual. We could've continued having children, but we left our existing lines to flourish—or die out —and focused on other things."

"What things?"

"Loa issues."

I was too tired to play games. "Just tell me what you're talking about. No more talking out of both sides of your mouth. I need to know what we're dealing with."

"That's against the rules." Brigitte was matter-of-fact. "We can't tell you. It will influence the game."

I wanted to hurt her. "You guys are the worst. You act as if you're using humans to play *Pokémon* or something." That's when it hit me. "That's exactly what you're doing." My gaze was accusatory. "You're using us to battle it out. Whichever side wins gets some sort of bragging rights in loa heaven, or wherever it is you hang out when you're not here."

"It's more like the underworld of mythology, but close enough," she confirmed. "I can't tell you about the game. That's breaking the rules. I can tell you that this game is not being played by two of us, as it was supposed to be. There's a third faction. That's who you have to worry about."

"Someone took over the game you usually play with your husband," I said. "You aren't in control. This is a different sort of game. You need me to level the playing field for some reason, but you won't tell me why."

"That's pretty much it." She smiled. "You might not feel fortunate to be involved, but I'm glad you are. This would no longer be anything other than a genocide if we didn't have people strong enough to play on board. You and your friends are the only ones standing between the game and real-world ramifications."

"Stop talking around the edges. Speak plainly."

She held out her hands. "I understand that it's frustrating. I understand that you feel you're being played with. I am on your side. I want you to win."

"But that means Baron wins."

"Yes, but it's either him or...the other. If he's leading you toward an outcome, do what he says. In this particular instance—and only this instance—he's right."

"But why this instance?"

"Because as removed as we are from the plight of the everyday man, we don't want to ruin it all. We understand what happens when faith is corrupted. If that happens, our entire way of life disappears."

"Is that what the third loa wants?"

She opened her mouth and then snapped it shut. "I've already said too much. I'm sorry. I can't tell you more than I already have." She stood directly in front of me. "This fight is not of your making and yet you have to win it. I'm sorry, but that's simply the way it is.

"Be prepared," she continued. "Prepare your team. The enemy will make a big move soon. You're the only one who can stop it."

"No pressure," I muttered.

Her smile softened. "You're up to the challenge. You do remind me of myself, after all. I was always ready for the big fight."

"How awesome for you."

"Bitterness won't change the stakes," she warned. "If you don't fight, the battle is already lost." With that, she disappeared, leaving me in the shrouded park with nothing but my frustration and anger.

Twenty-One

Max was at our bistro table when I went outside with my coffee the next morning. Normally I would spend some time chatting and flirting with Kade, but he was still dead to the world. My mind refused to rest, so rather than toss and turn and wake him, I went outside...and found his father waiting.

"Where have you been?" I demanded as I sat in the chair across from him.

Max chuckled. "You know I have friends in New Orleans and stay with them whenever we're in town."

"But we've been dealing with stuff." I tried to refrain from sounding bitter.

"So I've heard. I didn't know any of this was going on until I got Kade's text last night." He turned stern. "Don't you think you should've contacted me right away, young lady?"

I hated when he used that tone of voice with me. I felt like a chastised child. "Maybe, but I thought we could handle a few zombies." I ran my finger around the rim of my mug. "How much did Kade tell you?"

"He asked me to stop by for a chat. I ran into Raven this morning, and she filled in the rest."

I glanced at the sky. The sun was just starting to rise. "Raven must've been up early."

"So, I hear you have some loa in you." He cocked his head as he regarded me. "I hate to say it, but it makes sense. I can't believe I didn't think of it myself."

"That answers that question," I said. "I didn't even know loas were real. I thought they were a myth."

Max leaned back in his chair. "Most religious legends have some basis in reality. Why would the loas be any different?"

I shrugged, noncommittal. "The loas are different. They're so much more...over the top."

"They do have that going for them. New Orleans has always been over the top. You know I lived here for a time when I was younger. That would've been long before you were born. The children of the loa were a bigger deal then. I was familiar with a few of them. Heck, I'm starting to wonder if I partied with your ancestors."

That struck me as funny. "Did you party hard back in the day?"

He bobbed his head. "I loved a good party. As for your lineage, your affinity for the dead and for standing up for the little guy should've been a giveaway that you were descended from Baron and Brigitte. I feel bad that I didn't consider it before."

"Well, you did your best. Nobody is perfect."

"Kade says you're perfect." Max's lips curved. "We haven't really had a chance to talk since the engagement...at least about wedding-related issues. I want you to know that I already consider you my daughter. Now that you're engaged to my son, you should know that you'll never get rid of me...even when we argue."

I knew what he was trying to say. We'd had an argument in Moonstone Bay, when I realized he'd been considering letting Mark take over the circus. We hadn't talked much since. "We're fine, Max," I reassured him. "I was angry in the moment, but I'm over it."

"Yes, you're good like that." He held my gaze. "You tend to get angry in the moment and then you're over it five minutes later. You've always been that way. If you still want to be angry for a few weeks, I'm okay with that. I deserve it. Considering Mark was a mistake. You were so young when you joined us I feared you might never mature in the way I knew you could. I was wrong. You're the best leader this circus could ever have."

My cheeks colored under the heady praise. "Thank you."

"You're welcome." He sipped his coffee. "How is your uncle?"

I laughed at his transition. I figured he had a list of things he wanted to talk about, checking them off in his head. Sidney was merely one entry on the list. "It's difficult," I admitted, my eyes drifting to the street. It was far too early for people to be out and about in this neighborhood. "He wants to keep in touch. I don't get the feeling he wants more than I can give. He's mired in guilt, and I have trouble accepting anything he has to offer."

"Perhaps you don't have to push yourself harder than is necessary," Max suggested. "You're allowed to set the guidelines. Start with what you can handle, whether that's one call a month or you controlling when calls are made. You get to set your own boundaries, Poet. Even though I don't know your uncle, it's fair for you to be in control."

I nodded. "There's more." I told him about Vanessa, about the napkin with the veve. He no longer looked relaxed.

"You think she's involved in this," he surmised.

"It's a possibility," I confirmed. "She's just...too much. It's as if she's trying too hard."

"That could be because she knows this is important to Sidney. Perhaps she doesn't believe Sidney is capable of moving forward until he makes peace with his past." Max took a breath. "Poet, I don't have specific knowledge of this situation, but I can imagine that Sidney has had more than one or two bad moments wondering what happened to you.

"You just told me that he was shocked when he realized you didn't find a permanent home after he let you go," he continued. "I'm guessing Sidney romanticized your journey in his head to get through it. When he learned the truth, that you'd disappeared from the system, that likely threw him."

I rubbed my cheek. "I just feel like I'm off my game. I don't want to be suspicious of her. Sidney genuinely seems to care about her. It's not as if I want him to be alone and miserable. Kade, Cole and Luke do, but that's not what I want for him."

Max's eyes lit with mirth. "Your protectors can't see past Little Poet. They want to avenge you. You're much more practical. You understand Sidney isn't a bad person. Your time on the street made you aware of just how limited humans can be. You learned not to judge."

"I feel as if I'm being tugged in multiple directions," I admitted. "It's...difficult...for me. On one hand I have Sidney, who is the lone tie I still have to my family. Yes, I believe there are a few other people out there, but it's not as if I'll find them. They were out of my life long before my parents died. But Sidney had a chance to change the course of my life."

"Sidney *did* change the course of your life," Max pointed out. "Had he kept you, I very much doubt you would've ended up here."

"I love it here. Shouldn't I be thankful he acknowledged he wasn't strong enough to take me? I love my life, and he put me on the path here."

"Thinking like that will make you crazy," he chided. "You can't go down those rabbit holes. Suffice it to say that you're where you're supposed to be. It's okay to be angry with Sidney and the choices he made."

I wasn't convinced but going in circles on the subject was getting me nowhere. "I don't know what to do about any of this. Vanessa is a problem, but I have nothing to prove she is a problem. I can't say to Sidney, 'Your girlfriend is likely evil' without proof."

"No," Max agreed. "Do you know which hotel they're staying at?"

"The Royal Sonesta. Why?"

"I'll see if I can get a feel for her. She won't know I'm with you...unless she's more aware than she should be. That will be a dead giveaway. I agree that you don't want to tell Sidney what he should and shouldn't feel without proof."

"You'd do that?" I was surprised.

"Of course. This situation is...not good. I've yet to see any loa running around. I'm sure that's by design. I'm familiar with their work, so they would want to avoid me to the best of their ability."

"Did you know Baron and Brigitte in your partying days?" I tried to tease him.

"I did. That was a long time ago, but it's neither here nor there."

Max was serious now. "They're game-players, but they usually don't play games like this. Whoever is playing with them is the dangerous one. We have to figure out who that is."

"Any suggestions how?"

"Go see Caroline. I assume she's not aware of any of this."

I frowned. "I saw her the first day. That was before the zombies...and loas. Ugh." I slapped my hand to my forehead. "I'm such an idiot. I should've involved her much sooner."

Max grinned. "You have a lot going on. While you see Caroline, I'll track Vanessa. Show me what she looks like."

I leaned forward, allowing Max access to my mind. He looked for several seconds, his hand pressed to my forehead, before pulling back. "I'll see what I can get from her. It might be easier for me to get past her barriers, especially because she seems so focused on you."

"What if she's dangerous?"

"I won't do anything without talking to you first," he reassured me. "This is a group project."

"Thank you." I could breathe so much easier. "I'm so glad you're here. I didn't realize how much I needed you."

Max's smile was serene. "Poet, even though you're the big boss now, I'll always be here for you. Even when the move to Moonstone Bay is complete, even though I'll only be spending a month or two on the island a year, you'll be one of the most important people in my life...and not just because you're marrying my son."

"I thought you would visit because Grandpa Max would want to spoil the eventual kids," I teased.

"Oh, well, that goes without saying. You'll always have a huge piece of my heart. It belongs to you and only you."

I blinked back tears. "I feel the same way about you."

"Of course you do."

ONCE KADE WOKE, WE SHOWERED and dressed quickly. Madame Caroline had an opening in her schedule, so she agreed to meet us for breakfast at Cafe du Monde. I thought about inviting Luke and

Cole—Caroline wanted to meet both Cole and Kade—but they'd be a distraction.

"She's your mother figure?" Kade asked as we waited at the intersection to cross to Cafe du Monde.

"Don't listen to Nellie." I made a face. "She's a lovely woman, but she's not my mother."

"I believe that's why he referred to her as your 'mother figure.'"

"Don't." I sent Kade to order for us and then I searched for Caroline. I found her at a table at the edge of the space. She already had her chicory and beignets, and she beamed when she saw me. "Sorry we're a few minutes late," I said. "Kade is slow when he wakes."

She chuckled. "Sure, blame your poor fiancé." Her gaze was expectant as she glanced around. "Where is he?"

I pointed to the line. "He's getting breakfast." I sat in one of the open chairs. "I was going to bring Luke and Cole, but I figured they would be a distraction."

"Isn't Luke always a distraction?"

"Yes. That's why I love him."

"He's an acquired taste," Caroline agreed. "Tell me what's going on. I've heard rumors—none from you, unfortunately."

I filled her in on everything that had transpired. By the time I finished, Kade had our food and was getting settled beside me.

"Wow." Caroline shook her head at the news. "That is just...wow."

I put my hand to Kade's back. "We should do some introductions." I found I was nervous. "Kade Denton, this is Madame Caroline. I met her on my first trip to New Orleans and I've loved her ever since."

She laughed as if that was the funniest thing she'd ever heard and then extended her hand. "I think she's exaggerating a bit, but I've been fond of her since that first meeting as well. She was a little rough around the edges back then, but she's smoothed out nicely."

Kade gripped her hand. "It's nice to meet you, ma'am."

Caroline made a face. "Oh, don't call me 'ma'am.' You make me feel old."

"I'm sorry." Kade was appropriately contrite. "I know you're important to Poet. I want to make a good impression."

"Oh, so cute." Caroline beamed at him. "Actually, you're ridiculously handsome. Max is his father?"

The question was directed at me, so I nodded.

"I can see it." She patted his shoulder. "I've always found your father handsome. It could be the power that he exudes—I feel some of that rippling beneath your surface as well—but he makes my heart swoon occasionally. I haven't seen him this trip. I expect that will change given what we're up against."

I plucked a beignet out of the container Kade had placed on the table. "It's a mess. I don't know what to do about any of it. I didn't even realize loas were real, let alone that I might be descended from them. I have no idea how we're supposed to tackle this problem."

"I think I should've realized you had loa in your blood," Caroline said. "Your personality indicated so, but I never put it together."

"That's what Max said," I acknowledged. "That doesn't matter now. We have to get ahead of this problem. We can't keep patrolling cemeteries until we leave. That won't solve the problem."

"Maybe not," Caroline said. "Or maybe you haven't been in the right cemetery."

"Do you know something?"

"No, but I think you're missing the obvious location to search," she replied. "You're going to the big cemeteries. Perhaps you should look at the smaller ones, the ones that were reserved for true voodoo believers."

That's when realization hit me, and I felt like an idiot. "A Haitian Creole cemetery."

She nodded. "There are several. I can email you the information. If Baron Samedi is setting up a base in this area, he'll go for one of those cemeteries. He's done it before."

"He has?" I was incredulous. "How do you know that?"

"I used to like to party in my younger days, and if there's anything that loa loves it's a good party." She smiled at the memory. "In fact, I think Max was at one. Those were wild days, and the people we surrounded ourselves with weren't always the best behaved."

"Sounds interesting," Kade noted as he sipped his chicory. "I wouldn't mind hearing a few of those stories. I can hold them over my father's head."

"Oh, what happens in Marigny stays in Marigny." Madame Caroline let loose an effusive laugh. "I might be able to come up with a story or two, though. You've made our girl happy." She winked at me. "That deserves a reward."

Kade was solemn when he answered. "You have that backward. She's made me happy. That's reward enough."

Madame Caroline sighed. "You definitely have your daddy's charm." She winked. "I have a few stories that won't break confidentiality rules. If Max has a problem, he can stop by and we'll hash it out over some moonshine."

"I have a feeling Max will be stopping by regardless," I said. "If you can get us a list of Haitian Creole cemeteries—the type that aren't on any tourist maps—that will be very helpful. We won't be able to check them out until tonight, but it's a good start."

"It's your best option," she agreed. "I have no idea who would want to mess with Baron and Brigitte. My gut tells me it's someone dangerous, so be prepared."

Twenty-Two

We made it back to the park ten minutes before the circus was set to open.

"Where's Max?" I asked as I hurried to our trailer to change.

"He hasn't been back," Cole replied. "If you need him I can find him."

"It's fine. He'll find me if he has something important to share." I raced into the bedroom and quickly changed into one of my trademark skirts and a matching blouse. To save time, I threw a scarf over my hair and was still arranging the shirt when I reemerged. "Everybody knows what to do?"

Luke grimaced. "We've been doing this for years."

"I meant about the zombies."

"Oh." Luke shrugged. "I was under the impression that we were supposed to kill them."

"That's the plan," I agreed, "but with guests present, we have to be careful how we proceed."

"I've got my men patrolling the outskirts of the park," Kade offered. "We shouldn't be caught unaware again."

"Here's hoping." I flashed him a tight smile and started toward the park entrance. "Nobody head out once we close tonight. I might have a mission. I'll know more in a few hours."

"What sort of mission?" Raven demanded. "Do you know where the loas are setting up shop?"

"No, but Madame Caroline had a good idea this morning. She pointed out that the cemeteries we've been checking out are the tourist cemeteries. This is New Orleans. There are smaller cemeteries—ones long since forgotten—that hold more appeal for the loas. She's sending a list."

Raven looked momentarily flummoxed. "That makes sense. I didn't think about it, but the Haitian Creole cemeteries from the early days would be the sort of places the loas would be comfortable in."

"Exactly. Just...be sharp today, okay? Hopefully I'll have a better plan in a few hours. Don't get distracted."

"She's talking to you," Nellie said to Luke.

"Um, I think she's talking to you," Luke shot back.

"I'm talking to both of you," I said. "Pay attention today. It's important."

"We've got it, Poet." Luke looked exasperated. "You don't have to worry about us."

"That would be a nice change of pace."

MY FIRST CUSTOMER WAS a pretty woman with dark hair and dark eyes. She worked on a riverboat.

"I don't know how to get my boss to stop grabbing my ass," she blurted as she sat.

I accepted the money she handed me but didn't immediately tuck it away. "What?"

"That's why I'm here. Oh, I'm Bethany. I've been working on a riverboat for two months. I love it except for one thing."

"Your boss keeps grabbing your ass," I said. I handed her money back.

Bethany's eyes went wide. "You won't help?"

"Oh, I'm going to help." I was grave. "You just don't have to pay for it. What's your boss's name?"

"Ed, but he prefers people call him Eddie. He makes 'fast Eddie' jokes all the time. Like that somehow makes him cool." Her eye roll would've had me smiling under different circumstances.

"To your knowledge, has Eddie ever pushed things further?" I asked. "Have any of the other boat employees told you about him forcing himself on current or former workers?"

Bethany's mouth opened and closed several times. "Oh, no." She fervently shook her head. "He's just a butt man, according to them. He's not a rapist or anything, at least that I know of. I think I would've heard."

I nodded. "Okay, well, we'll handle Eddie."

She blinked several times in rapid succession. "That's it?"

"Yup. He'll be taken care of by this afternoon." I pinged Nixie with my mind, hoping she wasn't busy. "When is your next shift?"

"Um...tonight." Bethany was understandably leery. "What are you going to do?"

Nixie breezed into my tent before I could respond. "You rang?" she drawled playfully.

"Yes." I nodded. "This is Bethany. Her boss has wandering hands. He works on a riverboat."

"Wandering hands, eh?" Nixie made a face. "How often do his hands wander?"

Bethany swallowed hard. "A few times a night."

"Well, don't you worry." Nixie's expression was unnaturally bright. "I'll take care of Eddie." She shot me a knowing look. "Jerky bosses and wandering hands are something of a specialty for me."

"Are you sure?" Bethany almost looked as if she might pass out. "I don't want him to die or anything. I just want him to keep his hands to himself."

"Oh, we promise he won't die," I intoned.

"There might be times tonight when he will wish he could die, but it will be a good lesson for him," Nixie added.

"Okay, um...are you sure you don't want the money?" Bethany held up the two bills I'd returned to her. "It doesn't seem fair that you're not getting paid when you're putting in the work."

"Some jobs are fun," I replied. "The joy we'll get from torturing your boss is payment enough."

"Thank you...I guess."

I grinned. "Don't worry, Bethany. Your working environment is about to get infinitely better." I waited until she'd disappeared to speak again. "I'm thinking that dust you have that makes private parts itch is the way to go."

Nixie snorted. "The one that leaves the pus boils behind if you scratch or the other one?"

"Which do you think?"

"Pus it is." She ducked out of the tent, and I called for the next customer.

This one was a teenage boy, and he looked unbelievably nervous. "I want a girlfriend," he blurted as he handed me his money.

I took the bills and studied him. He was filled with longing instead of the usual curious perversion that attended teenage boys. I tucked the money into my metal case. "You don't want any girlfriend," I noted as I shuffled my tarot cards. "You have a specific one in mind."

The boy nodded. "Anna. She's my best friend."

"Ah." I smiled. "What's your name?"

"Andre."

"Well, Andre, how long have you and Anna been best friends?"

"Since kindergarten."

"That might make a relationship more difficult," I noted. "Have you considered that she might only have feelings of friendship for you?"

"That's why I've kept quiet the last two years." He looked miserable now. "I didn't want to lose her as a friend if she didn't feel the same way. The thing is, two days ago, Becky Boston told me that she wanted to ask me to the school dance, but Anna talked her out of it, said that I was afraid of girls and to leave me alone. There's only one reason I could think she would do that."

"Because she likes you," I deduced as I extended the cards. "Cut them."

Andre did as instructed, swallowing hard as I began doling out the cards. "I think we're supposed to be together forever. My mom says I'm stupid, that I'm too young to be thinking stuff like that, but it works for some people." He almost seemed to be begging me for confirmation.

"It does indeed." I studied the cards, opening my mind. Andre seemed like a good kid. He loved his best friend. He was also terrified of making the wrong choice. If I could help him, I would. "You and Anna met when she broke the green crayon," I said.

Andre's eyes went wide. "How can you know that?"

"It's part of a ballad your heart sings when you think about her," I replied, smiling. Anna was all over the tendrils of Andre's life. She wasn't going anywhere. "So, here's the thing." I licked my lips. "You're right about some relationships holding strong from a young age."

"But you don't think that's in the cards for Anna and me," Andre surmised, his shoulders sinking.

"Actually, quite the opposite." I chose my words carefully. "Some things are meant to be. You and Anna are meant to be."

The hope reflected back from his eyes squeezed my heart. "So I can ask her to the dance?"

I shook my head. "Not yet." I kept my voice soft. "That fear you've been feeling the last two years? Anna is feeling it now. She's afraid that if you guys screw it up, you'll only have the one shot and it will be over. That sort of fear can crush a person."

Andre was back to looking miserable. "Then what do I do?"

"You must be patient. This dance isn't for you and Anna."

"Should I go with Becky?" He looked horrified at the thought.

"Do you really need a date? Maybe go stag."

"I'll get laughed at because I couldn't get a date."

"If you take a date, you'll be there with someone, and Anna will not. She's not ready to go to a dance with you, but she is ready to sit next to you and make fun of the other people at the dance."

"Oh." Realization dawned on Andre's face. "We'd both be there without dates."

"And you wouldn't be a couple, but there's no reason friends can't dance," I said.

"That means we'll get together after the dance." Andre looked so happy I was reticent to crush him. If I could ease what was to come for him and Anna, I had to do it. They were truly destined to be a great couple.

"No. Not yet. You must be patient. The next few weeks, you're going to be friends with Anna. You're sixteen and it's okay to keep doing friend things."

His forehead creased. "When do we get to the good stuff?"

"In a few months, when spring begins to lead into summer, Anna's family is going to have a rough time of it."

"And then we're together?"

"You're going to be the best friend she's always needed," I clarified. "You're not even going to have to force yourself or think twice about acting. You're going to take care of her in a terrible time. You're going to be there for her."

"And then we're going to get together?"

"Eventually."

"Ugh. You make it sound like I'm going to be pining for her forever."

"Pining is an interesting word."

"That's not what I want to hear."

"I know." I was sad for him. "Here's the thing: When Anna gets past her sadness, the first thing she's going to see is you. She's going to know, because she'll have already lost something very important, that she doesn't want to lose you. She'll also know that some things are worth the risk."

Andre's forehead creased in confusion, and I instinctively reached out to touch his hand, transferring an image of his future into his mind. I rarely did that because I worried it would affect the outcome of relationships. In this instance, there was no stopping the freight train that was Anna and Andre.

"Do you see?" I whispered as Andre's mouth went slack.

"That's us," he gritted out.

"It's you...and what's to come."

He blinked so many times I thought he had something in his eye. Then I realized he was trying not to cry.

"You're going to be her hero forever, Andre," I promised.

"Together, you can overcome anything. Right now, she needs you to be her friend. The rest will happen when it's time. You're not there yet."

Andre let loose a choked sob. "Is that really going to happen?"

I nodded. "Some things are meant to be. You're right about that, but you must be patient."

He snuffled and then squared his shoulders. "I can be her friend until she needs me to be something more."

"You're a rare find, Andre." I watched him go, and then almost came out of my skin when I heard a throat clear behind me. I expected to find Baron waiting for me. He was getting adept at crossing our borders without setting off the dreamcatcher. Instead, I found Sidney. "How did you get in that part of the tent?" I demanded.

"Max brought me," he replied, eyes misty. "I lost track of Vanessa and was looking for her when I ran into Max. He said he would find her and directed me here to get out of the sun."

"That sounds like Max." I gestured toward the open chair. "Take a load off in front of the fan." My mind was busy with possibilities. Had Max purposely separated Vanessa and Sidney? Under those circumstances, it was likely Max wanted me to keep watch over my uncle. It was best I not disappoint him.

"I don't want to interrupt your work," he hedged.

I waved off his concern. "It's fine. I was about to take a fifteen-minute break anyway. Andre there about broke my heart. I need to compose myself."

"I saw at least part of his reading," Sidney acknowledged as he sat. He seemed grateful for the fan. "Was all that you told him true?"

"What do you think?"

"Are you asking if I think you're the real deal?"

"I guess."

"I've always known you're the real deal. Your parents knew you were different. Nobody understood how different, but you grew stronger with each passing year. I expected the things I saw in the street the other night, the way you took out the zombie. That was the type of thing I always imagined you doing. But this was something else entirely."

"A good something else or a bad something else?"

"Good. You didn't tell that boy what he wanted to hear. You gave him a map to a happy future. I don't think you realize how important that is."

"Oh, I know how important it is." I grinned. "Andre is going to grow into an amazing adult. Anna is just as amazing. They're going to do good things in the Quarter, like running a homeless outreach program and helping at-risk kids who wind up on the street. I wouldn't have done what I did for just anybody. Knowing the future is dangerous for most people, but Anna and Andre are destined for greatness. I needed him to see that, if only to make things easier on himself."

"Did anybody ever make things easier on you?" Sidney asked, his eyes glassy when they locked with mine. "Were you ever the person who received the help you needed?"

"Oh, Sidney." I shook my head. "You have to stop flogging yourself."

"I shouldn't have let you go. I...freaked out. I should've done right by you."

"You did the right thing for you," I countered. "It's okay. I ended up where I was supposed to be. If you'd kept me, there's no way I would've ended up here, and here is where I belong."

"That doesn't change the fact that I failed you."

"You failed Little Poet." I made an attempt at a smile as I reached over to pat his hand. "Big Poet is happy. She has a family and job she loves. She has a plan for the future. Focus on that."

Before I could pull my hand away, he flipped his over and gripped mine tightly. "I'm sorry. I have all these horrible pictures in my head of what your childhood must've been like. I can't shake them."

Curious, I allowed myself entrance into his mind. I wanted to ease his guilt. As I wandered through his head, I discovered another problem.

"Oh, Sidney." My stomach clenched so tight I thought I was going to be sick.

"Just put me out of my misery," he said. "I can't take this feeling."

I used my magic to glaze his mind. "Just stay there a minute," I said to him as I slid my hand free and stood. He was frozen in place, his mind serving as a jail cell of sorts. I pulled my phone from my pocket and called Kade. "Find Max," I ordered when he answered. "Get him to my tent. There's something wrong with Sidney."

Kade's confusion was obvious. "Like...he needs an ambulance?"

"Like somebody has messed with his memories. There are gaping holes in his mind. I need Max. I've never seen anything like this."

"Okay." Kade sounded unsure. "Last time I saw him, he was with Vanessa."

"I would rather she not be part of this," I said. "If you have to, take over the tour and send Max here. Be discreet. I need him to look without her knowing."

"I'll handle it," Kade promised. "Give me a few minutes. I'll have him there before you know it."

Twenty-Three

Max arrived ten minutes later, hair windswept, but unflappable as always despite my urgent request for his presence.

"What's this?" he asked as he stepped in front of an unmoving Sidney.

"I put him under," I replied. "There's something wrong with his head. There are huge gaps in his memory. I think they were made magically."

Max's eyebrows hopped and he leaned over to stare into Sidney's vacant eyes. "Let's see what we have here, shall we?" He placed his hands on either side of Sidney's head and slid inside.

I watched him rather than my uncle for a reaction. Sidney was officially dead to the world until I released him from the spell. Max drifted in and out of Sidney's mind for several minutes before dropping his hands.

"Well, that's interesting," is all he said.

My impatience got the better of me and I planted my hands on my hips. "Is that seriously all you're going to say?"

"I don't know what else to say," he admitted. "His mind is holier than the pope on Easter Sunday."

I didn't want to laugh, but that was such a Max thing to say. "I'm being serious."

"Of course you are." Max rolled his neck. "There are huge memory gaps. Memories about your childhood, the times he should've spent with you and your family, are awash in confusion."

"I didn't get that specific," I said, gnawing my bottom lip. "I just noticed the holes."

"I can't be positive, of course, but I'm almost certain all the missing memories revolve around you. There's one in particular that looks as if someone tried to remove it, but he refused to let it go. The memory is almost battered in some ways."

"Which memory?"

Max's eyes softened. "The day he said goodbye to you."

"I don't understand, Max. Why would someone want that memory?"

"Because whoever did this was trying to create a specific storyline in his mind."

I slid my gaze back to Sidney. "Is it possible that it was Vanessa?"

"Anything is possible. I have to say, though, I've spent several hours with her and Sidney today. I met them at the hotel bar. Initially I pretended that I didn't know you, but eventually I owned up to who I was. I decided to play things a little differently."

"And?"

"I explained how I plucked you from the streets of Detroit. I positioned myself as your father figure, explained I was being protective, and drew them out in conversation that way."

"What did they say?" I asked.

"Sidney was very forthcoming. He thanked me profusely for saving you. Guilt practically rolled off him in waves. He was very uncomfortable to be around."

"And Vanessa?"

"She's another story. She was very interested in my relationship with you, even going so far as to ask if we were romantically involved at any time."

I made a face. "Well, that's gross."

Max chuckled. "It is indeed, especially given the fact that I've always looked at you as a daughter."

"Vanessa's line of questioning was very...pointed," he continued. "I tried to get a read on her, but I couldn't get past her mind barriers. She's either incredibly adept at natural shuttering or she purposely tried to keep me out. I'm not sure which direction I lean right now."

"Isn't it obvious? She's somehow involved with the loa."

"Perhaps."

Frustration bubbled up. "What other explanation is there?"

"That she's magical in origin and has absolutely nothing to do with the loa," Max replied.

"How does that work?" I demanded.

"I don't know. I pinned Sidney down on the timeline of their relationship. They met in Boston months ago, long before Sidney even knew he was coming here."

"That doesn't necessarily mean anything," I argued. "It's possible that she led Sidney to New Orleans."

"Of course it's possible. But let's say she is involved with the loa. How does any of this benefit her? She hasn't managed to get too close to you. She doesn't even appear to be trying to forge a relationship with you."

I hated that he had a point. "She has to be the one who messed with Sidney's memories. It's the only thing that makes sense."

"I lean toward that hunch, but we don't have proof."

"So, what do we do?"

"I think we have to let it play out. I can implant a magic alarm of sorts in Sidney's mind. It will tell us if someone tries to enter again. Other than that, I honestly don't know what to do."

That wasn't enough. "Sidney—"

"Poet." He was firm. "I don't like the gaps in your uncle's memories any more than you do, but we can't force the issue. We can only play it out as we're supposed to."

I pressed my lips together, debating, and then nodded. "Sidney wasn't perfect," I said. "He doesn't deserve to be played with like this. If we find out this was done to him because of me, I'll finish the job."

Max looked momentarily sad. "You'll completely wipe his memory of you."

I nodded, fighting back tears. "I won't let him be used as a weapon against me. He deserves some peace. Right or wrong, I ended up where I was always supposed to be. Sidney is partially responsible for that."

"Even though it wasn't necessarily a decision made for the right reasons."

"Yes."

He let loose a long sigh. "We'll play it by ear. Don't make any decisions until we know more. For now, let Sidney believe you had a lovely conversation. Wake him, and I'll take him with me to continue the tour."

"Keep an eye on Vanessa."

"That is the plan."

"Madame Caroline is putting together a list of cemeteries for us. She thinks we're looking for the loas in the wrong ones."

"She's probably right. I'll go with you this evening. It's time I remembered I'm part of the group."

"We'll be glad to have you."

Max pressed a fatherly kiss to my forehead. We weren't big on displays of affection—either of us—but occasionally he took me by surprise. "We'll figure this out, my girl. You have my word."

I SPENT THE NEXT SEVERAL HOURS reading mundane fortunes. When it was time for the last reading of the evening, I was beyond happy to embrace the absurd, but I wasn't prepared for the individual who poked his head into my tent.

"Oh, good grief," I moaned at the sight of the man in the top hat. He wore skull makeup like Baron Samedi, but his hair was longer. He was also smoking a stinky cigar. "Get that thing out of here."

The loa smirked before waving his hand and causing the cigar to disappear. "Better?" he asked in a rich baritone voice.

"I can still smell it," I groused as he sat in the chair across from me.

"You'll live," he replied. "Do you know me?"

"I'm guessing you're Papa Legba." It was the only thing that made sense. "I've heard about you. You're not who I expected."

"Are you disappointed?" Papa Legba looked amused. "I would've thought anything would be better than that last woman who wanted to know if her best friend was stealing her cookie recipe."

I'd found that reading torturous. That didn't mean I was going to agree with Papa Legba. "I would take her over you."

"Lies." He leaned back in his chair. "I hear you're the granddaughter of an old friend."

I shrugged. "That depends. Who are we talking about?"

"Really?" He almost looked bored with my response. "That is not the answer I was expecting."

"Well, I'm sure you'll forgive me my trepidation. I don't know you. I've met two loa. They both claim ties to me. Before this trip, I didn't even know loa were real, let alone that I was descended from them. It's a lot to take in."

He bobbed his head. "Should I take that to mean they've both come calling?"

"Yup. And they're delightful. They think humans are beneath them and that we should all shut up and allow ourselves to become zombie food."

He chuckled. "That's not what they believe."

"That's what they said."

"Yes, well, Brigitte and Baron are known for posturing. They are two of the stubbornest individuals I've ever met. When they're both around, it's like being trapped with teenagers at summer camp."

The comparison threw me. "When did you go to summer camp?"

"I hear things...and watch movies. I also have an employee who reminds me very much of a teenager. If you would've asked me six months ago if I would miss her should she disappear from this plane, I would've laughed. Now, her absence from my life is disconcerting."

He was much more forthcoming than Baron Samedi and Maman Brigitte. "I don't understand," I said.

"I have a bad employee. Harley. She's on my mind of late, which frustrates me. I should be dealing with her situation. Instead I'm here, dealing with this situation."

"Dealing with?" I was still behind. "Aren't you causing it?"

He blinked several times. "Causing what?" he asked.

"The zombies. I was told there is a third loa mucking things up, that Baron and Brigitte enjoyed celebrating their anniversary with a game, but an outside force had slipped in to foul up the game. That's you."

"Ah." His eyes sparked with understanding. "I see why you would believe that, but it's not the case. I'm not responsible for the game careening out of control. There is another power here, but it's not me. I'm here to make certain this situation is addressed."

"Meaning?"

"Baron and Brigitte believe you can end this. I'm here to make sure you understand your responsibilities."

I groaned. "Seriously? They're really putting this on me? They caused it."

"They did. Unfortunately, they need help to fix it. That's where you come in."

"Maybe I don't want to help," I shot back. "Maybe I think you guys should pick up your own freaking mess."

"Oh, you're so cute." Papa Legba almost looked amused. "You remind me of my missing demon. She's been gone for weeks now. Not only do I have to pick up her slack with her charges now that she's gone, I also have to protect her favorite charges. It's a nightmare." He kicked back in his chair and rested his feet on my table. "I don't have time to babysit Baron and Brigitte on top of everything else. I would like to cede that duty to you."

"You would like to cede loa babysitting duties to me?" I was flabbergasted. "I can't control them. They do what they want, when they want. On top of that, there's another freaking loa out there wreaking havoc. I have no idea who that even is."

"Yes, it's troublesome." Papa Legba's smile fell. "Whoever it is hides behind magic and haze. They're close—I can feel them—but they refuse to move into the open so we can battle it out in proper fashion."

I was almost afraid to ask what that meant. "What do you want me to do?" I was determined to end this conversation. "If you have a plan, tell me. I won't guarantee I'll follow your wishes, but I'm as eager to end this as you are."

"Oh, I have no doubt." Papa Legba sighed. "Baron and Brigitte have always been...tempestuous." He smiled at his word choice. "They fell in love hot and fast. The air around them almost caught fire they were so enamored. Unfortunately, they allowed lust to cloud their minds and never once thought about the fact that they were incompatible.

"They're too much alike," he continued. "They both want to win. They're not willing to sacrifice for the other. The further they're removed from humanity, the worse it gets. Despite that, they still love one another—and they're not your problem."

"They sure feel like my problem."

He chuckled again. "I'm sure they do. The thing is, even when they play their games, safety precautions are taken. They also work together when necessary, like when a hurricane slams the city and they hold the levees together through sheer strength of will."

"They do that?"

"They love this city, perhaps more than they love each other...and they love each other a great deal. Don't let them fool you."

I didn't know how to respond.

"Things are out of control here. Brigitte may have set things in motion, but she's no longer in control. That's difficult for her to admit. And, however gleeful Baron is whenever Brigitte loses, he recognizes the trouble we're all in."

"Exactly what is the trouble?" I asked.

"We're only as powerful as those who believe in us," he replied. "Despite our bold words, we don't want our disciples to fall. Brigitte and Baron talk big, but in the end they'll protect their worshippers. Whoever is doing this does not share that feeling."

"You have no idea who is wreaking havoc on New Orleans," I said.

He gave me a charming wink. "Essentially. I need you to figure it out." Slowly, he stood. "You're a child of my brother, a granddaughter of my sister. I'll protect you."

"I still don't know what you want me to do," I said.

"Find out who's behind this," he replied. "We're stuck until we know who it is. The protection spell hiding his or her identity is profound. We're dealing with one of the stronger members of our tribe. It might take all of us working together to take this individual down."

"That's all well and good, but I still don't know where to look," I groused.

"Oh, I don't believe that." Papa Legba clucked as he moved toward the open flap. "You're a child of my brethren, one of the few who wasn't wiped out over the centuries. You're special."

"Or lucky."

"They're one and the same. I've learned that humans are not the fragile creatures we always assumed. They have evolved, and strong magic-wielders live in their midst. You're but one in an army...and yet you're one of the most important warriors the humans have. They need you now."

He was so serious a chill went down my spine. "What if I fail?"

"Then we all lose." He was grave. "Remember what I said: We are only as strong as those who believe in us. This is the capitol of voodoo, at least on this continent. If most of our believers fall...."

That's when it hit me. "Whoever is doing this isn't after the humans —at least not as their primary goal. They want to eradicate you."

"Very good." He beamed. "You need to ensure that doesn't occur. If we fall, you ultimately will. I think you're already aware of that. There's a balance in this world, a reason for everything. If you take away the reason, chaos will eat us all...and we'll still be alive and screaming when it happens."

"Kind of like zombies eating your intestines," I mused.

"Exactly like that."

I frowned. "I was being facetious."

"And yet you're right. Fancy that." With that, he disappeared through the tent opening, leaving me with worry pooling in the pit of my stomach.

Twenty-Four

"'m sick of these loas," I groused to Max as he helped me close up my tent. "Just sick to death of them."

Max smiled as he double-checked the ties of the tent flap. "Loas are like anything else. They have big personalities and small personalities. Unfortunately, you've met three of the bigger personalities."

"I'd hate to know who the fourth one running around is," I muttered.

"Yes, that's worrisome. The fact that the three of them don't know —and that Papa Legba has decided to insert himself in this situation— means we have big issues."

"Yeah, what's his deal?" I couldn't contain my annoyance. "He made it sound like he was busy with other problems and didn't have time for us, something about one of his workers running off the rails and getting trapped on another plane."

Max looked intrigued now. "Did he say which worker?"

"I can't remember." I shifted my full attention to him. "Why? Do you know his workers?"

"I know a few." His smile was soft. "I tried to recruit one a few years ago."

"You tried to recruit a loa?"

"Harley isn't a loa," Max said. "She's a crossroads demon."

That wasn't any better in my book. "How would a crossroads demon help us?"

"She has a certain spark...and a mouth that would make Luke cry. I'm extremely fond of her. Unfortunately, she has her own plans. I hope she hasn't gone missing."

I had questions, but this wasn't the time to ask them. "What's the hierarchy here? Is Papa Legba in charge? Does he boss the other loa around?"

"They don't have a hierarchy. They're all supposed to do their own thing. If there was a leader, I guess I would assign that role to Papa, but he's never been keen on responsibility. If he's here, he must be worried."

"Will he align himself with us or this mysterious fourth loa?"

Max lifted one shoulder in a shrug. "He came to you. If he was working against us, he wouldn't have revealed himself."

"Okay, but I still have questions. Is he friendly with Baron Samedi? What about Maman Brigitte? How do they all deal with each other?"

"I don't know." Max was rueful. "I'm sorry I don't have the answers you seek. They're private beings. They don't volunteer information. They consider themselves above it all."

"Ugh." My attention was drawn to the rear flap as Madame Caroline entered. She smiled at Max in greeting and then looked to me. There was an emotion in her eyes I couldn't identify. "You know something," I surmised.

"I have a lead," she replied. "McDonough Cemetery, or McDonoghville Cemetery, depending on your age. It's across the river...where a lot of former slaves were laid to rest."

"What can you tell us about it?"

"It was located on the McDonoghville plantation. It crosses into Algiers. There are a few tombs, but more graves than you're likely to find here." She hesitated. "It's surrounded by a wrought-iron fence. Inside, at one time, there was a fence erected to separate the races."

I made a disgusted face. "Of course there was."

"It's gone now," she reassured me. "The locals won't take kindly to us running around their cemetery. That's a historic place, and it's full of sadness. If they think we're in there screwing around, it could start an incident."

I looked at Max. "I think we're going to need a storm as cover."

He nodded. "And we need to drive. That's too far to walk."

"Where is it?" Kade asked. "I'm not that familiar with New Orleans geography."

"We have to go to the Pontchartrain Expressway and cross there," Madame Caroline said. "The cemetery is in a mostly residential area. It has a long history and the residents are extremely protective of it."

"What sort of history?" Max queried.

"Well, for example, in 1890 the mayor of New Orleans took on a man who was taking care of the cemetery. The individual caring for it said his father was a former slave and belonged to the man who owned the plantation. He said the cemetery was left to him and he was selling lots, but he didn't have a title. The mayor ordered the relocation and racial segregation of the graves."

My mouth dropped open. "Are you freaking kidding me?"

Madame Caroline patted my shoulder. "I share your outrage. It was a different time."

"I don't care. I can't stand that crap." I kicked my chair.

She was matter-of-fact. "Since that time, officials have taken a more hands-off approach to the property. They don't want to incite an incident. I haven't been to the cemetery in a very long time. I went as a child, but I don't cross the river much now. It's not that I don't feel comfortable there, it's just that I work on this side—and there are marvelous restaurants in the Quarter."

That drew a smile. "We'll have to go, and we'll have to cover ourselves with a storm. I think it makes sense as a gathering place."

"So do I. What will we do if we find this other loa there?"

It was a question I dreaded. "I guess we'll have to play it by ear."

"We have a strong group," Max said. "If the loa is there and attacks, we'll deal with it."

Kade didn't look convinced but nodded. "Okay. I'll gather the troops. As soon as the park is empty we'll head out. I'll leave my men in charge of watching for wayward zombies—something I never thought I would say a year and a half ago."

Max laughed, delighted with his son. "You're adjusting quite well. I'm very proud of you."

Kade's cheeks colored. "Um...thanks."

Max shifted his gaze back to me. "Let's do this."

WE PARKED OUR SEVERAL VEHICLES two blocks from the cemetery. Naida used her magic to conjure a terrific storm. We waited until the rain came down in torrents to exit our vehicles.

"Let's go," I said as I moved to the front of the group.

Madame Caroline had chosen to come with us. I never questioned why she wanted to be part of the group. This town was her home, and of course she wanted to keep it safe.

I used my magic to unlock the cemetery gate. Kade and I stood shoulder to shoulder to usher our people inside, counting heads, and then closed the gate behind us.

"What do you think?" he whispered. "Did we manage to get in without the locals seeing?"

I shook my head. "No. This sort of neighborhood pays attention to outsiders. I'm sure somebody saw us."

He nodded in understanding. "Let's get this over with." The words were barely out of his mouth before a terrific strike of lightning filled the sky.

I forgot what I was going to say when movement on of one of the mausoleums caught my attention. Maman Brigitte watched our group. She didn't appear bothered about being discovered when I whipped out a scowl for her benefit. "Why am I not surprised?"

She flashed me a smile, but it faded fast. "You're in the right place," she noted.

"Does that mean we're ending this now?" I was hopeful.

She held out her hands. "It means you're in the right place. As are we all."

Another flash of lightning illuminated the grounds, and when I looked to the left, I found two more figures on well-spaced mausoleum roofs. The hats were dead giveaways. Papa Legba and Baron Samedi were also in attendance. My blood ran cold when I realized we were all in the same space together. "What's the plan?" I demanded. "If you think you're going to use my people as fodder you've got another thing coming."

The laugh Brigitte let loose was mirthless. "Oh, little one, this...situation...has grown to epic proportions. It's no longer a game."

"Was it ever really a game?"

"Yes."

I glared at her. "Only in your head." I pushed past Nellie, who was seemingly in awe of the elevated loas, and took my place at the front of the group. "Keep your eyes open," I warned. "Just because these three have shown themselves doesn't mean they're part of the team."

Max seemingly felt differently, because when he moved up beside me he was grinning at Brigitte. "You look lovely as always," he said. "Black has always been a good color for you."

Brigitte laughed gaily. "Oh, Max, you always were a silver-tongued devil."

"Yes, and I look forward to cutting your tongue out of your mouth if you don't stop flirting with my wife," Baron snapped. "Can you not be...you, mage?"

Max was unbothered as he looked to the other side of the aisle. "Age hasn't been as kind to you," he noted. "Of course, I often wondered what she saw in you. That hasn't changed."

Rather than be offended, Baron grinned. "I've often wondered that myself."

"Can we stop the lollygagging?" Papa Legba demanded. He seemed much more agitated than his counterparts. "We can't move any closer to the mausoleum. Tell us what's ahead."

I narrowed my eyes. "Why can't you do it yourself?"

Frustration sparked in his eyes. "Because there are rules. Just tell us who we're dealing with. We'll handle the rest."

I didn't understand any of this. I found it unlikely they would deal with anything. If we wanted to ensure the safety of the people of New Orleans, we would have to do it ourselves.

The rain made the walkway slick, and I carefully picked my way through the headstones. I couldn't make out the names, but a feeling of despair clung to the property. I'd often thought of cemeteries as sanitized death. They were for the living, not those who had passed on. This place, however, felt like a true monument to the dead...and it was chilling.

We kept moving forward to roughly the center of the cemetery. There, a familiar face, zombies surrounding her on every side, awaited, her smug smile directed at me.

"You're late," Vanessa trilled. "I expected you an hour ago."

My voice was raspy. "Well, you know, traffic." I glanced around, uncertain. "Are you in charge here?"

"Of course." She clasped her fingers in front of her and smiled as an owl screeched in a nearby tree. "Who else?"

I glanced at Max. He didn't seem surprised to find Vanessa at the center of things.

"Oh, you don't have to pretend," she drawled. "I knew you were on to me." She wagged her finger in playful fashion. "The tour was very nice, Mr. Anderson." She grinned at Max. "I know darned well you don't give just *anyone* so much of your attention."

I glanced around. "Where's Sidney?"

She screwed up her face. "I didn't bring him. Why would I? He's no longer important. He was simply a means to an end."

"You only hooked up with him because of me," I said.

She nodded. "Finding a child of the loa is not easy in this day and age. Apparently the lines have almost completely died out. I fought for the idea that we should recharge our lines centuries ago. We don't want to completely die out and fade from memory. But I was shot down."

I glanced over my shoulder, to where the other loas remained on top of their mausoleums.

"Don't worry about them." Vanessa dismissed them with a wave. "There's nothing they can do. I was well prepared for their incursion. I needed them to kick things off—and they didn't disappoint. By the time they realized something was afoot, it was too late to stop what I'd set in motion."

"Who are you?" I asked, making sure to keep distance between the horde of zombies and my group. I had no doubt Vanessa was using them as a form of protection. She would unleash them as a distraction when she decided to run.

"Does it matter?" she asked.

"It does to me."

"Then you should already know the answer to that question."

I didn't realize Madame Caroline had moved next to me until she spoke. "Marinette," she intoned in a dark voice.

I jolted when I realized how close she was, but I was more interested in Vanessa's reaction to Madame Caroline's drawn countenance.

"I see someone has been doing her reading," Vanessa sang out.

"Who is she?" I asked.

"She's the loa of power and violence," Madame Caroline replied. "Her...shell...is artifice. You know how the other three paint their faces to resemble skulls? Her real face is that of death. This is just a costume she put on to hide her true self."

"Oh, that's not nice." Vanessa protested. "Beauty is what you make of it. Look at this one." She jerked her thumb at me. "She's very pretty. She doesn't use it to her advantage and is forever mired in a life that most people would kill to avoid. A circus?" The curl of Vanessa's lip told me exactly what she thought. "You could do so much better, my dear." Her gaze went to Kade. "Well, in some respects."

"What do you want?" Max demanded as he appeared on Kade's left. His attention was solely for Vanessa. "You obviously didn't set this in motion because you were bored."

"Never say never," she drawled.

"Stop." Max sounded downright testy, rare for him. "Tell us what you want and we'll see what sort of arrangements we can come to. That's the best offer you'll get. If you drag this out, things will end badly for you."

Vanessa snorted. "So full of yourself." She shook her head. "You're not even a concern for me, mage," she said when she'd finished rolling her eyes. "You mean nothing. I'm here for the girl—and them." She inclined her chin toward the loas on the mausoleums. "They're going to learn that they're not the center of everybody's world."

I couldn't understand what her beef was with the other loas, and I really didn't care. "Just tell us what you want," I insisted. "We can't negotiate if we don't know your demands."

Vanessa was haughty as she regarded me. "There will be no negotiation." She almost looked as if she pitied me. "You don't have a say in how this plays out. I'm in charge."

With that, she turned on her heel. "When the full moon comes, then you will understand the true breadth of my power."

"Wait!" I started to give chase, but it was too late.

"*Ingredior*," she hissed to the zombies, who stopped shuffling in place and turned in our direction. Their eyes were no longer white and milky. No, they were red hot and full of fury.

"I'll see you soon," Vanessa called out. "It's already too late for you. I'm here for my people. I don't care about yours."

I had so much I wanted to say to her. I had so much I wanted to do to her. But she was gone, and we had another problem.

"Here they come!" Nellie called out, brandishing his axe. "They're going to wipe us out. We're too close."

Twenty-Five

"Move!" Kade roared as he swaggered forward, his hand immediately landing on the nearest zombie.

He never saw two more zombies swooping in to cut him off from his plan of attack. "Kade!" I jolted forward and grabbed one of them around the throat. I couldn't grab the other, and my heart fluttered at the thought he would be bitten.

Thankfully, Cole wrangled the other zombie before it could tear a chunk from Kade's arm.

"Do it!" he ordered when surprise registered on Kade's face.

Kade's magic exploded, a zinging racing through the cemetery. When the zombies froze an underlying current that hadn't been there before flowed through them.

"What is that?" I demanded, breathless.

"*Marinette,*" a male voice growled from directly behind me. "She's changed the game—again."

I slid my eyes to the left, not releasing the zombie I had a hold of even though he'd frozen in place. My glare was dark when it landed on Baron Samedi. "I can't help but think this is your fault," I snapped.

"Yes, well, even though you have my blood running through your veins, you're still human," he replied breezily. "You can't help your whining."

I wanted to hurt him. Badly. Beneath my fingers I felt movement. "What the ...?" When I turned back to the zombie I realized the spell was breaking. "She did something." Horrified disbelief washed over me.

"She did indeed," Papa Legba agreed. "You need to burn them like you've been doing. No dilly-dallying now."

My rage wasn't solely focused on Baron because I had plenty in reserve for Papa. "I hate both of you," I growled as I reached around Kade's back and clasped hands with Cole. "I just want to rip you from groin to sternum."

"She gets that from me," Brigitte said behind us. She almost sounded proud. I couldn't focus on her because the zombies were close to breaking free of Kade's spell.

"Son of a...!" Cole viciously swore. "Poet, leave that one and come here. She's somehow made them stronger. I need you."

He wouldn't have said it if he didn't mean it. I released the zombie I was holding and hurried to him.

"Help," Cole ordered, making room between himself and the zombie in his grip. "We need as much magic as we can muster."

I started funneling what I could into the zombie, a gasp escaping when Cole's hands caught fire and landed on top of mine.

"Concentrate," he gritted out.

I doubled my efforts, but the amount of energy I was expending was enormous. The fire flowing from Cole through me into the zombie turned a molten red. I held my breath when I felt the magic looping backward. The zombies had absorbed everything we had but were still standing. And then there was a pulsing sound.

Once.

Twice.

On the third pulse, the zombies exploded.

My instinct was to cover my face with my forearm. I felt bits of flaming zombie blow past me. After a few seconds, I found the courage to lift my head. There were flaming hunks of...well, zombie...everywhere.

"Oh, this is so gross," Nixie complained from behind me.

"I think there's an eyeball in my hair," Naida announced.

"It's cool," Nellie said. When I risked a glance I found him covered in goo. He looked a little too happy about it as he stared down at his black romper. "It's like a Halloween costume."

I rolled my eyes. "It is not like a Halloween costume!"

"What happened to the crazy loa?" Dolph asked. "Did we lose her?"

"No, I have her in my pocket," Luke shot back. "Of course we lost her. She set the zombies on us so she could escape." He glared at me. "Why didn't you just kill her the night we met her? That would've solved all of our problems."

Rather than respond, I pressed the heel of my hand to my forehead.

"It's not like Poet knew she was evil," Cole argued. The rain was still coming down in sheets, which at least helped wash the zombie out of our hair and the blood from our faces. We looked like cosplayers on the make. "Give her a break."

"I can't give her a break," Luke whined. "I'm pretty sure there are teeth in my hair...and you have an extra finger." He reached over and plucked something from Cole's shoulder. "Ugh, we'll have to burn everything we're wearing...and I really liked this shirt."

The complaint would've been funny under different circumstances. Now it was just annoying. "I don't suppose you guys have anything you'd like to tell us?" I turned to the loas. They looked none the worse for wear.

Papa wrinkled his nose and darted a look at Baron, who offered up a blasé head bob. "Let's head back to the park, shall we? There are some things we need to discuss."

I wanted to press them to answer our questions here, but if the neighbors hadn't seen us entering the cemetery they certainly knew we were here now. "Fine. Thirty minutes. Be in that parking lot." I extended a warning finger in Papa's face. "Don't make me come looking for you."

Papa broke out into a wide grin and then reached for my hair. I refused to pull away from him. When his hand swam into view, he had what looked like an ear clutched between his fingers. "I'll bring the bourbon."

. . .

I STRIPPED IN THE PARKING LOT RATHER than enter the trailer wearing my ruined clothing. Kade did the same. In fact, all around the lot, as the rain began to diminish, I watched as my friends dropped everything but their underwear into heaps outside their trailers.

Kade and I showered together. By the time we exited the trailer, the rain had stopped, and somebody had lit a fire in a barrel in the middle of the trailer area.

"Don't worry about the police," Baron called out as he dropped ruined clothing into the barrel. "We've made sure they'll be otherwise engaged for the evening."

I was instantly suspicious. "What is that supposed to mean?"

"It means that we cranked up the revelry," Brigitte replied. She was already sitting, her legs crossed at the ankles, and an evil glare on display for Baron, who was apparently doing his best to pretend he didn't notice her. "Nobody will be hurt. You have our word."

I folded my arms over my chest and flipped my wet hair over my shoulder. "No offense, but your word doesn't mean much."

"No, I don't suppose it does." Her gaze was impassive as she slowly turned to me. "Sit down, little one. You've had a long night."

"Maybe I don't want to sit down," I shot back.

"Sit. Down." Baron brushed past me, a bottle of bourbon in hand, and headed straight for Max, who had been oddly quiet since the scene in the cemetery had played out. "Hello, old friend," he drawled. "It's been a long time."

Max mustered a smile. "I would say it's been too long, but you've thrown my team into a tizzy. We might've been able to forego this visit and nobody would've been upset about it."

Baron snorted. "You know me – a creature of habit." He glanced at Brigitte, who continued to smolder. "I had to celebrate my union with this glorious creature."

"You remind me of rancid pig intestines," Brigitte shot back. "That's how much appeal you hold for me."

Baron grinned at the insult. "She is the true joy of my life." He threw himself in one of the open canvas chairs. "When we first married I thought the day would come when I would decapitate her and wear her head as a hat. I guess I'm still hoping for that sort of love to be reciprocated."

"You're worse than vomit on a scalding sidewalk," she sneered.

"You're both worse than a sword in my gullet," Papa snapped. "Shut up. We have humans to grapple with. Show some manners."

Baron and Brigitte straightened in their chairs.

"Tell us about Marinette," Max instructed, taking control of the conversation.

"Marinette is...well...." Papa Legba scratched his chin.

"She's worse than Baron," Brigitte offered.

I had to fight back a laugh as I sat in a chair. Rather than accept Baron's bourbon, I took the White Claw that Kade handed me and popped the tab.

"We're like any other family," Papa Legba explained. "We have ups and downs."

"Marinette would be a constant down," Brigitte supplied.

Papa Legba shot her a quelling look. "Must you always make it personal?"

Brigitte didn't as much as blink. "Yes."

Papa Legba's sigh was long and drawn out. "Marinette has never been what I would call friendly. The rest of us—even these two—have embraced periods of calm. We've partied together throughout the years even when fighting. All of us...except Marinette."

"That's why we couldn't ascertain her identity," Brigitte explained. "We haven't seen her in centuries. She does her own thing."

"That includes hating us," Baron added as he swigged straight from the bottle. His eyes drifted to Raven, and he winked at her. "Lamia. It's been a while. Do you want to show me your tail?"

A full can of White Claw whizzed through the air and smacked Baron in the side of the head. I was stunned, until I realized Brigitte had thrown it.

"Leave her alone," Brigitte warned. "Nobody needs your version of flirting to bring down the party, you perverted old billy goat."

"Don't be jealous, my love." Baron ruefully rubbed the side of his head. That was a great shot." He almost sounded encouraging. "I appreciate you still care enough to try to hurt me."

"Yes, that is my lot in life." Brigitte rolled her eyes and then turned serious. "Marinette has always been difficult. She's feared and rides those she possesses as if they're cattle. She's not always evil. She's been known to free people from bondage a time or two."

My mind drifted to those interred in the cemetery. "Is that why she picked that cemetery?"

Brigitte nodded. "Yes, and we really should've taken her background into consideration when we were trying to pinpoint her location."

"Does that mean you always knew it was her?" Cole demanded. "If so, you guys suck. You could've told us what we were up against."

Baron shook his head. "Oh, don't be such a whiner, my little flame." When Baron winked at him, Cole wrinkled his nose. "We didn't know it was her."

"We *suspected*," Brigitte corrected. "We didn't know for certain, not until tonight."

"She aligned herself with my uncle," I volunteered. "She sought him out months ago, long before he contacted me. Why would she do that?"

"I can't know for certain," Brigitte hedged. "I think she was looking for you."

"Is that what you wanted to hear?" Papa Legba challenged.

I narrowed my eyes. "I want to know why my uncle was chosen, why his life was derailed. I want to know why he has gaps in his memory. What was she looking for?"

"Gaps in his memory?" Brigitte shifted on her chair. "Why would she do that?"

"I'm asking you," I snapped.

Kade slid his hand to my knee to still me. "It's okay, baby," he whispered. "Take a breath."

I refused to meet his gaze out of fear that I might start crying, but I did as he instructed and forced myself to regulate my breathing.

"I don't know why she would go after his memories." Brigitte appeared sincere. "What little I know about you suggests you weren't raised by your family. I didn't even realize you had an uncle."

"When my parents died, he put me in the system rather than raise me," I explained. "Other than this trip, I haven't seen him since I was a teenager. I don't understand how Marinette could have known we'd cross paths again, and here of all places."

"Unless she set it in motion," Papa Legba mused. "Do you know where they met?"

"Boston. Several months ago."

"When did your uncle set up this meeting with you?" Brigitte asked.

I slid my eyes to Kade. "The letter arrived in Florida in December, right around Christmas. He tracked down my address there and said he knew I would be in New Orleans in a few weeks. He requested the meeting then."

"How would he know you planned to be in New Orleans?" Baron asked.

"How did *you* know?" Brigitte shot back. "You obviously had knowledge of her arrival before she set foot in the city. You were using her against me from the start."

"That's a bit of an exaggeration, my love," Baron said. "I simply sensed her when she appeared and opted to appeal to her baser urges to ruin your fun."

"I truly hate you," Brigitte growled.

"You're lying," Papa Legba argued. "You never stumble across luck. You make your own. You knew she was going to be here. How?"

Baron let loose a tortured sigh, as if he was suffering from a mortal wound and yet somehow managing to stay on his feet. "I've been watching her for a long time," he said finally.

"How long?" I asked.

He shrugged. "By my standards? About five seconds. By yours, since you were scamming people out of their money in Detroit. Maybe even a little bit before that. I sensed you working your magic there. I went to take a look and watched you for weeks. I was about to intervene, offer you a job because you were that impressive, but someone beat me to it." His eyes drifted to Max.

"You were there," Max said. "You saw me recruit Poet."

Baron nodded. "I was considering breaking my own rules to adopt her because she was stronger than any of my remaining kin, but then you came along and I figured it was a better fit. She's always been headstrong. She needed someone with patience to train her." He winked at me.

"You've been keeping tabs on me this entire time?" I had no idea what to make of that. "Why didn't you say something?"

"What should I have said?" he demanded. "You needed responsibility to mature. Max could provide that. Besides, I couldn't give you the life you were seeking. I was just amused watching you work."

"That's the answer," Brigitte announced. "Marinette knew about Poet because Baron knew about her. She's always been obsessed with him."

It took me a moment to understand. "Wait...is this all about a love triangle?"

Brigitte snorted. "She can have him."

"I have a way with women," Baron noted, his expression whimsical. "They throw themselves at me constantly."

"He's making that up," Papa Legba countered. "That's his way. He tells stories about himself, and people believe him. That's how he became the favorite loa."

This was all too much. I rubbed my forehead, exhaustion threatening to overwhelm me. For the first time in a very long time, the thing I wanted most was sleep. "What do we do to stop her?" I asked. "She's obviously figured out a way to combat our magic."

"Which is why I believe she was at the cemetery," Papa Legba replied. "She clearly used the blood of those interred there, the magic from the cruelty perpetrated on them, to fight what you've been doing to rein in her creations."

"My creations," Brigitte countered bitterly. "It was my spell that raised them. She hijacked it."

"Fine. Your creations." Papa Legba looked as tired as I felt. "Either way, she's in control now. She enhanced the spell. The next time she unleashes the zombies, we won't be able to use that spell to stop them."

My heart skipped. "So what are we going to do?"

Papa Legba shrugged. "She's spoiling for a fight. We need to figure out her end goal and get ahead of her. I don't see any other way to fix this."

"Great." I held out my hands. "How do you suggest we do that?"

"I was kind of hoping you had an answer."

"Ugh." I wanted to crawl under my covers and block out the world.

Twenty-Six

We talked for a long time without deciding anything. Marinette was out there, but we were no closer to figuring out her plan. Eventually, the loas took their leave and we retreated to our trailers.

Waking the next morning was like forcing myself to wade through quicksand. When I finally opened my eyes, I found Kade watching me with quiet contemplation.

"What?" I instinctively wiped at my mouth to see if I'd drooled.

"Good morning to you too," he drawled, kissing me before I could get my bearings.

"You're in a surprisingly good mood for a guy who had brains in his hair last night," I said.

"If traveling with the circus has taught me anything, it's that there's no reason to dwell on things I can't change."

He was far too upbeat. "Something bad is going to happen today," I reminded him. "We still have no idea what her plan is, but we know Marinette is going to move today. Our trick with the zombies no longer works. We're screwed."

"Wow. Somebody is in a good mood." He leaned back against his pillows and dragged a hand through his disheveled hair. "Can't we have a restful few minutes together before you start with the doom and gloom?"

I was about to tell him where he could stick his rest when I realized he had a point. "I'm sorry." I leaned my head against his chest. He held me tight. "It's just a lot to deal with."

"It is," he agreed, resting his cheek against my forehead. "I'm a little worried."

"Just a little?"

"I'm not worried about the fight. Well, I am, but I know we'll get through it. We always do."

"What are you worried about?"

"You."

I pulled back to look directly at him. "I'm fine. Why are you worried about me?"

"You've been through a lot the past few days. You found out you're part loa. The uncle who abandoned you is back. Now we learned his memory has been messed with, and that means you're not allowed to feel the anger you should be allowed to feel where he's concerned because he's suddenly a victim. That's too much weight for those diminutive shoulders of yours."

The way he phrased it made me laugh. "You've been spending too much time with Luke," I complained as I closed my eyes and listened to his heart. "That sounds like something he would say."

"Luke is a smart guy."

"Since when do you think that?"

"Since you started comparing him to me."

"Ah." I brushed my fingers over his firm chest and tried to lull myself with the sound of his heart.

"It's okay to feel overwhelmed," he said in a soft voice after a few seconds of silence. "You don't always have to be the one who holds it together."

"If not me, who?"

"Me. I can hold it together. Or we could do it together," he said after a beat. "You, me, and Cole. We'll hold it together for everybody else and save the day."

"We don't know what we're dealing with," I responded. "She's going to try to wipe us off the map today."

"That's a bit dramatic. Now who's channeling Luke?"

I ignored the dig. "That doesn't make me wrong. She has a specific plan. She outsmarted the others and she knows it. Now she's coming for us."

"She outsmarted the others because they didn't see her coming," he countered. "She segregated herself from them for years, lulled them, and now she wants to lord it over them. It's possible this is her version of a game. She could take whatever this is to the edge of oblivion and then pull it back."

"What are the odds of that?"

"Probably not good," he conceded. "I just hate when you take all this on your shoulders, as if there's nobody here to help you carry the burden. Because there is, baby. I'm here...and I'll always be here."

I kept my eyes closed. "How about we take ten minutes for ourselves, just...do this, and then we'll deal with the weirdness that is our lives. For ten minutes there will be no loas...no weird uncles with holes in their memories...no loas telling each other how much they hate each other. It will be just you and me."

"That's the best offer I'm going to get all day."

EVEN THOUGH I WOULD NEVER ADMIT IT, the quiet few minutes with Kade were exactly what the doctor ordered. I took solace in his strength, and he reassured himself that I wasn't yet ready to run headlong into danger. By the time we joined the others at the picnic tables, we were much more centered.

"No loas?" I asked, glancing around.

Raven shook her head. "No, and we can't count on them." She was matter-of-fact. "We have to come up with a plan on our own. If they show up to help, great, but we can't assume they will. Loas are nothing if not predictable."

I surveyed the faces at the tables. "Where's Max?"

"Getting breakfast," Nellie replied. "He wouldn't even let us place orders." He looked sullen. "He said he had it under control. Knowing him, he'll probably bring back grits and force us to eat them against our will."

Nellie was not a fan of grits. To be truthful, neither was I. Still, choking down grits was hardly the worst thing we would face today. "Something tells me you'll make it through the day no matter what he brings," I replied, patting his hand as I sat at the table. "I don't suppose anybody came up with a foolproof plan to keep us safe from a rampaging loa overnight?"

To my utter surprise, Luke's hand shot in the air.

I was understandably dubious. Luke wasn't a great strategic thinker when it came to battles. "Would you like to share with the class?" I prodded when he didn't immediately volunteer his idea.

"We should turn the dreamcatcher into a zombie trap," Luke replied.

"Zombie trap?" I arched an eyebrow. "Is that a technical term?"

"I want to make a trap for zombies. I want them frozen in place when we spring the trap. We need to use a different sort of magic than Kade used when he froze them. She won't expect that."

I opened my mouth to thank him for his input—and then immediately dismiss it—but snapped it shut, my brow furrowing. I looked to Raven, who appeared as surprised by the suggestion as I was. "Is that possible?" I asked.

"I don't know," she said. "I was about to tell him to keep his idiot mouth shut, but I'm not so sure he's being an idiot today."

Luke beamed at her. "Oh, that could be the sweetest thing you've ever said to me."

"*Today*," she stressed. "You're still an idiot most of the time."

"I choose to believe you don't really mean that." Luke sipped his coffee again and then smiled at me. "Go ahead and tell your best friend how much you love him. I'm ready."

I worked hard to hold back a smile. "We'll see how I feel when we reach the end of the day. Right now, that's an excellent idea. The dreamcatcher is still up. There's a gap, but we can fix that—and maybe enhance it."

"Maybe we should glamour it while we're at it," Naida suggested. "Make the evil loa believe that it's still broken when she arrives."

"That's not a bad idea. We need to figure out how to freeze the zombies in the trap before we do anything. We can't use Kade's magic because she has figured a way around it."

"She has," Raven agreed, her expression thoughtful. "In fact, she used every trick in her arsenal to combat the previous spell. If we change things up, she shouldn't be able to combat it because she shot her wad with the first counter-spell."

"We could set a trap." Ideas were swirling in my head. "That handles the zombies, but what about her?"

"I have an idea about that," Max offered as he appeared, bags of food in hand. I had no idea where he'd spent the night since his trailer was in storage. "There's more food in my truck, Dolph and Nellie."

Even though Nellie normally complained about having to follow orders, he didn't give Max any lip. He understood the trouble we faced.

"Where did you come from?" I looked around.

His smile was enigmatic. "I haven't been far, my dear. I picked up breakfast. I thought they would've told you."

"I didn't see you drive up." Now that I looked, his truck suddenly appeared at the far end of the parking lot.

"You were likely distracted." He winked. "As for where I was overnight, I've had my ear to the ground. I tapped a few sources to see if they had any ideas on where we might find our missing loa. They didn't, but they're on the hunt. I've also been lending my considerable services to the security detail at the Royal Sonesta."

I was taken aback. "Sidney."

He nodded. "He's fine. He's in his room. Our suggestion that he stay in his room wasn't too much for him to bear. He's so confused I'm not sure he even realizes Vanessa is gone."

"He didn't act confused when we met with him," Kade said.

"Probably because Vanessa was with him," I said. "She's had control of him this entire time."

"I think she's had control of him almost from the moment they met," Max added as he placed the bags on the picnic table. "My guess is she arranged the meeting in Boston, used her considerable charms on him, and then started invading his memories."

"To what end?" I demanded. "It makes no sense that she would be interested in me."

"She knew Baron was interested in you," Max pointed out. "You heard them last night. Even though they're keen to hold their cards close to their vests, it's apparent Marinette has been interested in Baron a very long time. I'm guessing she hasn't really been separate from them as much as behind them."

"All because she was in love with him?" The notion baffled me. "I don't get it. Why not just tell him?"

"Do you really not know?" Max's gaze was almost pitying. "Come now, Poet, you must see the truth of Baron. He might be a braggadocios pain, but there's one thing that's obvious whenever you look at him."

That's when it hit me. "He truly loves Brigitte."

Max bobbed his head.

"He loves her and loathes her at the same time," I said. "Nobody else can hold a candle to her."

"Exactly." Max sat across from Kade. "Love does funny things to people. It has made Brigitte and Baron the worst kind of lovers. They hurt each other just to stay close to one another. Make no mistake, though, there's still a relationship there...and it's more than they show on the surface."

"Are they into some funky sex stuff?" Luke asked, his face awash with horror. "If so, for once, I don't want to hear about it. I have no interest in the loas and their sex games."

Max laughed. "I think we all agree on that. It's a triangle, but all sides are not reciprocal. Baron loves Brigitte. He also loves to torture her. Brigitte loves Baron. She wishes him harm on a daily basis. Nobody loves Marinette – and that has made her bitter.

"She's not here to kill the people of New Orleans, no matter what her actions indicate," he continued. "She's here to get Baron's attention. I'm guessing she feels the only way to get him to notice her is to threaten the one thing he loves more than Brigitte."

"Himself," I surmised.

"He is a bit of a pompous jackass," Max confirmed. "He'll do what he wants, when he wants. Marinette doesn't stand a chance."

"But why would she dig so deep inside Sidney's head?" I asked. That was the part I kept circling back to. "What does she hope to accomplish with that?"

"It's possible that Marinette didn't understand Baron's interest in you," Max said. "She might've thought his feelings for you were something other than what they were. When she realized who you were she must've figured you had something Baron wanted. It's possible she simply wanted to take possession of that something herself to make herself just as important."

"So she maneuvered us all into position in New Orleans and then took control of the game," I said, my head hanging low. "What a mess. But why create gaps in Sidney's memory?"

"She might not have meant to leave gaps," Max replied. "She might've been mainly interested in knowing what he knew about you. The gaps might be a result of Sidney doing his best to protect you."

I fell quiet, mostly because I didn't know what else to say.

"Is there a way we can help him?" Kade asked. "I know I've been the one saying Poet should cut him loose, but I'm starting to think I was wrong. If we can help, we should."

"That's on the agenda after breakfast." Max rummaged through the contents of the bag before coming up with a container and handing it to me. "You need to fortify yourself. Once we're done here, we're going to Sidney. We're going to figure out what he was hiding...and hopefully what Marinette found when she was digging around in there. After that, we're going to set the trap that you were talking about and bring her to us."

"You make it sound so easy."

"I don't think this will be easy in the slightest," he said. "But we have to deal with it." Max's hand landed on mine, and he gave it a hearty squeeze. "I know this is going to be difficult for you. I have no doubt that you're going to struggle with what we find out. I'm sorry you have to go through it, I truly am."

"But it's necessary," I finished.

"It is," he agreed. "You can't run from this part of your past any longer. You need to know the truth. You need to hear it from Sidney. We also need to help him if we can. We can't leave him in this state. It seems that without Marinette's influence he's falling apart."

Briefly, I pressed my eyes shut. Then I nodded. "Okay, I'm up for it. I need to know. You're right about that." I darted a look toward Kade. "I have a future I'm looking forward to. I can't do that if I allow the past to keep haunting me."

Max broke out in a genuine smile. "That's my girl." He released my hand. "We'll do this together. We all have a future we're working toward. We lean on each other for strength."

"While you guys are handling Sidney, we'll figure out the logistics of the dreamcatcher," Raven offered. "I already have some ideas for building the trap. Marinette won't know what hit her."

"I certainly hope so," Max said. "Even if we take out her minions, she's going to be hell on wheels when it comes to the final battle. We need help."

"You mean the other loas," I deduced. "What if they don't want to help?"

"They don't have a choice."

Twenty-Seven

Luke tagged along with Max and me to the Royal Sonesta. Kade was furious about being cut out of the action, but he was needed at the park. Raven explained that his magic was key to their plan. I reassured him it would be fine, but in truth, I wanted him with me. So when Luke volunteered to serve as a chaperone—his word, not mine—I didn't protest.

I loved Max, but I needed someone to coddle me...just in case.

Max strolled through the hotel as if he owned it, and no one questioned our presence or direction. Once on the seventh floor, he led us to Sidney's room and used his magic to get us inside.

It was a standard hotel room, a king-size bed in the middle, and my gaze immediately fell on Sidney, his eyes glazed, hair disheveled. He was dressed in cotton pajamas, his skin sallow.

"I don't understand why this is happening," I said as I studied him. He didn't even resemble the man I'd eaten dinner with several times since our arrival. "How could she do this to him?"

"She doesn't care about him," Max replied. "She never did. This was always about you."

"That doesn't make me feel better."

"Well, we're going to fix him." Max was calm. "I promise we'll do right by Sidney, even if we have to completely wipe his mind of you. We'll put him back together first."

My heart constricted at the thought of sending Sidney out into the world with a modified memory. It was always a measure of last resort. Ultimately, however, I nodded. Max was right. We had no choice.

"Let's do this." I sat on the bed next to Sidney and gathered his hand. Slowly, his eyes traveled to me. Maybe it was wishful thinking, but I found a hint of recognition buried deep in his somber eyes. He didn't speak but I knew he was aware of my presence. "Hi." My voice was soft. "I'm sorry this happened to you."

He blinked but didn't respond.

"I need to get inside your head, Sidney. I need to fix whatever she did."

His expression didn't change.

"Just go in," Max instructed as he sat next to me. "I'll follow you. Luke, try not to be a distraction."

"When am I ever distracting?" Luke whined.

Max and I pinned him with twin looks of annoyance.

"Fine." Luke threw up his hands. "I'll sit in the chair quiet as a mouse. You'll be sorry for doubting me."

"There's a first time for everything," Max said. His hand landed on my shoulder. "Go ahead, my dear. This is your show. I think you're the key to unlocking the things he's protecting with his sanity."

I pressed my hand to Sidney's forehead and closed my eyes. There were no initial walls up to guard his mind, so it was easy to waltz in and take a look around. What I found threw me for a loop.

"Sidney?"

From his spot on a leather couch inside a huge library, my uncle turned his attention to me. He seemed surprised at my appearance. "Hello, Poet. Look how nice you look in your dress."

Confused, I glanced down and found I was dressed in an old frock I remembered from the day I'd been removed from Sidney's care and taken to my first foster home. A glance in the mirror on the wall told me I was a teenager again.

"This is how he sees you," Max explained. He'd followed me into the library but stood several feet away from Sidney. "This is how he's always remembered you."

I battled back my annoyance at being put in this position again and sat next to Sidney on the couch. "Do you come here often?" I tried for levity. "I don't recognize this place."

"This is my safe place," Sidney explained as he shut the book he'd been reading and placed it on the table next to the couch. "This is where I come when the guilt about what I did to you overwhelms me."

"You don't have to feel guilty," I assured him. "I'm fine. I don't look like this any longer—my fashion sense has grown by leaps and bounds. You can let it go."

"Your fashion sense still sucks," Luke called out from beyond the library.

I ignored him and kept my focus on Sidney. "I was angry the day you let me go," I admitted. If I was going to do this, I needed to get it all out. "I was hurt. But I saw things from your point of view. I understood why you didn't want me."

"It's not that I didn't want you." Sidney looked pained. "In fact, I was trying to figure out a way to keep you. He said I couldn't."

Confused, I asked, "Who? Who said you couldn't keep me? Dad?"

"Not your father." Sidney vigorously shook his head. "Your father would've been so angry with me. I know that if I see him again in the next life he'll want nothing to do with me...and I won't blame him." A lone tear slid down Sidney's cheek. "Your father was my best friend, and I betrayed him."

"That's not true," I protested. "You just couldn't do what he wanted. That doesn't make you a bad person."

"I *am* a bad person. I let you go, and I will never forgive myself." He dropped his head into his hands and cried.

My heart went out to him. Did he torture himself constantly over this one decision? "Sidney, I need to know who told you keeping me was a bad idea."

He didn't respond.

"Sidney." My voice was so soft I wasn't sure he heard me.

"It was me." Baron Samedi, in all his glory, stood in front of one of the bookcases and gave me a rueful smile. "If you have hate in your heart, direct it at me."

I was dumbfounded. "You told him to let me go? Why?"

"Stay back," Max warned, taking an aggressive step forward. The look he pinned Baron with promised retribution if his wishes weren't followed.

"I'm not going to hurt her, Max." Baron looked weary, beaten down. When he sat in one of the antique wingback chairs across from us, he also looked apologetic. It was a far cry from the blowhard I'd become accustomed to dealing with. "She's one of the few children we have left. The others, almost all of them, are mere shadows of what we wanted them to be. She's the only one with enough power to be considered a rightful heir."

"An heir to what?" I demanded.

"I knew Marinette was searching for our offspring," he admitted. "She's been wiping them out. That's why I started my own search before your parents died."

"She killed them, didn't she?" I don't know how I knew, but I did.

"She is responsible," he agreed. "You were supposed to be with them that day. You were supposed to die. I changed your mind, had you remain at the house. You probably don't remember."

"I don't ever remember meeting you."

"It was just a little push." Baron was inexplicably sad. "I had a feeling. I would've protected your parents had I known, but I couldn't shake this feeling that something bad was going to happen. I protected you above all else. She went after your parents because she's barred from going after you explicitly. We have rules. You weren't in the car with them, so there was nothing she could do. After that, I did the only thing I could. I made you strong."

I had no idea what to make of that, so I turned to Max. "Do you understand what he's saying?"

Max nodded stiffly. "You convinced Sidney to put her in the system."

"He was ill equipped to deal with her," Baron insisted. "Marinette would've kept coming for her through him. I thought he was weak. Now I know he's not weak. He protected her to the best of his ability long after she was removed from his life. The holes in his memory prove that. Marinette still would've won. That's why I had Brigitte use her powers to hide her in the system."

His eyes were clear when they landed on me. "Brigitte helped you make your decision to move to the streets. I knew it would be a tough time for you, but I knew you were resourceful. Once there was no record of your location, Marinette couldn't find you. Do you understand?"

I did...and it made so much sense. "You hid me from her."

"And made your life difficult in the process," Baron added. "Then, when I knew Max was close, I pushed him to find you." He smiled at the memory. "It didn't take much. All I had to do was put you on the same street. You were like magnets, and I knew when Max sensed your power that he would protect you. I knew it was going to be okay."

"That doesn't change the fact that you put her in an awful position," Max snapped. He looked furious. "She was a child."

"With a legacy to uphold," Baron shot back. "She's so much more than a child of a loa. You can't see it yet. Her destiny is upon her, and it will be fulfilled today."

My heart hammered. "I don't understand. What's happening today?"

"Marinette hasn't only been taking out my children," Baron replied. "She was unnaturally focused on me because she convinced herself she had feelings I didn't reciprocate, but that's not what was going on. She was always unbalanced, and because of that, our entire belief system has been thrown into flux."

"Meaning what?" I demanded.

"Marinette has decided that if she can't have what she wants she's willing to take everybody down with her. She thinks that's her destiny. She's vengeance. We need a child of the loa not just to take her down but to become her."

I reared back as if I'd been smacked. "No." I shook my head. "I won't become a loa."

Baron let loose a low chuckle. "You won't become a loa," he agreed. "You're just going to take on the power of a loa."

"Is that somehow better?"

"Nothing lasts forever in this world." He appeared to choose his words carefully. "Beliefs change. They...evolve. That's what's happening here. We need you to help us with the change."

"I don't understand." I was beyond frustrated.

"I think I do." Max looked much more relaxed than he'd been when the conversation with Baron first started. "The loas aren't going anywhere, Poet. He doesn't expect you to become a loa, but you're uniquely bred to handle the loa power.

"Marinette needs to die today," he continued. "Her power has to go somewhere. He wants it to go to you."

"She's pure of heart," Baron said. "She can accept the power without using it to destroy the world. Instead, she'll dole it out to another group of ancestors moving forward. Given who your son is, and what he can do, it will be like starting an entirely new line. They will be more than what we are—better."

I couldn't believe what I was hearing. "You want Kade and me to start a new line of what?"

"Heroes?" Baron laughed at his own joke. "I don't have a name for what we're doing today, or for the children you will bring into this world. I only know that it's what's supposed to happen."

"How do you know?" My voice shook.

"Brigitte saw it. We don't often agree on much, but she showed me what she saw when looking at you...and we knew. Marinette has been a threat for a very long time. You're going to help us eradicate that threat. As for what comes after, it's impossible to say, but I expect great things."

"Will I still be human?" My voice cracked.

"Of course. You will be what you were always meant to be. At your core, you've always been human. Yes, you can do extraordinary things, but you can't be anything other than you are. You won't lose sight of the necessity of being human like we did because you understand what being human really is. Your time on the streets molded you. I look forward to seeing what you'll become."

"But I'll be different," I insisted. "I won't be the same."

"Your heart will not change." Baron got up from the chair and approached me. "You are who you are. I don't think you understand that you get a choice. You get to decide who you're going to be. I know you'll choose to stay human.

"You love hard, and with your whole heart," he continued. "Believe it or not, that's what's kept Brigitte and I sane through all these centuries of games. You'll be different. You'll become more powerful, but you won't become a threat. You'll be you...with a little something extra."

"How will it work?" Max demanded.

"It's already set in motion," Baron replied. "Your people are building a trap." He almost looked amused. "They're very good. Marinette assumes she's outwitted us. She was ahead at the start, but she became greedy. She tipped her hand. Now we know how to defeat her."

He sounded so certain. I couldn't help being afraid despite his bravado. "I won't lose the people I love." I was adamant. "I won't lose the life we've planned."

"Of course not," Baron reassured me. "I haven't protected you all this time for you to suddenly become someone else. You're the culmination of our line. I won't let you be hurt."

"What about Sidney?" I gestured to my uncle, who remained on the couch, seemingly bewildered. "Will you fix what she's done to him?"

"It's already done." Baron waved his hand, directing a kind smile at Sidney as my uncle's eyes widened. "He was never meant to be a sacrificial lamb. I knew leaving you would torture him, but I never thought it would get this bad. I was protecting him as much as you, Poet. When Marinette falls, he will be free."

"Marinette would've killed him in another attempt to get to me," I surmised. "You knew that, so you forced him to let me go."

"We suggested it," he clarified. "Rather strongly. He still fought us. It took a great deal of effort. We didn't want to torture either of you. We did our best. We might've gone about it the wrong way, but we really did have your best interests at heart."

"What happens when Marinette is gone?" I pressed. "Will I have to stay here? Will our other plans be derailed?"

Baron was solemn as he shook his head. "You won't be a loa, Poet. You'll be something more...and maybe something a little less. The time of gods has passed. It's time for you to be you. Something tells me the new world you build will be something fantastic."

I hesitated and then nodded. "I'm going to be really mad if you're lying to me."

He chuckled. "You remind me of my Brigitte. So forceful, so blood-thirsty when you want to be."

"I know what I want. I won't let this change me."

"That's why it was always meant to be you."

Twenty-Eight

Max stayed with Sidney as Luke and I headed back to the park. He promised to join us shortly, after arranging for one of his friends to stay with Sidney. We couldn't fix the damage completely until Marinette was gone. Sidney was already on his way to recovery, and we now had to remove the final obstacle.

I was lost in my head during the walk. Luke, for once, was silent. He didn't say anything until we were on the sidewalk that led into the park.

"Are you okay with this?" he asked finally. "You can still say no. I mean...we'll find another way to defeat Marinette if you don't want to do this."

In truth, I didn't know how I felt about it. "I didn't expect to start the day finding out that there'd been some grand plan in place for my life since the start," I admitted. "I don't know what to make of it."

"Then say no." Luke's disdain was obvious. "You don't have to do what they want."

"What if I do? What if this is what's supposed to happen?"

"Then I think you should have more than an hour to think about it," he huffed. "I hate these stupid loas."

That made me laugh. "I'm not a big fan either. That doesn't change the fact that Baron saved me when I was a kid. If he hadn't intervened and influenced my decision that day, I would have died."

"I still don't understand that," Luke said. "If the loas can't mess with the offspring of other loas, how could Marinette go after you?"

"She didn't go after me. She went after my parents."

"Wouldn't one of them have been in the same position as you? I mean...you inherited the loa gene from one of them."

He had a point. "Yes, but she likely focused her efforts on the other one. I'm guessing my mother was the loa. She targeted my father, who always drove. My mother died because Marinette targeted my father, not because Marinette went after her."

"That seems like a crappy loophole." Luke scuffed his feet. "These loas are buttheads."

"They are, but the fact remains that I believe Baron did what he thought he had to do. He protected me."

"By forcing you to navigate the foster care system on your own."

"I survived, Luke." My voice was soft. "I made it here, and this is where I belong. He made that possible."

"I still don't like him."

"That's allowed." I slid my hand into Luke's as we emerged in the parking lot. "Thank you for going with me. I'm glad I had you."

"You'll always have me, even if you turn into some crazy hell beast with unlimited powers bent on destroying the world. I'll always be your ride-or-die guy."

I kissed his cheek. "I will never want anybody other than you as my ride-or-die."

"Even Kade?"

"Oh, don't even." I shook my head as the rest of our group came into view. "I want all of my boys with me."

"I'm still your favorite, right?"

He wasn't going to let it go, so I simply nodded. "You're my best friend for a reason." I headed straight for Raven when she appeared at the edge of the group. "Where do we stand?"

She looked me over, head to toe, and nodded. "The trap is set. We used pixie magic and fluffed it with Kade's magic to serve as a distraction. It will draw in the zombies, and when we spring the trap the loa will have no natural defense against it."

"Good." I flashed her a thumbs-up and braced myself for what was to come. "So, there have been a few developments. Everybody should sit down."

"I'm going to hate this," Kade muttered as he plopped down on one of the picnic table benches. "Be gentle, baby. I can't take bad news."

"I don't know that it's bad news. It's just not what we expected." I laid it all out for them. I chose my words carefully but went into great detail about what was expected. When I finished, Kade and Cole were swearing. Raven, however, looked intrigued.

"It's time for the evolution," she murmured, cocking her head and studying me as if for the first time.

"What is that supposed to mean?" Cole demanded. "What evolution?"

"It's something that happens naturally with religions," Raven replied. "With every evolution, the corresponding gods become more human. It's natural...and it makes sense in this case."

I found I was hopeful. "I'll still be human."

She smiled at my worry. "Of course you'll be human. That's who you are. Your loa blood makes you uniquely qualified to absorb the overflow of power that Marinette will surrender when her time ends. But there's just one thing."

"What?" I was almost afraid to hear her question. Obviously we'd missed something when talking things out in the hotel room.

"We can handle the zombies," Raven replied, "but how do we kill Marinette?"

"Oh, *that*." I gave a dismissive wave. "We can't beat Marinette. Our job is to handle the zombies. The other loas will tackle her. They'll be here shortly. In fact, they could be waiting in the wings now. Baron said it's inevitable she'll come here, but not because she's moving on me. She wants the zombies to take over. She feels she needs to start with us. She can't move specifically on me, but she can unleash the zombies and hope they finish me off. That's the plan...and after that, when the power of the other loas is diminished, she'll move on them."

"We have to stop the zombies here," Raven said.

"She's expecting a battle," I explained. "Our trap should ensure it never gets that far. We'll draw the zombies in, spring the trap, and then the loas will come in to end her."

Raven blew out a sigh. "I'm ready to see it finished. I'm also dying to see what your power boost will look like."

That was the part I was most nervous about. "This plan is set in stone now. We need to follow through." I held Kade's gaze and saw absolute terror reflected back at me. "It's going to be okay. I promise."

"We're with you," Nellie said as he grabbed his axe from the table. "Let's just get it over with. I think we're all ready to finish this."

"Yeah." I dragged a hand through my hair. "Let's finish this, for better or worse."

"For better," Luke insisted. "I always knew you were a goddess. It's time to ensure your destiny."

THE CIRCUS WAS SUPPOSED TO OPEN at ten o'clock, but we cast a spell repelling people. Then Raven threw a glamour over the park grounds to make it appear as if it was bursting with guests.

Then we waited.

It was almost noon before we saw any movement.

It's happening.

The voice that spoke in my mind belonged to Raven. I nodded to Kade, who was in my tent with me. He'd had a lot of questions about what was going to happen, and I wasn't sure how placated he was by the answers. Ultimately, he stopped resisting. At least with me, because I knew he would never stop fighting alongside me. I couldn't tell whether it was because he agreed with my decision, or he simply felt he had no say in the matter. Either way, I recognized there would be some long discussions later.

"Are you ready?" I asked him as I stood.

He nodded, his expression unreadable.

"It's going to be okay," I reassured him. The more I said it, the more I started to believe it. "I know it's weird to say, but I think this is what's supposed to happen."

He stroked my hair and offered up a soft smile. "Well, since this is also supposed to happen, you and me, I'll take your word for it." He graced me with a quick kiss. "Let's end this. If all goes as planned, we'll still have a few nights in the city to enjoy without zombies hanging over our heads."

"That sounds fun, doesn't it?"

"As long as I'm with you I'm happy."

I squeezed his hand and then exited the tent. The second I was outside I felt the change in the atmosphere. The air had turned oppressive in the blink of an eye, and the wind was beginning to whip.

"Is that us or her?" I asked Raven, who appeared between two booths.

"Us," Raven replied. "I thought it best we make it look as if our guests were running into tents. You know, congregating in one place."

As if on cue, the fake people Raven had conjured started shouting and broke into brisk jogs at the moment the sky opened up.

I smirked, amused when I saw a woman slip on the ground before her husband caught her and dragged her in the direction of the tent. "Very realistic."

Raven returned my smile. "I'm nothing if not gifted. Just ask Percival."

My smile disappeared in an instant. "Let's not go there. I'm still scarred from the chaps incident."

Her laugh was light. She was having a good time. "Let's finish her."

We moved in tandem toward the tent. We took only a few steps before the first zombie shambled into view. It was a woman, bottle-blond hair standing in a million different directions as she shuffled toward us. She was missing an eye.

I glanced over my shoulder at Kade. "We can't spring the trap until we know how many of them are on the grounds. Take out the first few through normal methods."

Kade produced a dagger from the back of his belt. "I've got it. Stay alert." He strode to the zombie and barely blinked before stabbing it in the head. "How are we going to know when it's time to trigger the trap?"

"We'll know," Raven replied, her eyes keen as she scanned the grounds. "They're everywhere now."

I nodded. I'd caught sight of more than a handful of them myself. "Where is Marinette?"

The question was barely out of my mouth before I felt movement to my left. I jerked my head in that direction, expecting a zombie. Instead, the loa in question crouched on top of the ticket booth, her eyes lit with amusement.

"Surprise," she trilled.

I stared at her, reminding myself she wasn't the human she claimed to be. If the legend was real—and I had no reason to believe it wasn't given everything we'd learned—beneath she was nothing but a skeleton. This was nothing but a fancy glamour.

"Why am I not surprised?" I drawled, giving her my full attention. Raven was in charge of springing the trap.

"You really didn't know I would be coming for you today?" she challenged. "Come on. You're not stupid. Naive maybe, but definitely not stupid."

"I knew you would come," I replied.

"And you know your little trick no longer works on my army," she said. "You can't stop me...and yet you still opened today." She clucked her tongue. "That's possibly incredibly brave or more likely a total waste. Either way, it's good for me."

"You seem to believe that," I agreed, rubbing my hands over the front of my damp pants. "Can I ask you something?"

"Do you really want to waste time on conversation?" Marinette almost looked disappointed.

"I just have a question," I pressed.

"Fine." She looked bored now, making a big show of checking her fingernails, but I knew she was curious.

"The day you killed my parents, did you talk to them first? Did they know what was going to happen?"

Genuine shock reverberated through her. She shuttered it after a few seconds, but not fast enough to cover what she felt. "Who told you that?"

"Baron." I saw no reason to lie. "He said he kept me from getting in the car with them that day because he knew you were after them...and me."

Marinette was incredulous. "I can't believe he broke the rule."

"What rule is that?"

"Loa business is not for outsiders." She shook her head, amusement now taking over her face. "Baron never did think the rules applied to him."

I risked a glance at Raven. Her attention was on the zombies. If she was listening to the conversation, she was doing it covertly. Kade was with her and they looked poised to strike. That left Marinette for me.

"He's an interesting guy," I replied in an attempt to draw things out. "He explained how things worked, how you couldn't come at me directly. I'm guessing you couldn't go after my mother directly either, which left my father. Timing must've been difficult, and once he intervened, I was all but lost to you."

"I have no idea what you're talking about," she lied.

"No?" I was determined to keep her attention. "Sidney was going to keep me. He was trying to figure it out. You know that, though. That's why you went digging in his head."

"Oddly enough, that was much more work than I thought it would be," she admitted. "He had a barrier, a wall he'd built around his memories of you. He was willing to die to protect them. I wasn't expecting that."

"Do you want to know why?" Now I was playing with her.

"By all means, illuminate me." Her smile was feral.

"Baron helped him erect that wall. He convinced Sidney to give me up. He also had a hand in almost every decision I made between the time my parents died and the day Max found me. He also had a hand in that meeting."

Marinette's eyebrows moved toward one another. "But...why?"

"Apparently I'm uniquely poised to do something he wants," I replied.

"And what's that?"

"Help end you."

Marinette blinked several times and then straightened. "Excuse me?"

"Now!" Raven roared.

Marinette raised her hand into the sky, as if she expected to take off flying, but when the trap kicked in, it was powerful enough to rock her back. She flew off the ticket booth and hit the ground with a resounding thud.

All around us, the zombies caught fire and blazed.

"What's happening?" Marinette rolled to her knees, her eyes wild. "How are you doing this? I circumvented the spell."

"This is a new one," I replied as I towered over her. "We have access to more than one type of magic. You probably should've taken that into consideration."

I sensed the moment the other loas arrived.

"Sometimes even loas outlive their usefulness," I said.

Marinette realized she was no longer alone when Papa Legba moved to stand on my right side. "No." She vehemently shook her head when she saw them. "You can't. It's against the rules."

"It's against the rules if we do it unilaterally," Papa Legba countered. He almost looked sad. "It's not against the rules when we take a vote."

"You really should've come to the tribunal," Brigitte trilled as she stepped behind Marinette, glee filling her eyes when the endangered loa snapped her head in that direction. "That will teach you to miss employee meetings."

"This really is on you, Marinette," Baron said as he joined the trio, his trademark smile back in place. "You forgot the one rule we all live by when you embarked on this vendetta."

Marinette was still defiant. "What rule did I forget?"

"That even though we're higher beings, we're still beholden to *them*," Papa Legba replied, inclining his head toward me. "The humans are as much our gods as we are theirs. It's time to end this."

"No!" Marinette scrambled to her feet, desperately clawing for purchase as she attempted to solidify her footing in the rain. "You can't end me without someone to take my place."

"Who says we don't have someone to take your place?" Baron demanded, his lips spreading into a wide grin. "All we need is someone with powerful loa blood. You might've wiped out a lot of our candidates, but you didn't get all of them."

"Not by a long shot," Brigitte agreed on a hiss as she moved to Marinette's back. The movement was so fast she was almost a blur, and she had the other loa by the neck, an odd bejeweled dagger at her throat, before Marinette could respond. "Your replacement is a child of my blood. You probably won't like that outcome, but I find it fitting."

Marinette opened her mouth, but nothing came out. Brigitte sliced across the loa's throat before she could answer, and then took a step back as plumes of black smoke escaped from the body. There was no blood, just magic, and it pooled on the ground, circling and swirling.

I tore my gaze from the magic long enough to focus on Marinette. She no longer looked human. She resembled a skeleton, sunken and hollow, and was slowly dropping to the ground, eyes as vacant as the soul I figured she lost long ago.

"Don't be afraid," Brigitte said to me as the magic rushed toward me. "This really is the best course of action."

I braced myself for impact, but when the magic hit everything went dark, like a candle being blown out. The last thing I remembered was my eyes rolling back into my head, and then there was nothing but the sound of Kade's voice.

Twenty-Nine

I woke in my bed. It was dark outside, not even a hint of color filtering through the blinds. I wasn't alone.

"Hello."

The lamp beside the bed flicked on, but there was nobody there to hit the switch. I found Baron sitting in one of the canvas chairs from outside. He'd moved it next to the bed. A book rested in his lap.

"How can you read in the dark?" I asked, my voice raspy.

He smirked. "I have many gifts. Besides, if you ask my wife, I only look at the pictures." He closed the book and put it on the nightstand. "How do you feel?"

I glanced around, my mind muddled. It was almost as if I'd been removed from my body. There were no dreams clouding my memory, no fears. Only a sense of calm.

"Where's Kade?" I demanded. There's no way he would abandon me. If history had taught me anything, it was that he would've sat vigil by my bedside forever if that's how long I slept. Something must be wrong.

"He's with his father," Baron replied. "They're outside dealing with...things."

"What sort of things?" I was suspicious. "What time is it?"

"Almost midnight."

That couldn't be right. "I slept the whole day?"

"I wouldn't call it sleep. You were adjusting. Now, let's get back to my original question: How do you feel?"

I was pouty when I answered. "Tired."

"That's to be expected. What else?"

"I...don't...know." I lifted my hand and stared at it. I felt normal, all things considered. "Did it work? Is she gone?"

"She's gone."

"And I'm still human?"

He chuckled. "You are. Even I'm not sure how your new powers will manifest. I don't suppose you could put on a demonstration for me?"

I glared at him.

"I didn't think so." He pushed himself to a standing position. "You have things to deal with. Your friends outside are furious I locked them out. They're trying to figure out a way inside even as we speak...and the little one wants to use his axe. They won't be able to overpower me, but if I want to stay in your good graces it's probably best I take my leave."

"That's it?" I demanded. "That's all you have to say?"

"What do you want me to say?" He sounded utterly reasonable, and it only infuriated me further.

"I don't think I like you." I folded my arms over my chest. "I just want to know what I'm going to be grappling with going forward."

"I don't have an answer." He shrugged. "This is a new world for all of us. I'm going to give you a bit of time to adjust and then I'll stop in for another visit. I believe you're going to Arkansas next. It's not a favorite locale, but I'll make an exception for you." He winked.

"I really dislike you," I grumbled.

"You'll learn to love me. Just ask your grandmother." He looked smug as he started for the door. When he turned back, he was solemn. "You took a leap of faith today. You trusted me when you didn't have to. I won't forget that you swooped in and saved us all. If Marinette had her way, we would already be fading into memory."

"I didn't have much choice. She was a threat."

"There's always a choice. You made the right one as far as I'm concerned, but you still could've fought me on it. Why didn't you?"

"Because, despite your many faults—*many, many faults*—I think you try to do what's right," I replied. "You still serve a purpose in this world. I'm not thrilled with your marriage games, but overall you don't seem the worst guy imaginable."

"High praise."

"You protected me when I was a kid."

"That benefitted me."

"You didn't protect my mother, and I might always be angry about that, but I see what you did with me," I said. "You extended your hand to push me in the correct direction on multiple occasions. You led me here, and I love my life."

He smiled. "You should. Your friends are loyal. This group of misfits is powerful. Now you're the most powerful one. I look forward to seeing your development." He turned to leave again.

"I can't believe you're going to leave without giving me more information," I complained. "That's a total jerk move."

"It is, but you need time to adjust. Besides, the mage and the wolf will melt down if I don't lift the protection spell. The elemental will start threatening to burn down the Quarter if I don't cede this space. I will be in touch."

"So...I'm just supposed to figure this stuff out on my own?"

"Who better?"

"What if I hurt someone?"

"You won't."

"How can you know that?"

"You're the most human person I've ever met."

I went warm all over at the statement. "How did you know that's what I needed to hear?"

"You are your grandmother's daughter. She's always been big on protecting the oppressed. You get that from her."

"When will I see you again?"

"Soon. Get some rest. Reassure your loved ones. We have nothing but time to see what you become."

"That's pretty vague."

"Yes, well, I'm nothing if not annoying. Just ask my wife."

"Oh, I don't need her to confirm it for me."

I stared in his wake for several seconds, and then heard the front door of the trailer burst open. Kade tumbled through the bedroom doorway first, followed closely by Cole and Luke.

"Baby." Kade practically choked on the word as he approached, his eyes wide. "Are you okay?"

I nodded and patted the bed next to me. "I'm fine. At least I think I am."

Kade gingerly sat next to me. Then he pulled me to him for the longest, hardest hug of my life. "I thought I would never see you again. He wouldn't let us in."

I patted his back. "He's a pain. I think he gets off on it."

"He's a total pain," Cole agreed. "How are you?" His eyes were contemplative as they looked me up and down. "How do you feel?"

"Honestly, I feel pretty normal." I nudged Kade back when it became apparent he wasn't going to stop smothering me. "I'm okay," I reassured him. "Just...don't freak out. I don't feel any different."

"Are you sure about that?" Luke challenged. "I don't want you to lose your head or anything, but you glowed gold for an hour after you were hit with that cloud of loa magic."

I stilled. "What?"

Kade nodded, solemn. "It's true. I swear it was as if you were on fire, but the flames were golden. We couldn't get close to you." He choked on the last part. He took my hand in his and squeezed. "It was the worst."

I smiled despite the serious conversation. "How did I end up here if you couldn't touch me?"

"He carried you," Kade replied. "That devil loa brought you in here. We thought we would be able to sit next to you once you were safely in bed, but he locked us out."

"For hours," Luke added. "It was torture."

I cocked my head, considering. "Where were Brigitte and Papa?"

"They left as soon as it was over," Cole replied. "They left Baron to clean up the mess. Brigitte said it was his penance for messing up the game."

"Interesting."

"Are you sure you don't feel any different?" Luke prodded. "You glowed, Poet. I definitely think something happened."

I snuggled closer to Kade. "Baron said it will be a learning experience for us to see how it plays out. I guess we're going to have to learn together, because I really don't feel any different right now."

"Well, I guess that's good." Cole said the words, but he didn't look convinced. "We have more good news. Sidney is awake and his mind seems to be fixed. Max spent part of the evening with him. He's coming tomorrow to hang out with you. We figured it was best we let you get some sleep tonight."

I looked to Kade. "I think I'm going to keep in touch with him."

"I think that's a good idea," Kade replied.

"Really? I thought you hated him."

"That was before I found out the loa pressured him into making that decision. Now I hate the loa."

I didn't bother to hide my smile. "I look forward to spending time with Sidney without Marinette's influence guiding him."

"Max said he seems pretty normal," Luke volunteered. "They're bringing breakfast tomorrow."

"Which is only eight hours away," Kade said, tightening his grip on me. "Can you rest?"

"Yeah. The rest we'll figure out in the morning."

"Oh, sure," Cole said dryly. "We'll figure out your new life as a loa over the course of one meal. Seems totally reasonable."

I shot him a quelling look. "You know what I mean."

Cole smiled and kissed my forehead. "It's a magnificent new world, Poet Parker. I'm kind of giddy to see how it all works out."

Giddy wasn't the word I would've used, but I understood the sentiment. "I really do feel okay," I said to Kade when they were gone and he was tucking me in at his side. "I don't want you worrying."

"Too late for that." He kissed my cheek and cuddled me close.

"I feel human," I reassured him as he shut off the light.

"Poet, I was never worried about you not being human."

"What were you worried about?"

"That loa running off with you. You're the most human person I know. Now, apparently, you're the most powerful too. I was afraid they would steal you."

"That's what he said to me. Not the stealing part, but the other part."

"Just because he said one smart thing doesn't mean I'm going to start liking him. I totally hate that guy. I'm going to pound him the next time I see him."

I closed my eyes, the weariness of the day overcoming me a second time. "Sounds fun."

"I'm serious. He scared the crap out of me."

I didn't have the heart to tell him that I thought a few more scares were in our future. For now, I decided to embrace the moment. "I'll see you in the morning."

"I'll be here all night if you need anything."

"I only need you."

He rested his cheek on my forehead. "This is going to be another adjustment."

"Yeah. Are you up for it?"

"As long as I have you, I'm up for anything."